FOR LOVE OR BUNNY

ELLEN RIGGS

BOUGHT-THE-FARM
MYSTERIES

FREE PREQUEL

For Love or Bunny

ISBN 978-1-998742-07-3 Paperback - D2D
ISBN 978-1-989303-95-5 eBook
ISBN 978-1-990613-26-5. AudioBook
ASIN B09FW2W8ZQ Kindle
ASIN 1989303943 Paperback
ASIN B0FJNPGJ4K AudioBook

Publisher: Ellen Riggs
www.ellenriggs.com
Cover designer: Lou Harper
Editor: Serena Clarke
2507281610

CHAPTER ONE

It was one of those crisp autumn days you want to hold onto with tooth and claw to keep it from slipping away into the relentless march of winter. The sky was blue, the trees ablaze with color, and the breeze a brisk slap to remind you of your good fortune.

Given a choice, I would have spent the day on chores. I loved chores, great and small. With eggs gathered, animals fed and stalls cleared I usually moved on to recreational chores, like turning manure and building fences. Checking things off a long list made me feel like my life was completely under control, which was rarely the case. Still, chores worked better than any of the myriad activities I'd used to manage anxiety when I worked in the corporate world. No amount of yoga, meditation or breathwork could conquer the stress that came with being the grim reaper of HR.

Today, my farm manager Charlie was getting all the fun while I stepped into my role as maid of honor for my best friend, Jilly Blackwood. The wedding was less than a week away and we had dozens of errands to run. A recent crime had put us behind.

Story of my life in Clover Grove.

Since leaving Boston and moving home, there had been more murders than I cared to count. Jilly and I had teamed up with Keats, my border collie, Percy, my ginger cat, and many others to help the police solve these mysteries. It was exhausting and yet somehow less grueling than planning a wedding. That didn't make sense, but there was no point pretending otherwise, at least to myself. With Jilly, I plastered on a smile and did my best because she was awesome in every way and deserved my full support.

The pets were already in the truck when she joined me. She was dressed impeccably but I could tell from her resigned expression that she'd rather be doing chores, too. Neither of us had been raised to dream about "the big day" or being the center of attention.

Marriage was different. We were in full support of making things official. The party was the problem.

I was thinking about how to shift the mood when I saw the rabbit. It was hopping slowly across the entrance to the long lane out of Runaway Farm.

Ambling, really, if rabbits could amble.

It was the prettiest gray rabbit I'd ever seen—nothing like the regular brownish cottontails that occasionally zipped across the lawn. I didn't see many of those, probably because my two furry passengers roamed the property freely. We'd also acquired some new barn cats, lately. Perhaps word had spread that my father, who practically lived in the hayloft, had a special fondness for felines. He was usually covered in hair of many colors.

"What's with that rabbit?" Jilly asked. "It looks like a pet."

"Exactly what I was thinking."

We shut the truck doors at the same time. There was a shrill whine from inside, followed by a plaintive yowl. The boys didn't like being left out of the action. While I trusted them not to hurt the rabbit, they both enjoyed a good game of chase and the rabbit wouldn't believe it was innocent. *Shouldn't* believe it was innocent. There were foxes around who wouldn't be so kind. They hadn't found a meal yet, thanks to Byron, the livestock dog, and the donkey thugs, who brayed threats and kicked fences as a "no trespassing" sign.

I started to walk toward the rabbit. Its casual bunny saunter certainly seemed like an invitation.

"Ivy, we don't have time to chase rabbits today," Jilly called after me. "Our appointment's at noon and you know what Rosalie's like. I'm already on her bad side and I can't afford to lose her so close to the wedding."

Rosalie Roarke ran Clover Grove's one and only flower store, called Rose to the Occasion. She had a flair with roses, but was known to be equally thorny. No one wanted to cross her by going further afield for their floral needs, which meant she was booked for major events a year in advance. Jilly had approached her a month ago and gotten a hard no. My brother Asher, the groom, dropped by in his police uniform to see Rosalie and worked his legendary charm to make sure there would be a bouquet in his bride's hand and a boutonniere in his tuxedo. Jilly had plenty of charm, too, but she didn't waste it on florists. My best friend probably would have been just as happy carrying a potted begonia up the aisle. She was the opposite of Bridezilla.

"I think this rabbit is trying to tell us something, Jilly," I said. "Like with Picasso, remember?"

Of course, she remembered. It had only been a few weeks since we'd followed a painted bunting through a swamp and stumbled into another mystery. Jilly had been just as eager to resolve that puzzle as I was. This time she had cold feet.

"Do you think we could take up the cause when we get home?" It sounded like it cost her something to ask. An animal in need was high on her priority list. "If this little cutie wants help, it'll stick around, right?"

"Probably." It was true that these odd situations rarely remedied themselves. Besides, we were supposed to be on vacation from animal causes. The Rescue Mafia, our animal advocate friends from nearby Dorset Hills, had vowed to leave us off the volunteer roster. Everyone agreed that a wedding gave us a free pass.

Everyone except me, it seemed. I didn't want a free pass. As much as I loved being Jilly's maid of honor, helping animals was my purpose in life. I didn't need a vacation from that.

Keats mumbled something from inside the truck. I shouldn't have been able to hear him through the glass, but he knew how to project and my ear was constantly attuned to his commentary. It sounded like he was telling me to stand down, so the situation couldn't be that urgent.

I walked back to the truck and Jilly said, "Shoo, little bunny. Just for now. We promise to listen to your story later."

It looked like the rabbit's long ears twitched an acknowledgement and there was more pep in his hop as he moved off the driveway and disappeared into the bush.

I kept a close eye out for the rabbit as we drove down the lane. "Maybe it was just a regular bunny doing regular bunny biz," I said. "If every animal we came across had a secret we'd never get anything done."

Keats mumbled again from the back seat, confirming my suspicion that it wasn't just a regular rabbit. That suited him just fine because he had energy to get everything done. Everything that mattered to him, that is. A wedding wasn't on that list. Our distraction annoyed him, but at least he got to drive all over town with us.

"We'll look out for the bunny later," Jilly said, as both the dog and the cat slipped through the seats and climbed into her lap. I knew she'd rather arrive at Rose to the Occasion without a layer of pet hair, but she didn't have the heart to disappoint the pets twice. "This won't take long. Although I was hoping we could stop at Clover Grove Gardens first."

That was my secret romantic getaway with my boyfriend, Kellan Harper, and I didn't recall Jilly mentioning the place before. "Sure. Why?"

"The photographer suggested it for the wedding pics. I'm wondering if there's anything left of the fall flowers."

"There's plenty left," I said. "The town's garden club does a great job planning out the full season."

Jilly turned to look at me. "You visit that often? I didn't think you were interested in flowers."

I gave her a grin. "I'm interested in Kellan and he's taken me there since we were teens. To canoodle, as Edna would say. He has a key so we can get in after hours. It's 'our place.'"

"How could I not know this?" Jilly said, grinning back at me. "I didn't think we kept secrets from each other."

"Very few, my friend. But it's nice to hold a little something back when it comes to romance."

"I agree," Jilly said. "Do you think he'll propose there?"

I shook my head as heat whooshed into my cheeks. I'd imagined the proposal more times than I'd care to admit, and the gardens used to be first on my list. Then Kellan and I started visiting Garnet Point, the "lover's lane" of earlier generations, and I thought it might happen there. He wasn't like my brother, who'd dropped on one knee in front of a small crowd to offer his hand to Jilly. Kellan was the Chief of Police and preferred some privacy. He would surprise me, and not until he was good and ready. There was no sense trying to predict it.

Keats mumbled something sassy, perhaps agreeing that I spent far too much time speculating about what he considered inevitable. I wasn't nearly as confident. Kellan and I had broken up once, and for many years. Perhaps we were still a little gun shy now.

"I don't know where, when or even if," I said. "But it certainly won't happen till your wedding goes off without a hitch. Kellan's not one to steal anyone's thunder." I turned down the side road that led to the gardens. "Besides, he's hardly had a spare moment to visit lately. There's some police business afoot he doesn't want to discuss."

"He's trying to keep you safe," Jilly said, as we parked in the spot nearest the gate. "And the rest of the town, too, I'm sure."

"I know. I'm just jealous. The other woman in this scenario is a crime he won't tell me about."

Jilly laughed as we got out of the truck. "Be thankful that's all you need to worry about. We found good men, Ivy."

Walking through the gate reminded me of that instantly. Kellan and I had been here at all hours through every season during the past year, and while I was hardly a horticultural buff, he was more inclined that way and I had learned a few things. The Clover Grove Garden Club marked everything well for the few visitors who came to enjoy their work. Part of me felt sorry the gardens weren't more appreciated. Mostly I was grateful it could be a private haven with Kellan.

Jilly stopped just inside the gate and clasped her hands. "Oh Ivy, it's perfect. Look at the colors!"

Red, yellow and orange leaves made a striking contrast to the dark firs lining the stone walls on all sides. Every flower bed still had brilliant blooms and Jilly spun in delight, like the star of a romantic comedy movie. My happiness over sharing something special with my best friend was mixed with a vague sense of disloyalty. What if Kellan wanted to hold our wedding here? He wasn't as sentimental as Asher, but the streak was still there.

Jilly must have noticed my hesitation because she stopped whirling around and came over to me. "There are half a dozen gorgeous backdrops in this town I could use for my wedding photos," she said. "If you want to keep this private, I completely understand."

I shook my head and smiled. "On the contrary. Consider it your 'something borrowed.' If Kellan and I decided to do a similar shoot here, it would look different with a new season."

"That's true," she said, scooping up Percy. "It had better not be a whole year away."

Keats mumbled his agreement. He liked having Kellan around,

especially now that the chief consulted him on important policing matters. When crime business was slow, the dog could taunt and tease my boyfriend, who still wasn't entirely confident around animals.

"Okay, so fair's fair," Jilly said. "Do you want to see *our* place? My romantic hideaway with Asher?"

"He managed to stay quiet about that?" My brother had always seemed incapable of keeping a secret. More recently, I'd uncovered a few, the biggest of which was staying in touch with our father. When it came to Jilly, however, he was typically an open book.

"It's hard to evade prying eyes in this town," she said. "When we found some privacy, even he knew better than to spill it."

I signaled for Keats to herd her up. "Color me intrigued. Let's go."

As we walked back out the gate, a rabbit darted into the bushes around the parking lot.

"Was that another bunny?" Jilly asked. "How strange. I've never seen one in Clover Grove until today. What are the chances?"

"If it were a regular cottontail, I wouldn't think much of it," I said. "But that one was mostly white with brown splotches. It looked like a pet, too."

Something shot out of another hedge and hopped a speedy zigzag into the fields beyond. The rabbit was black, and considerably larger than the two we'd seen.

Jilly and I watched it go and then turned to stare at each other.

"That's odd," she said.

"One pet bunny on the loose is odd," I said. "Two is a coincidence, and three... a conundrum."

Keats gave a happy pant as he jumped into the truck. Wedding planning was boring. A conundrum, he could get behind.

CHAPTER TWO

"Where to?" I asked, as we drove back to the main road. The dog had his paws on the dashboard, pounding out directions. "Has Keats ever been on one of your romantic rendezvous? Because he seems to know where we're going."

"Never," Jilly said, as the cat coiled around her shoulders. It was neither comfortable nor safe having him as a headrest, but I doubted we had far to go. "Percy has. Asher doesn't particularly enjoy feline competition, but the purring calms me."

I glanced sideways. A fluffy tail flicked across her face and obscured her green eyes. "Are you so worried about the wedding that you need a fur buffer from the groom?"

She sneezed a couple of times and patted her nose with a tissue. "You know I thrive on organization and this event feels like it's spiraling out of control. What started as an intimate affair for forty has a guest list of two hundred and it's growing by the day."

"I wish I'd envisioned the event within walls instead of in the orchard," I said. "Then Asher would have had limits. Kellan told me he invited the entire police department, including Bunhead Betty."

Jilly leaned back into Percy's warm embrace. "Betty, too? He knows how you feel about her."

"Right? He's out of control."

By all accounts, the police receptionist continued to disparage me after an embarrassing incident involving a femur. She didn't deserve my hospitality but there was no stopping my brother. Despite the tragedies he witnessed as a cop, nothing could close his open heart. He was unlike anyone else in our family. Mom, Dad and my sisters were shut down in various ways, and I pretty much expected the worst from human nature, thanks to a decade in corporate HR, followed by a dozen run-ins with criminals and psychopaths. That said, I expected the best from animals and my heart was wide open in that department.

"He can't help himself," Jilly said. "We're so different that sometimes I—"

There was a sputtering sound as the fluffy tail choked off her words.

"Have doubts?" I asked. Alarm bells went off in my head. I probably knew my best friend better than my brother did and I always worried his relentless cheer and faith in humanity would wear on her. I hoped she wasn't regretting her choice because Asher would never recover from a breakup with Jilly, no matter how many eager women were ready to take her place. Jilly represented the stability and happiness we never had growing up, and he desperately wanted to right that wrong with children of his own.

Finally, she started speaking again. "I have no doubts about loving Asher. He brings out the best in me in so many ways. But I still worry about whether I'll be the wife he needs." After a long moment she added, "I'm not sure he sees the real me."

"He probably doesn't," I said. "He sees an idealized version of you. The smart, capable, talented woman who helps run an inn, cooks like a celebrity chef and sleuths a little for recreation. Oh, wait... that is the real you."

She smiled in spite of herself. "I'm not sure he's capable of seeing my other side. The one *you* know. I'm cynical and jaded from my childhood and our corporate work."

"I know, my friend. I am, too." I patted her arm. "A year ago, I'd have said my brother couldn't adapt or accept that. But he's changed, Jilly, and that's mostly because of you. He's still sweet, but he isn't naïve. Or *as* naïve. I'm pretty sure he's going to keep surprising both of us. Haven't you surprised yourself lately?"

"Shocked, more like." She rested a hand on Keats' back. "The day we decided to rescue this guy changed everything."

"Exactly. That's when the little bit of darkness in our hearts became... well, an asset, I suppose. Without it, we couldn't do what we do here."

"But Kellan sees that in you and accepts it," she said. "He's not going to wake up one day and have second thoughts when he realizes who you really are."

I sighed. "Kellan's jaded enough himself to have those thoughts up front. Maybe that's why the proposal hasn't made a landing. He probably wonders whether we can have a normal life. Let's face it, with sixty head of livestock and sundry other animals, normal isn't in my repertoire."

"Yet he adores you for who you are. It's obvious."

"I'm not the girl he met in high school." I reached out and touched Keats' ears. "I worry one day he'll realize that girl is gone forever."

Keats mumbled something impatiently. He was my emotional support dog, but also a busy border collie. There was only so much angst he could handle.

"So, we both have the same worries," Jilly said. "Do you think they'll ever subside?"

I shrugged. "I like to think that a bit of darkness means we can be better partners, especially to the men we've chosen. Hill country can be a dangerous place. Cynicism is a strength here."

My turn signal was on before she raised her hand to point. Keats knew exactly where we were going.

Jilly laughed at my expression when I saw the discreet sign at the entrance to the parking lot for the Clover Grove Cemetery.

"Your secret romantic getaway is a graveyard?" I asked.

"Asher's choice," she said. "It's far from the prying eyes and loose lips of the rumor mill. Especially the original smaller cemetery way down the back. There's an old stone bench and perennial gardens. It's incredibly peaceful, as long as you don't think about it too much."

I pulled into a space in the empty parking lot. "Tell me you don't come here at night."

"Never," she said. "Although Asher's suggested it several times."

"Huh. If I'd known that, I probably wouldn't have doubted my brother's capacity to see the dark side." I turned off the ignition and let the pets leave through my door. "Thank goodness he didn't suggest holding the wedding here."

"I would have drawn the line at that," she said. "Even I have limits."

We strolled through the arching iron sign over the gate and my head swiveled as I took the place in. I could only remember being here once as a child when our school principal passed away. The new part of the cemetery had been spartan and uninviting, from a landscaping perspective alone. That had certainly changed now. The trees had developed a beautiful canopy and someone had the good sense to plant plenty of Japanese maples to lend their scarlet brilliance to the autumn palate. There were at least a dozen garden beds that seemed faded now. Many of the graves, however, were adorned with bouquets and larger arrangements. All in all, the place appeared to be as well tended as Clover Grove Gardens and any of the parks in town.

Jilly walked ahead of me, carrying Percy. "Wait till you see the old section. It has the best gardens. I've never seen anyone working on them but they're weeded and watered and things bloom as if they were scheduled to the minute."

"Sounds like the work of the garden club," I said. "You can compliment Rosalie Roarke later, because she's the president. Maybe it'll win you some points."

"Except something's changed." Jilly's voice trailed off and her feet slowed as we passed under an old arbor and into the original cemetery. "It looks like someone's taken a chainsaw to the flower beds. Or run over them with a thresher."

The beds had taken quite a beating, no doubt about that. For the moment, however, my eyes were drawn to the old tombstones. Many were covered in moss and looked ready to keel over and join their owners.

"Maybe they do that in autumn," I said. "To give the plants a fresh start."

She shook her head. "Asher and I were here last fall and the gardens were gorgeous until the first frost. This looks like the work of vandals, I'm afraid. We've been too busy to come for a few weeks."

"I wonder if Rosalie knows. We may not want to break it to her today, when there are wedding bouquets at stake."

Jilly turned to walk back under the arbor. "How awful. It feels like I've lost someone." She hugged Percy so tight that he squawked a protest. He didn't fight to get down, however. The cat was tough, and he knew when he was needed.

After a few minutes, my friend straightened up. "I suppose I should focus on the people we lost more than the plants. Let's go over and pay our respects to Imogen Pigeon."

I had missed the interment after the funeral and never thought to visit afterward. Ima was on my mind often and I didn't particularly want to associate her with a headstone. Her granddaughter, Teri Mason, had recently given me a pendant with a garnet chip that had lived a long life in Imogen's brooch. Ima herself had given me her wedding ring, so there were happier reminders of the friend who'd bound me with a deathbed promise to solve an old crime.

Still, I followed Jilly as she wove through the headstones. It was clear she'd visited Imogen often. Before we arrived, she paused and pointed. About 10 yards away was a plot with fresh sod and an understated headstone.

"What's wrong?" I asked.

"It's Verna Rae Cobbler. It must be. She's the only one who's passed this month."

"Ah. And there's a stone already. Let's pay our respects to her, too."

Vernie's life had ended in violence and we'd worked hard to resolve that crime. She was an artist who also loved gardening and I was glad the cemetery's foliage had matured and become worthy to be her final resting place.

We took another few steps and stopped again. A large, extremely ornate floral arrangement rested on the grass near Vernie's headstone.

Well, "rested" was the wrong word.

As we watched, the arrangement was being vandalized... by a rabbit.

"Shoo," Jilly said, running the rest of the way. "You leave Vernie's flowers alone."

I gestured for Keats to stay back. A chase through the cemetery would be unseemly. We could replace the bouquet.

The rabbit turned sideways but didn't run. It was gray and sleek, very much like the one we'd seen in the farm's lane earlier.

"That couldn't be the same rabbit from home," I said. "There's no way it could hop a couple of miles in the time we've been gone."

"Seems unlikely, although I don't know much about rabbits." Jilly turned and then gasped. "Hey! Get off there, you!" Releasing Percy, she darted through the stones to a different plot. "There's another rabbit eating the flowers I left for Ima last week."

A white rabbit with pink eyes hopped away slowly. Like the others, it seemed unfazed, not only by us, but by my pets.

"This really is a conundrum," I said. "The rabbits must have escaped from someone's farm. They're obviously domesticated and breeds I've never seen." I pointed out a few more hopping casually through the headstones. "It reminds me of the breeders' show at the fall fair."

"Someone needs to do something about it," Jilly said. "They're eating all the flowers. I'm guessing that's what happened to the garden in the old section."

I nodded. "The vandals are rabbits. Some arrangements have survived, though. They must not be tasty."

Jilly finally smiled. "That's because they're plastic. Bright and cheery year-round."

Keats whined, pleading with me for permission to round up the long-eared trespassers.

"Not right now," I said. "What would we do with them? Toss them in the back of the truck?"

Pulling out her phone, Jilly started texting. "This is a case for the Rescue Mafia. Domesticated rabbits need to be rehomed. They don't even have the sense to run from a cat and a dog. Talk about easy targets for predators."

She stared at the phone waiting for a response, and I put Keats into a down stay. Then I picked up Percy and walked back to Vernie's headstone. The gray rabbit continued to decimate a lavish bouquet adorned with opalescent angels and small pinwheels. Seemingly oblivious to an audience, the rabbit nibbled a black parasol, jerked it out of the bouquet and dropped it on the grass.

"Can you just leave that one alone?" I asked. "Vernie was a friend to animals and she deserves better. Go on, now."

The rabbit turned and seemed to stare at me with one big brown eye. Whatever the breed, it was very attractive. The rich grey of its coat was offset by delicate white circles around the eyes and pale fur under its belly. The inside of its ears was a light, delicate pink. Halfway up one ear was a small V-shaped cut. The rabbit had been injured at some point, but the wound had healed completely.

For a minute or more, it just sat there, twitching its nose. Maybe it was deliberating on my request. I glanced around and saw the pickings were getting slim. Likely most of the blooms in view were plastic. This small but ravenous army hadn't left much behind.

I stomped my foot to show I meant business. The rabbit stomped its foot, too, and several others I hadn't noticed started to hop in the direction of the original cemetery.

"Yeah, go," Jilly called after them. "Varmints."

"They're just being rabbits," I said, smiling. "They don't know their appetite is killing the romance for you."

She sighed. "I suppose that's the risk you take when you choose a graveyard as your special place."

"Hopefully we can do something about it before they infiltrate Clover Grove Gardens," I said.

"*We're* not doing anything. Bridget and Remi reminded me that our honeymoon from rescue has already started so they'll investigate at dusk. That's when rabbits are usually active."

"If they're nonchalantly grazing at noon, there's got to be a lot more of them," I said.

Coming over, she took Percy from my arms. Then she glared at the gray rabbit, who seemed to wait for its cronies to clear the area before finally turning to hop after them. I gave another stomp and it took a huge leap and shot off.

"We can leave it in the Mafia's capable hands and get on with our day," Jilly said, clearly still disgruntled. "I don't know if I can look at wedding flowers in the same way, now."

"Let's not mention this to Rosalie until we have a handle on the issue. I have the feeling it wouldn't end well for the rabbits."

Jilly walked ahead of me, grumbling. She didn't care about the rabbits in that moment, but I figured she'd relent later.

As Keats herded me briskly along, I caught up with Jilly and touched her sleeve. Sitting right in the middle of the arching exit was the same gray rabbit. The little V in its ear was a giveaway.

"It's the same rabbit again," I said. "She must be trying to tell us something." I guessed it was a female, perhaps only because it was so pretty.

Jilly pulled her sleeve away. "I'm trying to tell *her* something. Leave my special place alone. Some of the most romantic moments of my life happened here. Strange as it sounds, this graveyard has always been balm for my soul."

"It's not strange at all," I said. "We need to spend time in nature to decompress from— What the heck?"

The parking lot that had been empty when we arrived was jam-packed now. Families spilled out of minivans and kids ran toward us.

"It must be a burial," Jilly said.

The gray rabbit leapt away into the bushes and we hurried to the truck. "Do people bring cameras and binoculars to burials these days?" I asked, sliding into the truck after Keats and Percy.

"Maybe." She sounded even more disgruntled as she climbed inside. "Social media turns everything tacky."

A man passed us cradling a camera with an extra-long telephoto lens in his arms. "Looks like paparazzi," I said. "Did we lose a celebrity?"

"Did we *have* a celebrity?"

"I'm sure we'd have heard about that. This day is getting weirder by the second. Let's shake it off and get back into our starring roles. You're the bride and I'm your maid of honor. Keats and Percy are your ring-bearers and now protectors of all things floral."

Some of the tension released from her shoulders and she allowed Percy and Keats into her lap. "Rabbits cannot ruin the runup to my wedding."

"That's the spirit," I said, gunning the truck toward town. "Even a whole horde of rabbits can't wreck an orchard. We're going to make this event magical."

Keats turned his blue eye on me and mumbled. It sounded like a suggestion to keep a lid on my expectations.

"Never mind your negativity," Jilly told him. "I'm marrying an amazing guy and nothing else matters."

"Nothing," I agreed, rolling down the windows.

Keats lifted his muzzle to sniff and then gave a hearty ha-ha-ha.

Jilly seemed relieved at the sound, but I had a feeling the laugh was going to be very much on us.

CHAPTER THREE

Rose to the Occasion Floral Designs had become an institution in town. Situated on the main strip, not far from the Berry Good Café, the small storefront was hard to miss. There was a flashing red rose that took up most of the window's real estate. That told customers all they needed to know about Rosalie Roarke's aesthetic before they walked through the door. Her arrangements reminded me of the ornate hats British ladies wore to weddings and horse races. Deliberately over the top. I knew Rosalie's choices *were* deliberate because she was also president of the Clover Grove Garden Club. In that role, she designed the layout of all gardens on township property. When it came to the public realm, her tastes were restrained, possibly even classic. With her designs for her private business, on the other hand, she let it all hang out. There were unfamiliar and often garish blooms combined with bric-a-brac. To my eye, her funeral arrangements were almost grotesque, with bits of black netting among white lilies. She reminded me of a trained artist who painted traditional pieces by commission and burst out with abstracts on her own time. They weren't to my taste, but what did I know about wedding fascinators or flowers?

When we walked inside today, the air was humid and fragrant. I tried to pick out roses, but my nose had been desensitized to finer things by quality time with manure. All I knew was that it smelled nice.

That's where "nice" seemed to end as far as Rosalie was concerned. Her involvement in the major ceremonies in town took her right into the dark heart of the Clover Grove rumor mill. She was usually the first to know and the first to tell. I knew that only by rumor since I had little reason or desire to see her.

Rosalie's central role as a purveyor of scandal typically attracted a crowd. Today, three other people stood around the counter among buckets of flowers. One was a silver-haired woman I knew I should know, but the only person I could name was a redhead named Tizzy Cousins, who had recently launched a cupcake bakery called First Frost. The other person was a slim, balding man in a striped shirt and jeans.

"No pets allowed," Rosalie said. She leaned over the counter to glare at Keats and I saw purple framed glasses studded with rhinestones nestled in her butterscotch bouffant. Then she aimed a sharp look at Percy, who was cradled in Jilly's arms. "I hope you're not planning to carry that fluffy thing down the aisle along with my creation, Jillian. I'll have something to say about that."

A glint appeared in my best friend's green eyes. The idea of carrying Percy to the altar hadn't occurred to her before, but now she was all for it.

The silver-haired bystander laughed. "Oh, Roz, you can design around orange, can't you?"

"I can design around anything, Lita Peeble," Rosalie said. "But my wedding bouquets are fine art. If she plans to carry that cat, she can shop somewhere else."

"There *is* nowhere else for fine flowers in the region," Lita said. "Or so I've heard. I'm still new, of course."

Lita had moved here a few years ago, but I supposed that qualified as new to the local populace. I was still considered new, despite being born and raised in Clover Grove. The clock started over again when I came back. Assimilation took time and was based on a secret code.

Keats mumbled something soothing and I touched his ears. Normally, I didn't care much about being accepted, but the little store was overcrowded with gossips and that awakened the butterflies in my stomach.

Percy struggled and Jilly set him down on the polished hardwood floor. He leapt into my arms, probably sensing I could use an extra shot of pet love.

"Rosalie, you don't need to worry about showcasing your bouquet," I said. "The bride isn't going to let this clawed fluffball destroy a dress she'll want to hand down to her daughters someday. But I like your idea, and I might very well carry this guy."

Jilly smiled and shook her head. "Orange doesn't pair well with the cranberry silk of the bridesmaid dresses."

Cranberry had been a compromise between my mom's vote for scarlet and mine for anything else.

Rosalie looked over the list Jilly handed her. "Pink roses and baby's breath? Too bland. Too cliché. I can't work with that."

"Roz, let the bride have a say." The voice came from the balding man. I noticed he had kind brown eyes and an even kinder smile. "It's her big day."

"I'm not in the mood to coddle anyone, Aubrey Wagner," Rosalie said. "How could I, in the face of such a tragedy?"

Crystals of fear formed instantly in my head. It felt like one of those ice cream chills minus the sweet aftertaste. With only a few days left till the wedding, there wasn't time for even a small tragedy. Our town was known to do tragedy on a large scale.

"Tragedy?" I asked. "Jilly and I are out of the loop. What's happened?"

"Rabbits," Roz said, letting her glasses slide down from her hair. The frames hit a bulbous bump on the end of her nose and stopped moving. She was an attractive enough woman of Mom's vintage. I suspected the big bouffant was intended to compensate for her distinctive nose.

"Rabbits?" I said. Her tone suggested it was a mild curse word, like Edna's "dagnabit." Based on what we'd seen earlier, however, I suspected it was more literal. Keats gave a mumble and his ears pricked curiously under my fingertips. "Tell us more."

Rosalie tossed a blue carnation onto the counter hard enough to damage the bloom. "For pity's sake, don't you read the paper, girls?"

"Actually, no," I said. "I thought the Clover Grove Tattler shut down."

There was an open box on the counter with six fancy, monogrammed cupcakes obviously from First Frost. As a nervous eater, I couldn't resist reaching out to help myself to the closest one, even though the scrolly letter R suggested it was meant for Roz.

Aubrey gently directed my hand to the cupcake with the letter A, which was gallant of him. I peeled back the paper wrapper and took a bite that nearly sent me into sugar shock. I loved sweets but this was almost too much. I set it down on the counter and returned Aubrey's smile as I swallowed.

"The last publisher at the Tattler left abruptly on stress leave," he said.

Roz stared at me accusingly through her glasses. "Everyone's stressed over the ridiculous rash of murders."

Aubrey slid the box of cupcakes toward Rosalie. She covered her mouth and shook her head slightly. Shrugging, he put hers aside, helped himself to Lita's and dug in.

Lita didn't seem to care. "This town's body count is ridiculous," she said.

"It's hard to see the humor in it," Aubrey said, around a mouthful of cupcake. "Especially for a reporter, I suppose. So the last one left, and a new one moved in a couple of weeks ago. Justine

Schalow. She's been snooping around for her first big story, and I guess she found it."

"She published an exposé about the rabbit problem," Tizzy said. "There's been explosive growth in their population and they've recently seized control of the cemetery."

"The garden club has been rocked to the core," Roz said. "Tizzy and Lita are members with me and Aubrey is a good friend to flowers."

"Isn't it a good thing to know about the rabbits?" Jilly asked. "Now something can be done about it."

"Gardeners throughout town were already handling it," Rosalie said. "We're used to dealing with pests. The reporter has called attention to the issue and regular folks will get all emotional about it. They think rabbits are cute."

"They *are* cute," I said.

"Cute is beside the point," Tizzy said. "What they've done to Rosalie's funeral arrangements is an absolute crime."

"I left flowers for Ima Pigeon last week," Lita said. "A fluffy white rabbit devoured it right under my nose. The little savage didn't have the decency to run when I threw my shoe at it."

"That's because they're pets," Tizzy said. "They have no fear of people."

"Pets?" I asked. "How can that be?"

Rosalie took up the tale. "Stupid homesteaders, that's how. Until they took over the town, all we knew in this region was cottontails, and predators kept their numbers in check. But these nouveau farmers don't know how to keep their animals confined."

"Some owners have been releasing their rabbits," Aubrey said. "Accidentally on purpose."

"Why on earth would they do that?" I asked.

"Because they start out thinking rabbits are mild-mannered pets who'll enjoy hugs from grimy toddlers," Rosalie said. "And then little Johnny gets bitten."

"Rabbits don't like to be held or cuddled," Aubrey added. "They'll fight if cornered."

That surprised me. I'd obviously fallen hard for Easter bunny hype, too, and assumed they were sweet, docile pets. "Domesticated rabbits will perish in the wild," I said. "There are foxes and coyotes and plenty of other predators. They won't know how to protect themselves like cottontails. A fluffy white rabbit can't blend in with fall foliage."

"They're not perishing," Rosalie said. "Like all leporines, they're proliferating at a furious rate. Anyone who has a garden knows it. We've been sharing stories all summer."

"My vegetables were decimated," Aubrey said. "I've spent all my free time building new fencing. I tried high-powered sprinklers and blew my romaine and kale to smithereens."

"I used loud music to drive them out of my flowerbeds," Tizzy said. "What they did to my lilies was a crime. Then my neighbors called in noise complaints." She glared at Jilly. "Your groom may be handsome, but he sided with the rabbits."

"Same with Chief Harper," Rosalie said, pinning me with a fierce stare. "I told him that flowers are not only my work and my art, but my pets. I had every right to do what I did."

"Which is what?" I asked.

"Borrowed my sister's fox terrier, that's what." Her teeth gleamed in a cruel smile. "Barney's an excellent ratter and he kept my property clear of all vermin until someone complained anonymously to the township."

"They threatened to have Roz ejected from the garden club," Tizzy said. "After all she's done."

"My business took a hit over it, too," Rosalie said. "Luckily, we've had an all-time high in funerals since you came home, Ivy. Thank you for that."

"No thanks required," I said. "But maybe I can help with this rabbit problem."

Every head shook in unison.

"It's hopeless," Tizzy said. "Justine Schalow's article proves that. There's a massive colony in the cemetery that needs to be cleared out. Animal Services has been ignoring the problem."

"No one takes gardeners seriously," Lita said. "Except other gardeners."

"The problem is the bylaws," Aubrey said. "The rabbits are considered pets so they can't just be exterminated. But Animal Services doesn't know what to do with them. Everyone has thrown up their hands while our crops and gardens suffer."

"There must be something we can do," I said. "I'll look into it, I promise." Jilly twitched beside me, so I added, "Right after the wedding. I'm good with animals."

"We don't need a pied piper of bunnies," Rosalie said. "It's my responsibility as president of the garden club to take a leadership role here. By the time you worked your wiles there wouldn't be a stem standing in all of hill country."

"A lot of our perennials are damaged beyond saving," Lita said. "It's just a matter of time before the little savages decimate Clover Grove Gardens, too."

"Maybe you'd care about *that*, Ivy," Rosalie said, proving she knew Kellan and I frequented the place.

I swallowed hard. Seeing the gorgeous flora I loved chewed up would be hard. But it wasn't the fault of the rabbits. They had either escaped or been released and multiplied beyond what the environment could support. Perhaps they stuck around because this was what they knew. Home.

"Of course, I'd care about that," I said. "I appreciate all the effort you and the garden club put into keeping it beautiful. For free, too."

"Not entirely," Tizzy said. "We get a small stipend from the township. And a generous budget."

"I'm sure it brings in business, too," Aubrey said. "A horticultural expert like Rosalie can never want for clients."

She gave Aubrey a nod. "Thank you. I'm sorry for the loss of your lettuce."

"And I for your irises," he said. "I put aside some bulbs to get you started again. Once it's safe."

"Maybe there's still time to plant them," Tizzy said. "If our team can get this problem resolved soon."

"What team?" I asked. "Can I join?"

"No." Rosalie's response was quick and decisive. "Gardeners only."

"We're dedicated to the preservation of hill country horticulture," Aubrey said.

"By taking any steps required," Roz said.

"No matter how lethal," Tizzy added.

"Tizzy." Rosalie turned sharp eyes on her friend. "These two girls are in cahoots with the police, and even the mayor. They're on the side of the rabbits."

"I'm biased toward animals, but I love flowers, too," I said. "They're living things."

"Then let's talk about killing some of them for the wedding," she said, changing the subject. "I'll need a final decision on bouquets, corsages, boutonnieres and table centerpieces immediately. This list won't do."

She opened a drawer under the counter and dropped Jilly's wish list into it.

My friend extracted Percy from my arms and walked to the door.

"Where are you going?" Rosalie said. "This is serious business, Jillian. The drop-dead cutoff is today. I need to place orders."

"I just need some fresh air," Jilly said. "All this talk of killing is making me queasy."

"Well, it's a dreadful situation," Roz called after her. "There's no point sticking your head in the dirt."

I walked to the door with Keats. "All we wanted to do was enjoy a wedding, Rosalie. It's a big day."

"Then enjoy your denial fully," she said. "But if I don't get a decision by tomorrow, the bride really will be carrying a cat bouquet."

"We've faced worse things," I said, following the dog outside. "Much worse."

CHAPTER FOUR

"I thought you wanted to be on vacation," I told Jilly, as we drove toward the cemetery just before sunset. "A honeymoon from rescue."

"Turns out there is no honeymoon from doing the right thing," she said. "Picturing that garden mob descending on the innocent bunnies sickened me. How could I enjoy my actual honeymoon knowing such an injustice had been done?"

I turned to smile at her. "That's why I'd marry you as a best friend all over again."

"Oh, get a room." The voice came from the back seat, where Edna Evans, my octogenarian neighbor, sat in fatigues. Her helmet was in her lap. It seemed like overkill for a scouting mission.

"Edna, weddings are an important rite of passage," I said. "You'd better get used to us emoting all over the place."

She gave her helmet a brisk slap. "Good thing I came equipped with brain protection. I don't want sentiment slipping into my mental landscape. I need to stay sharp. A battle has begun."

"Against rabbits? They seemed pretty friendly."

"Against so much more," she said. "Visions of bouquets are dancing in your heads, girls, and you're missing the obvious."

Driving on, I considered whether to indulge her. I was happy she agreed to come with us to assess the rabbit situation with the Mafia. The more the better, especially in a cemetery at night. I was already nervous because several victims of crimes I'd help solve resided there permanently. Post-traumatic thoughts plagued me at the best of times, without tiptoeing among graves. At least with Edna along, I could coast on her courage. Thank goodness we'd put our recent tiff about her SurvivalDare prepper course well behind us. True friendship meant trying to understand different perspectives without judgement. Edna was eccentric, but when the chips were down, she had my back.

"What are we missing here, Edna?" I asked. "Some thoughtless people released domesticated rabbits into the wild and a newspaper article has divided the town. Half the people want to exterminate the rabbits and the other half want to bring their kids out to take photos, like it's Easter all over again in October."

"It's not about the rabbits," she said. "You know how I feel about them. They're best deployed in a good meal or a nice coat."

Jilly raised her hand between the seats. "Stop that. I'm already queasy."

There was a pause and then Edna leaned forward. "Are you with child already, Jillian? Is there a bunny in the oven?" She chuckled. "Joking. About the oven."

Now my friend turned to cast what was likely a cold stare at Edna. "Baby Galloways aren't currently on my radar."

"They're on Asher's radar," Edna said. "He was the strangest lad, talking about family long before any of his peers. The revolving door of girlfriends were all beauties, so I wondered if they were poor prospects in the maternity department."

Jilly continued to stare back at her. "I'm rethinking your role in the wedding. There's a vacancy at the punch table."

"Perfect place for me," Edna said. "Throwing punches and

taking a few hits for your burgeoning family. I hope my dress suits someone else. Perhaps one of the other Galloway nesting dolls cares to look like a distinguished senior citizen."

It was rare that Edna referred to herself as a senior or acted like one. Since launching her prepper course, she'd evolved from the lady of the recliner I met a year ago. The one who brought her rabbit pelts out of mothballs for formal occasions.

Keats mumbled something from Jilly's lap, and then gave me a long look with his cool blue eye. He wasn't impressed with our banter. The mission appeared to be taking on significance for him. I'd assumed rabbit reconnaissance would be a fun romp for my easily bored sheepdog.

"What's bothering him?" Jilly asked. "Aside from Edna being rude."

I laughed. "He doesn't mind if Edna's rude. But he thinks we should be presenting a united front tonight. At least, that's how I'm reading him."

The dog mumbled a short affirmative and gave me a shot of warmth from his brown eye.

"Edna, I'm glad you're here," Jilly said. "And I'm honored to have you as a bridesmaid. You'll wear that dress like no one else could."

"Thank you, Jillian," she said. "I know you both worry I've gone feral, but it's not true. Being mindful of the perils ahead doesn't mean ignoring the pleasures of the present. I look forward to dancing at your wedding. Harvey Dunbar and I can out-foxtrot anyone."

"Harvey's your date?" Jilly asked. "Why didn't you say so earlier?"

"Technically, he's Asher's date," Edna said. "The police went to the smithery for a weapons consultation and Asher invited both Harvey and his apprentice. Plus a random client who happened to be getting fitted for a blade."

Jilly slouched in her seat. "He's incorrigible. Our guests are like the rabbits."

Keats mumbled again, perhaps suggesting I circle back to the problem at hand.

"Speaking of rabbits," I said. "I'm assuming the Mafia will come up with a plan for extraction. We can help protect the critters in the meantime."

"Protection is where I shine," Edna said. "Although I must admit I'm not fully committed to rescue in this case. An overpopulation of any creature tips the ecosystem out of balance. My garden was stripped, too, but I wasn't around enough to see the perpetrators. I lost enough produce to feed my troops for weeks. If I didn't have a full set of fur, I'd be—"

"No pelts in my wedding photos," Jilly said. "Ideally we can find a solution that saves the gardens *and* the rabbits."

"I have news for you, Jillian. If rabbits are hopping around in broad daylight, it's the tip of a long-eared iceberg. There's a colony somewhere that could house a hundred of them."

Jilly gasped. "How could that be? The news article suggested the problem started with a couple of broken rabbit pens back in March."

"There's a reason people joke about how fast rabbits breed," I said. "I did a little research earlier, and they can have up to twelve large litters per year. Plus, the youngsters can breed by the time they're four months old. The growth can be exponential."

"But what about the different breeds we saw?" Jilly said.

"They aren't choosy. Interbreeding is totally fine, just not with wild rabbits or hares."

"Clearly someone needs to do something," Edna said. "After the end times, this would be a boon, but not in modern-day Clover Grove."

"Most of them probably wouldn't survive the winter," I said. "Or the predators that get hungrier in cold weather."

"Then you end up with too many coyotes or foxes," Edna said. "It's a boom and bust cycle. Nature at its finest."

"Let's focus on the immediate problem," Jilly said.

I turned into the cemetery parking lot. "Which is getting the bunnies out."

My friend shook her head and pointed. "Which is getting *us* in."

CHAPTER FIVE

S tanding in front of the iron gates at the entrance, I sighed. "Why didn't I anticipate this?"

"Because you're not prepper material." Edna's helmet was firmly in place over her permed curls. "Luckily, I anticipated your failure to anticipate. So I stuck a ladder into the back of the truck. Along with sundry other tools."

When she went to get the ladder, I turned to Jilly. "Why didn't you mention they lock the gates? You and Asher canoodle here in the evening."

"The gates have never been locked before," she said. "I guess town council is trying to keep the rabbits in."

"Good luck with that," I said, pointing at a chubby black-and-white rabbit hopping along the wall. "They'll have more success in keeping rabbit killers out, I guess. Rosalie and the rest of her garden cadre will have trouble scaling an eight-foot brick wall with ironwork on top."

"So will we," Jilly said, pulling out her phone. "I'll let Cori and the gang know what to expect. We're half an hour early."

Even so, the shadows were already long in the parking lot. Assessing the scope of the rabbit problem wouldn't be easy in darkness, let alone finding a colony, if one existed. The reporter hadn't taken her research that far, but someone else would. Like Tess Blade from Animal Services. Or any number of local hunters willing to settle for easy pickings.

"I hope Cori and Bridget have a solution, and a quick one," I said. "That reporter blew everything up. If the situation had been handled properly and early, this could have been an easy enough extraction."

"I suppose she was looking to make a splash, being new to the local journalism scene," Jilly said. "It can't be easy to beat the rumor mill."

"The only difference from gossip is that she gets people on record," I said. "I asked Asher about her and he said she's paying the print costs out of pocket, so she's probably looking to build subscribers."

Edna came back and propped the ladder against the brick wall beside the gate. There was a rope attached and she tossed it over the top. "We'll need to haul over the ladder when we're inside and come back for the Mafia," she said. "Leaving the ladder would invite others with more sinister goals. Although some people just come here to smooch on a tombstone."

Jilly gasped. "You followed us?"

"Tracking practice," Edna said. "Thank you for keeping things G-rated. Even sharing a seat is risky with the fertility problem around here. That's why I asked about baby Galloways. I didn't mean to suggest a white gown is inappropriate."

"Edna, sometimes I don't know whether to slap you or hug you," Jilly said.

"Sparring is hugging to me," Edna said, placing a combat boot on the bottom rung. "Are you planning on making the climb with the cat-baby, Jillian?"

"I don't want to leave him in the truck," she said. "There's a high chance of hooligans in the forecast."

"Starting with us," I said, taking the cat from her arms and putting him down. "If the rabbits can find their way out, Percy can find his way in. Both animals understand we're here to help, not hunt."

"You're a trusting soul," Edna said, scaling the ladder easily. "They're animals, and never forget it. Just like the rabbits. I advise you girls not to let your maternal hormones take over. You cannot save all the vermin."

She hoisted herself over iron spikes shaped like arrows, dangled for a second and then dropped on the other side. I seriously hoped I had the strength and coordination for the same move.

Jilly went next, grumbling. "For the record, Edna, Asher and I never smooched on a tombstone. That would be totally disrespectful."

"No one underfoot would mind too much," Edna said. "This town has always been full of romantics. Look to Garnet Point for proof. Love and violence are in our blood."

Jilly managed to get up and over with more ease than I expected. Apparently, her skills went far beyond scaling corporate ladders.

Both women came back to the gate to watch me.

"You had your share of both love and violence, Edna," I said. "In your wild youth."

"Perhaps even beyond," she said. "I'll take the stories to my grave. Which won't be here, by the way. I don't intend to spend eternity lying beside people I didn't like while living. Perhaps you girls can sprinkle my ashes with yours on the farm someday."

Jilly went for the hug. "We'd be honored to spend eternity with you, Edna."

I expected Edna to shrug her off, but she patted Jilly's back. A little too hard, perhaps, but fondly. "I'm pleased you know how to see a compliment. So few people truly understand me." Turning, she shook off the sentiment. "We don't have all day, Ivy. In fact, there's no daylight left. Get a wiggle on it."

"I'm wiggling," I said, kneeling on the pavement. "Someone else refuses to move."

Edna had brought my go-kit along with the ladder, and it contained the doggy backpack I occasionally used to transport Keats in tricky situations. As usual, he went limp the second he smelled it. By the time I pulled it out of the pack, he was flat on his side with his eyes closed. It was as bad as trying to get him into a winter coat. The indignity was such that he couldn't muster a mumble of reproach.

"On your paws, soldier," Edna snapped, as I shoved a second paw through the loop. "Pretty soon Clem will be here with Cori. Do you want to be the leader or the follower?"

Keats' eyes opened as he contemplated. Then he jumped to his feet and I had to start all over.

"You really speak his language, Edna," I said, finally easing the straps over my shoulders and standing. "A true motivational leader. No wonder your class is such a hot ticket."

"Less jawing and more climbing," she said, as I carried the go-kit back to the truck and locked the tailgate. "The rabbits await."

My maneuver over the top was considerably less graceful than anyone else's, but I blamed it on the unwieldy backpack and the 40-pound dog, who didn't take the ride lying down.

"Now I get a sense of what it's going to feel like being pregnant," I said, sighing in relief as Edna and Jilly helped me down. "Ungainly."

"I didn't expect talk of breeding from you, Ivy," Edna said. "You can't win a sword fight with a baby throwing you off balance."

"Oh yeah? Challenge accepted." I released Keats and he raced in a wide circle. It wasn't his usual joyous romp, I noticed. His nose was down and his tail started to puff. Maybe he didn't like the idea of a graveyard at night, either.

"All you need to do is talk Chief Haughty McSnobalot into taking that risk," Edna said, pulling the ladder over and sliding it into the bushes. "That's probably why he hasn't pulled the marriage trigger. He doesn't want to see his offspring in battle underage."

"Can we argue about this later?" I said. "Because Keats is telling us there's something wrong."

Indeed, one snowy paw came up and he stared in the direction of Verna Rae Cobbler's grave. Dusk was upon us now, but I could see the distinctive silhouette of a rabbit.

"I guess it's back to finish off Rosalie's arrangement," Jilly said. "Probably brought friends."

"Her arrangements deserve to be eaten by rabbits," Edna said. "She refuses to listen to customers and puts her elaborate spin on everything. I say, let the flowers do the talking and leave the doodads for kids' parties."

Jilly started walking down to the original cemetery, where we figured the rabbits were most likely to hole up. There was more foliage for cover there, and fewer visitors.

"All I wanted was pink roses and baby's breath," Jilly said. "A classic bouquet, you know? And Roz outright refused. Too cliché, she said. It's not as if she weren't charging me a bomb." Percy zipped up behind Jilly like a bolt of lightning, hit her mid-back and climbed the rest of the way to her shoulder. "I'm glad she fired me today."

"She was just upset about the rabbits," I said. "You'll get your bouquet."

Jilly turned and then sneezed as she got a nose full of orange fluff. "Did you call her?"

"Nope. You told Mom and Mom told Asher. He went down there in uniform with two other cops and either charmed or threatened her to provide his bride with exactly what she deserves."

"That's heroic," Edna said. "But we've circled back to romance again. I tend to agree with Keats that it's not the time or the place." She stopped suddenly. "Would you look at that?"

We turned and saw a large group of rabbits perched beside a marble marker. I switched on my phone and directed the light at them. They didn't move, either frozen in fear or completely blasé. There were two gray rabbits, a white one, a brown one and several with patches of other colors. The smallest had a calico coat and droopy ears.

"It really is like the rabbit show at the fall fair," Jilly said. "I can't believe someone deliberately set them free."

"Asher said it happens all the time," I said. "People just get tired of pets and don't even bother to drive to a shelter. They leave them to fend for themselves. A little research would have shown them rabbits are affectionate in their way, but not cuddly. It's heart-breaking."

Edna pulled off her helmet and ran her fingers through her curls. "This is a problem I didn't foresee. I fully support the food chain, as you know, but even I can't imagine eating a bunny that once lived in little Jimmy or Janie's bedroom." She gestured toward Jilly and Percy. "It would be like eating—"

"Never mind," I said. "No one is eating pets of any kind, Edna. We're here to *save* the rabbits, remember."

Keats gave a rumble that suggested we were actually here for a more ominous reason. When I didn't respond immediately, he gave me a nip in the calf to drive me on to the old graveyard. Once I was moving, he circled back and herded Edna and Jilly into line behind me.

The walk felt much longer than it had this morning. I couldn't help looking at the tombstones looming out of the darkness on either side. There were familiar names I'd heard growing up.

"Keats must be leading us to the colony," I said. "Rabbit head-quarters. Judging by his hackles, however, someone may have gotten there first."

Edna smacked her pockets. "I'll outman them. Man or woman."

"We should have brought Gertie, too," I said. "I expected the Mafia to be here by now."

A few more yards revealed what Keats was concerned about.

Someone's feet stuck out from behind a tall tombstone that bore the family name "Kinkaid." The person was wearing black pants and sensible black upscale sneakers. The shoe size suggested a woman.

"Uh-oh," Edna said. "I told you the garden club wasn't fit to climb that gate. Someone's had a heart attack."

I ran the last few yards and bent over. The woman was lying on her back with her arms crossed over the large funeral arrangement we saw on Vernie's grave earlier that day. I recognized the angels and pinwheels. There was enough greenery left to conceal her entire head but something glittered through the leaves.

Rhinestones, I guessed.

"Is it possible she fainted?" Jilly whispered.

Keats' eerie blue eye left little question about her condition.

Percy was the one to make an official pronouncement, however. He scraped at the exposed soil around the woman's head in his litter box move. It was just enough to reveal the halo of a butterscotch bouffant.

A shudder ran down my spine. Finding a body in a graveyard kicked the drama of our lives up a notch.

"Should we move the arrangement?" I asked. "Just a bit?"

"No." Jilly's voice was a faint rasp. "Let's not disturb the crime scene."

"We don't know it's a crime scene," I said. "Like you said, she may have fainted."

Jilly pressed numbers on her phone. "Percy has spoken."

"Percy just calls a death," I said, taking a photo to send Kellan. "It's not always a murder. Is it?"

Her fingers paused and we all reflected.

"Pretty much," Edna said, putting her helmet back on. "More the rule than the exception."

Percy took matters into his own paws and swatted the arrangement aside, sprinkling the victim's face with dirt.

There was no doubt in my mind that it *was* a victim, now.

Rosalie Roarke's eyes stared sightlessly through purple glasses at the sky. Her mouth was open and full of leaves and berries.

"Yew," I said.

"She can't hear you, Ivy," Edna said, rather gently. "Not anymore."

"Yew as in the toxic Christmas plant," I said.

"Well, no one's feeling festive now," Edna said, leading me away. "Except possibly the rabbits."

CHAPTER SIX

The Rescue Mafia arrived before the police. If we'd had enough time to warn them they would have been able to walk through the gates after the police arrived, instead of coming over the spikes the hard way, like we did.

When I aimed my phone light their way, both Cori Hogan and Remi Malone were wearing empty doggie backpacks like mine. Bridget Linsmore's stately black dog, Beau, was too big to hoist over and without him, it was like she was missing a vital appendage. Evie Springdale, on the other hand, was pet-free as usual, because she liked to be able to film without worrying.

Keats normally ran over to bow respectfully to Cori's border collie. Clem was the only dog that garnered much interest from Keats, yet tonight, he barely acknowledged him. Cori's dog might be an award winner in herding trials but mine was the expert in murder. Right now, that meant Keats had no time for idle mingling. All his senses were engaged as he monitored our surroundings. His hackles and tail still bristled and his teeth gleamed as he scanned the cemetery. The one blue eye seemed to glow.

Jilly leaned in and whispered, "Do you think the killer is still here?"

The others were still about 10 yards away and Edna had gone to greet them.

I gauged the state of Keats' flags. "Gone, I think, but not far ahead of us." Keats lifted his front paw in a point and peered deeper into the old cemetery. "That was probably the escape route."

"If only we'd gotten here a bit sooner," she said. "Do you think Rosalie came in to rescue her arrangements?"

"Looks that way." I shone my phone light around. "Maybe she was planning to deal with the rabbit problem, but I don't see any tools."

Jilly picked up Percy again. "Poor Rosalie. This is awful. I guess I'll be going with the cat bouquet, after all."

"We can find flowers in time," I said. "But I'm not sure we can salvage your happy place with Asher."

"Uh, no." She turned her back on the body. "That ship has sailed."

The Mafia stayed well back from us. At first, I assumed Edna was preserving the crime scene, but then I saw that she was trying to pull Cori forward. The tiny, fierce trainer refused to budge.

"Oh, come now," Edna said. "With the trouble you ladies get into, surely you've seen something like this before."

Remi clutched Leo, her emotional support beagle, with the same grip Jilly had on Percy. As a gentle, sensitive soul, I expected Remi to be the most affected by what had happened here, but her feet started moving before anyone else's. "No, Edna, we've never seen a body before. I speak for all of us in saying we'd have preferred to keep it that way."

"Yeah," Bridget said, fingers reaching for the empty space where Beau's head would normally be. "I guess you never forget your first."

"I feel sort of numb," Evie said. "I hope I don't faint."

"Don't faint," Edna said, with a trace of a smirk. "Because your head would hit a tombstone."

Cori, normally so vocal, was the last to find her voice. "I suppose this was inevitable, spending as much time with Ivy as we do."

"What's that supposed to mean?" I said, glaring at her.

"For you, murder is like flies on manure," Cori said. "No offense."

"Offense taken," I said. "But not really, because now isn't the time to worry about my feelings. Plus, I can see you're in shock, Cori. There's no glove commentary."

Her trademark black gloves with orange middle fingers dangled at her side. They'd lost their personality.

"It's not your fault," Remi said. "The murder problem, I mean."

"Well, sometimes it is," Edna said.

Jilly turned on her other bridesmaid. "Edna! Whose side are you on?"

"Settle your veil, Jillian. All I mean is that people who volunteer to help with things like this rabbit debacle risk stepping into the very manure of which Cori speaks." Edna raised her wispy eyebrows. "The bigger surprise is that others haven't done so earlier."

Cori took tiny steps toward us, perhaps not noticing it was Clem's doing. The dog was herding her into the circle of crime-solving, it seemed. Perhaps his already busy life needed a new challenge. Sheepdogs rarely declined an exciting plot twist.

"We've encountered a lot of people behaving badly," Cori said. "Just not quite that badly. Where do we go from here?"

"Nowhere," Jilly said. "The first rule is to avoid disturbing the crime scene, which we've already done, of course."

"Percy moved the flower arrangement," I told the others. "But I got photos beforehand."

"I'd hate to see your photo roll," Remi said. "With all the crime scenes you've witnessed."

"And meddled with, according to Kellan," Cori said.

I stared at her. "He told you that? And since when do you call him by his real name?"

"We've had a meeting of minds," Cori said. "He's still a thorn in our side with his holier-than-thou attitude, but I've come to realize the benefits of a relationship with the police. And Dog Town's finest aren't as fine as Chief Hottie."

"She doesn't mean that the way it sounds," Remi said.

Cori blinked a few times. "Right. I don't care how hot the cops are in any jurisdiction. But I suppose it doesn't hurt when the thorn in your side is easy on the eyes. I'm only human."

Remi stepped in front of her friend. "Cori, be quiet. You're in shock, like the rest of us, but blurting random thoughts won't help."

"It's okay, Remi," I said. "I remember exactly how I felt when I discovered the dogcatcher in my rye field. I blurted plenty of random thoughts to Chief Hottie, which got me in hotter water. It's a natural reaction."

"Exactly," Jilly said. "Let's all just take a few deep breaths and stay calm. I hear sirens, so the matter will be in good hands shortly."

"I'm not taking any deep breaths," Cori said. "It smells like death."

"It doesn't smell like death," I said. "Unless you mean dead flowers."

"Well, something stinks," Cori said. "Look at Clem. And Keats. Even that beagle handbag of Remi's is sitting up to take notice."

"They're taking note of the rabbits," I said, observing Keats closely. With the immediate threat gone, he could afford to shift his attention to our long-eared audience. "You should take note, too. Isn't that why you came tonight?"

"How can I focus with... with *that* in the middle?" Cori asked. "Do you know who she was?"

"The town florist," Jilly said. "Rosalie Roarke."

Putting a name to the body made Cori step backward.

Edna reached out and poked her hard with a camouflage index finger. "Special Agent Hogan. Get a grip on yourself. You've got a leading role in my militia and I didn't expect you to crumble like this."

That seemed to snap Cori out of it. Her slim shoulders straightened, and she turned to Edna. "I am not crumbling. I'm superb in a crisis. Ask anyone."

"No one rappels into a situation like you do," Edna said. "Even me. But if you're babbling about hot cops, you're crumbling. And you'll be of no use whatsoever after the apocalypse if you're still ogling men."

Cori reared back as if she'd been slapped. "Stand down, Edna. We needed a moment to shift gears, that's all." Her gloves came up and flexed. She cracked her knuckles and the sound was oddly loud. "Rabbits. That's why we're here. To find out why *they're* here." Glancing around, she added, "That reporter wasn't kidding. They're everywhere."

Several of us flashed our phone lights around and at least two dozen eyes gleamed back at us. A few of the rabbits hopped among the old tombstones, idly nibbling what was left of the grass. Most just sat like stone garden ornaments.

"They're adorable," Remi said. "Is it okay to say that?"

"Of course, it is," Evie said, taking some photos with her flash. "We came to help the rabbits. The rest is just... unfortunate."

"Take a moment to appreciate them," Cori said. "But then we need to start figuring out how to round up a herd of adorable rabbits and relocate them."

"Fluffle," I said.

"Pardon me?" Cori said. "Are you in shock too?"

"A fluffle is what a group of rabbits is called."

Her birdlike eyes were pools of darkness. "I don't think fluffle suits the scope of this problem. Let's go with colony."

"Sure," I said. "I can't wait to hear your plan to gather a colony of crepuscular critters who are living their best life right now."

"Don't ask," Edna told Cori. "Why inflate her Google-loving ego even more?"

"I know rabbits are more active at dawn and dusk," Cori said. "Which adds to our challenge. The light will never be on our side for extraction." She clapped gloved palms together with a soft thud. "The Mafia never backs down from a challenge, right Bridget?"

Bridget's eyes were still on Rosalie, and I wished for her sake that she'd been able to bring Beau inside, because she needed him. As always, Keats kept me grounded by cycling back from his investigations to infuse me with calm through my fingertips. Remi must have read my mind because she offered Leo's back end to Bridget, and the tall, reserved woman grabbed hold of his paw.

Bridget cleared her throat. "This rescue is definitely going to be one for the books."

"Or the movie," Evie said. "It's only a matter of time before someone tries to buy the rights to our story."

"We're not for sale," Cori said. "The money we just raised through the antiques auction will buy us our privacy for years to come." She glanced in the direction of the new part of the cemetery. "Thanks to Verna Rae Cobbler."

"I guess we owe it to Vernie to try to restore the peace in her final resting place," Evie said. Of all the Mafia, she was now the most animated, darting around to capture images of the rabbits. I wasn't surprised she'd adjusted. There was a sleuthing streak in Evie nearly as deep as my own. Two years ago, she'd risked her life to break up an exotic pet ring. "Once we get the rabbit problem solved, we can pitch in to figure out who killed the florist."

"The police will have that part well in hand," Jilly said. "At least I hope so, because I'd like my groom to get a week off. We booked the prettiest inn for our honeymoon. Remote, yet upscale. I intend to borrow their best ideas."

"Leave it to Jilly to do market research on vacation," I said. "I'm sure Kellan will give Asher the time. He's doubled his staff lately."

"Why is that?" Bridget asked. "Is there a problem we should know about?"

I shrugged. "There's a problem he doesn't want anyone to know about. Something that came to light while investigating Vernie's murder. So far, he's being very tightlipped."

Evie crept closer to the rabbits. "I guess it's a good time for you to build an auxiliary team. You're honorary Mafia, and we can be honorary crime-solvers."

"If Chief Hottie is always this slow to respond, you'll need the extra hands," Cori said.

Lights flooded through the tombstones and heavy boots thudded on the turf.

"They set up outside while someone collected the key from the groundskeeper," Jilly said, checking her phone. "They knew nothing could be done for Rosalie."

Asher led the pack. Several phone lights hit his blue eyes at once, nearly blinding him. "Jilly," he called. "Jilly! Are you okay?"

Reaching her was like running an obstacle course through tombstones and finally my athletic brother started leaping over them like hurdles. He was gaining ground quickly when he noticed a half dozen rabbits frozen in his path. To avoid landing on them, he lurched sideways at the last moment and landed hard on Benjamin Pilcher, one of Clover Grove's early mayors. Then he flailed away over the grass, moving like a crab into the path of his colleagues.

"That's gotta hurt," Cori said. "You still have time to back out, Jilly."

"I keep telling her that," Edna said.

"Something I don't need to hear from my bridesmaid," Jilly said.

"Poor Asher," I said. "Benjamin Pilcher was in cahoots with the Milloys and the Swensons. I wouldn't have wanted to land on him, either."

"He was trying to spare the rabbits," Jilly said. "A man who cares that much about rabbits is exactly the man for me."

"All of our men care about rabbits," Remi said. "Jilly, you chose a good one. Cori and Edna... your turn will come."

"Mine came and went," Edna said. "Now I can focus on what's truly important in life."

Asher reached Jilly at last and hugged her as if she were a life buoy in a stormy sea. "I'm so sorry, sweetie," he said. "You shouldn't have to keep seeing things like this."

"I'm fine," Jilly said, easing him away. She glanced at Kellan, now crouched beside Rosalie, and added, "As fine as we can be in such circumstances."

My boyfriend's eyes looked darker than blue when he flicked them in our direction. "It sounded like a tea party from outside. Your voices carried more than you expected."

"Sorry," I said. "We were just trying to keep each other calm, Kellan."

"Well, I hope the killer didn't overhear you talking about kerfuffles of rabbits."

"Fluffles," I corrected. He was normally curt around crime scenes but seemed especially so tonight. "And I would imagine the killer hightailed it out of here fast. I have no idea how, though."

"There was a ladder at the far end," Kellan said, pointing deeper into the old cemetery. "Hopefully there's some DNA evidence to make this simple." He directed a glower around the semicircle the Mafia had formed with us. "Don't get any ideas about airlifting these rabbits out of my crime scene. Not a thing can change until I'm good and done. Got it?"

"Far be it from us to get in your way, Chief," Cori said, adding some glove commentary to show him she wasn't cowed in the least.

Edna crossed her arms and glowered back at Kellan. "You may well appreciate a hand, young man. The time for an independent gunslinger attitude passed several murders ago. Even a loner like me knows the value of a big team in tough times."

"I have plenty of trained professionals on staff, Miss Evans," he said. "The last thing I need is to chase a bunch of would-be detectives as they hop around like bunnies chasing clues."

Edna tipped her helmet. "If I'm not mistaken, there's a wedding at the end of the week, in which you play a key role. How much merrier it would be if this case were put to rest with Rosalie. Some of us called her the Tyrant of Tulips, but she didn't deserve to die beside Sarah Pilcher. She was the wife of Benjamin, and as bitter as you might expect a mob boss' wife to be. I had to see Sarah out of this life when I was just a student nurse. It was a relief to relinquish her to this plot." She scuffed at the turf underfoot gently. "Let's pull together on this one, young man."

Kellan's lips pressed into a thin line and he mirrored her posture. He didn't appreciate being called "young man" in front of his staff, particularly the new ones. Until they knew and understood Edna—and her history of saving lives—they might believe he tolerated disrespect from just anyone.

"I hate to be the bearer of bad news," he said, looking sideways at Asher, whose arm was still around Jilly's shoulders. "But if we can't put this to bed quickly, the current plan isn't feasible."

"What plan?" Jilly's voice had a shrill note. "Our wedding?"

"Not necessarily the wedding," Kellan said. "But the reception in the orchard. It wouldn't be safe to hold an event like that outdoors with a killer on the loose."

My brother's mouth opened and closed a few times and his arm dropped from Jilly's shoulders and then inched back up again. He was caught between his boss and a hard place.

Jilly's green eyes grew steely under the police floodlights as they came on. I'd seen that expression any number of times in corporate negotiations, and even reps from a big company like mine had quailed.

"Chief Harper, there's nowhere to relocate an event of this size at the last minute. Our guest list has quintupled, and I think it's widely viewed as a town celebration." Jilly crossed her arms, too.

"I'm not thrilled about the size, to be honest, but we've made a commitment now. I don't think you'll want to disappoint the community during these turbulent times."

Kellan's expression softened and he turned into Asher's best man. "I don't want to disappoint anyone. Especially you and Asher. But I need to put public safety first. We'll find another solution."

"The other solution is right under your nose, Chief," Edna said. "You have a strong auxiliary team and it's time to deputize them."

"I have faith it won't come to that," he said.

"I don't," Edna said. "Because I knew Roz a long time and she had nearly as many enemies as I do. So unless you get a nice fingerprint off that ladder, there's going to be a lot of legwork."

"If it means saving the wedding, I absolutely need to pitch in," I said. "As maid of honor, it's my duty to make sure these two are happily wed on Saturday."

Asher looked relieved I was taking on his boss for him.

"Ditto," Edna said. "Chief, I wouldn't give Jillian a chance to change her mind. Think about the effect on the police force."

"Edna!" Jilly said. "Stop that or face a demotion."

Kellan took a little leap as Keats delivered a nip on his calf to add his two cents to the discussion. "Well, I could definitely use the help of the furry ringbearers," he said. "As annoying as they are, sometimes. So, if it means accepting a little help from their handler, I'll permit it. In consultation."

"Of course," I said. "I'm an open book."

Keats gave a ha-ha-ha and Kellan nearly smiled, and then shook his head instead. It wouldn't do to smile over a victim. "I mean it, Ivy. Take unnecessary risks and Edna could get promoted into your dress."

"Young man, hers is strapless," Edna said. "Completely inappropriate for a warrior of my vintage. However, it would put me on your arm for much of the event. So, I defer to your judgment."

Kellan's Adam's apple bobbed and there was a low murmur as

his team tried to fight a snicker. Asher was less successful and got an elbow in the ribs from his bride.

"We need to solve this crime fast," I said. "Together. That's what friends do."

Dodging out of Keats' way, Kellan shook his index finger at Cori. "No Mafia. Understood?"

"We'll stick to rabbits," Remi assured him. "Murder is out of our current scope."

"Help your rabbits after I say so," he said. "Not a second before."

"We need to get in here," Cori said. "This cemetery is fluffle headquarters."

"Rappel and risk a night in the slammer," Kellan said. "Officer Galloway, see them out. I permit use of force."

Cori easily outmaneuvered my brother, being very light on her feet. "You can't tell me what to do. And for the record, you're not as hot as everyone says."

I thought about correcting her but that was only going to undermine my boyfriend more.

Kellan had grown in wisdom in the past year and proved it now. He signaled Keats and Clem to herd us out.

"Hey," Cori said, jumping just as Kellan had earlier. "You can't tell my dog what to do either. Clem! This is an outrage."

Clem and Keats continued to do what border collies do best and we stayed well ahead of them. Cori's squawks of protest made me smile.

"They take direction that keeps us safe, Cori," I said. "Consider them deputized."

CHAPTER SEVEN

Turning out of the farm's lane the next morning, I smiled at the orange paws propped beside the white ones on the dashboard. Keats rarely allowed a copilot, but there was enough excitement to go around. A rabbit problem and a murder problem. On top of a wedding with hundreds of guests to herd. It was an embarrassment of riches for an ambitious sheepdog, and he was willing to permit all paws on deck.

"I don't think Kellan actually meant he welcomed our help," I said. "He just wanted to get rid of us so he could focus." My boot got a little heavy on the gas as we passed the speed limit and prepared for liftoff. "Sending Asher home with us to comfort Jilly was just a ruse. He wanted to keep me from getting started on our investigation. You know how I know? Asher was supposedly comforting Jilly from the living room couch while she slept upstairs. There was no way we could get past him."

Keats mumbled his agreement. He'd left me several times in the night, no doubt to check on our chance of escape. We were prisoners in our own home until Aladdin, the rooster, extracted my brother from the leather cushions and sent him off in his police SUV.

"To be fair, Kellan may want to protect Asher from himself, too.

The wedding hangs in the balance and he'll be a lot more upset if it's canceled than Jilly will be. There's a good chance he could get reckless, and he'll need to be on a tight leash."

Keats gave a ha-ha-ha, possibly over the concept of my brother leashed. It was rare that my dog wore one, although I kept several on hand. I also had a harness and a crate for Percy with me. Recklessness ran in our family, but with my animals, I did pay some attention to safety.

"You know what really bugs me?" I slowed on the approach to Mandy's Country Store. "That Kellan's staffed up with half a dozen cops, most of them rookies, and seems to think they'll do a better job than we would. What do these newbies know about the way this town works? You boys and I will have at least one clue by noon. Guaranteed."

Keats mumbled another affirmative, but his monologue didn't end there. He was trying to get me to focus. Sometimes my thoughts climbed onto a train and started chugging down the track without a conductor. That was an unfortunate legacy of getting clobbered by Keats' previous owner. Before that, I was at the other end of the mental spectrum: hyper-focused. That's how I survived a life of corporate misery as the grim reaper of HR.

"You're right," I said. "This is no time to sweat the small stuff. Kellan's doing the best he can in difficult circumstances. There's something he's not telling us, but it'll come out in time. Meanwhile, we'll do what we always do. Go around him for the greater good. This time he actually said we could, so we'll ignore the cop on the couch and carry on."

The dog gave a hearty yip to endorse that idea. He sounded pleased that he'd herded my thought train onto the right track, and the truck into our favorite parking spot under the trees. Here, it was almost invisible from the highway and gave us a bit of a head start over the rumor mill.

Percy stepped inside his crate on the back seat when I opened the door. He accepted and understood that a cat couldn't always have the same freedoms as a support dog. He still got to join me on the bulk of my missions.

I touched Keats' ears for a moment before we got out. "I'll probably need some extra help this week, buddy. Even before the rabbits and the murder, it was an emotional time. Silly as it sounds, I'm feeling anxious about losing Jilly. Just knowing she's at home packing makes my throat tighten."

The dog mumbled something encouraging.

"She'll only be twenty minutes away, I know. And I have you and Percy. But Jilly was a calming influence in my life before I even knew I had feelings. I think she'd say the same about me." Opening the door, I let him out. "They call it codependence, just so you know. Now we're working toward healthy interdependence."

He grumbled a complaint about the psychobabble. Despite being a willing agent of my personal growth, he didn't really want to hear about it. In his view, growth came through action, not navel-gazing.

"I bet you're a little more sympathetic, Percy," I said, collecting the cat carrier. "You're Jilly's cat-baby and this transition will be hard on both of you. Understand that I'll be okay if you want to split your time between us. We both need you."

Percy gave a soulful yowl. I already suspected he'd elected to stay with me, because no cat liked to walk away from a room full of empty boxes. Coming along today suggested he deemed me more in need of support than Jilly right now. I wanted to be the bigger person and make the sacrifice but decided becoming the best possible version of myself was probably the greatest gift I could give Jilly. And the rest of the people in my life.

"Oh my gosh, I forgot," I said. "I still haven't shopped for a wedding gift. No matter what happens this week we need to find the perfect thing for Jilly. Forget Asher. He won't care as long as she's happy. In that my brother and I are in full agreement."

Keats let out a little blat that sounded like "piffle."

I laughed as I let him walk ahead of me into the store. "Weddings are important for us humans, buddy. We can't let that fact get mixed up in the problems at hand."

"What's this about mix-ups?" Mandy asked. She'd already come around the counter with a big mug of coffee and led us to our favorite seat at the counter. The store wouldn't open officially for half an hour, and we'd have time to pie-up before getting started on our full to-do list.

"Mixers," I said, setting Percy's carrier down before sliding onto the stool. "Do you think Jilly would like a really fancy one as a wedding gift? I feel like I should go with something that speaks to her as a chef. It's a tribute to the year we've spent together at the inn."

"My mixer is a cherished pet," Mandy said. "But Jilly's more of a cook than a baker. Think about what she loves most about her work in your kitchen and what she'll miss when she moves to Asher's. It should be something that reminds her of her calling every time she touches it."

"So, no pressure," I said, grinning.

"Lots of pressure on you right now, from what I've heard." She turned to go back to the counter. "I've already plated the pie in expectation of your early call."

"I wish more people understood the power of pie. There would probably be less violence in the world." I thought about that for a moment and called, "Depending on the pie, naturally. I've had pie that could provoke violence."

"I hope it wasn't cream cheese apple crumble pie," she said, coming back with a delectable slab.

Mandy's creations were a feast for the eyes and nose, as well as the taste buds. It felt like a crime to cut into its perfection, but that didn't stop me. Until the sugar melded with caffeine in my bloodstream, my brain wouldn't come fully online. I'd had very little sleep, despite Officer Couch Surfer keeping the inn safe.

"Superb," I said after the second bite. "Just what the doctor ordered."

"Along with a side of gossip?" Mandy took her usual stool, twisting slightly so that she could keep an eye on the parking lot for other early arrivals.

"Yes, please. I'll take all you've got. Every murder is important, but this one is holding Jilly's wedding hostage."

She turned back and her brow furrowed. "No! Why?"

"Public safety, Kellan says. If there's still a killer at large, we can't gather in the orchard. When the guest list was only forty, we could have probably moved it inside. Now it's quintupled, thanks to Asher."

"And Dahlia," Mandy said. "Yesterday she walked in here and invited Justine Schalow."

I set the fork down with a clatter. "The reporter who broke the rabbit story?"

"That's the one. She was sitting here holding court with the garden club just before closing time and your mom came in to second-guess Jilly's decisions about the dessert table."

"Mom doesn't get a say on the dessert table," I said, picking up my fork. "And the last thing Jilly wants is a reporter at her wedding. Even Asher would draw the line at that."

Mandy nodded. "That's why I'm telling you. So that you can handle the situation."

Keats mumbled from around my shins. "You got that right, buddy. There are a lot of situations to handle right now. But we'll focus on the most important, which is the garden club. Who was here and what were they saying?"

"Lita Peeble, Tizzy Cousins and Rosalie," she said. "They were grilling Justine about the rabbit situation. Pressing her for details and photos."

"What were they plotting?"

"Whatever it was, they were being cagey about it with the

reporter. I saw a lot of significant looks pass between them. Roz got so agitated at one point that she was nearly shouting. She said, 'These are my babies.' I'm assuming she meant her flowers, since she's childless."

"Roz died with an arrangement clutched to her chest," I said. "It humanized her that she cared so much. But she wasn't kind to us yesterday. Basically she told Jilly to take what she was given or carry the cat." Percy meowed from inside the carrier. "Jilly decided to go with the latter."

Mandy couldn't help smiling. "It needn't come to that. There are other florists around. Roz chased two of them out of town with her ego and skilled rumormongering."

I took a deep sip of coffee, feeling it warm me from the top right on down to my chilly toes. When I was nervous, my feet were always cold. "Really? When?"

"The first was about ten years ago. Roz set up shop right next door and staged a fierce siege on the woman's business. Ultimately, the original florist moved down the range and set up shop there— apparently successfully. More recently, a naïve upstart found a space in the old cigar store and Rosalie started a vicious gossip campaign about her. Someone threw a rock through the store window and she vacated. Kevelyn Welsh was her name. Not sure what happened to her."

"That's nasty business," I said. "Maybe Rosalie's death has nothing to do with the rabbits after all. I just assumed, based on the timing and her outrage yesterday."

"Rosalie's normal setting was outrage." Mandy blinked pale blue eyes at me and then let out a long sigh. "When did I get so judgmental? And so vocal about it?"

I patted her arm. "Shortly after you got played by a loser and betrayed by your own grandmother, probably. Thank goodness you found your voice, Mandy, because the information you share has helped Kellan and me put nearly a dozen killers away. Don't forget that. It's an incredible public service that should fill you with pride."

Her eyes closed for a second and she took a deep breath. "How is that possible? That it's a dozen, I mean?"

"That's a very good question. I feel like there's an answer floating around just out of reach, but for now we need to take it one crime at a time." Her eyes opened and I asked, "Have you had some pie today?"

"Sugar and caffeine get me more jangled than I already am," she said. "And I don't want to lose track of my tidbits of information. Sometimes, it's like catching moths around a light at night. Unpleasant, but necessary."

I shoveled in another mouthful, mindful that people usually arrived on the dot of eight. "There's more?"

She shrugged her slim shoulders. "Leads you'd likely pursue anyway, but if it can speed things along, I want to help. I'm invested in making Jilly's wedding a success, too. There's a gorgeous cake out back with her name on it. Literally."

"Tell me quick," I said. "There's a car signaling to turn into the lot."

"The garden club," she said. "Their mandate was about creating beauty, but there was backstabbing in the ranks. I can't even name the flowers they argued about but a few years back, Joyce Hustings tried to oust Rosalie and replace her as president with Tizzy."

"I haven't met Joyce," I said, scraping my plate and then chasing the last bits with a few gulps of coffee.

"Exactly. Driven out of town by a scandalous and likely unfounded rumor that she was harassing a town councilor. Honestly, she seemed like a nice lady but Rosalie made her out to be obsessive and dangerous."

I slid off the stool and bent to collect Percy's carrier. "This is way more than I bargained for. And we haven't even touched on the rabbits."

Mandy glanced out the window and pointed. A woman with a scraggly light brown ponytail was taking a photo of my truck's license plate. Her jeans were baggy enough to fit a whole other snoop. "Stick around if you want to question Justine Schalow yourself. You can uninvite her to the wedding at the same time."

Backing away from the window, I waited long enough to get a good look at Justine as she headed toward us. I had a feeling I'd need to spot her at a distance.

Keats circled and pressed me toward the kitchen.

"Right you are, buddy," I said. "We'll show ourselves out, Mandy."

"Say hello to the cake while you're there," she called after me. "No touching. I'm letting it set before putting it in the cooler."

I did pause long enough to admire the three-tiered wonder on the counter. Then I filched a little pink rose made of icing from the bottom row and popped it into my mouth.

No one would miss a single flower now that Rosalie Roarke was gone.

CHAPTER EIGHT

E dna and Gertie Rhodes met me at Rosalie's quaint cottage on the outskirts of Clover Grove. I'd expected a more lavish home, given that she was obviously making a good living, but when we walked around the cottage and used a ladder to enter the back yard, I saw why this house had made the cut.

It was all about the gardens and landscaping. There were several tiers on three sides, each with flowers of different heights in complementary colors. It reminded me of a floral version of the wedding cake I'd just seen in Mandy's kitchen.

"Seems like her gardens are in great shape," I said, as Keats and Percy fanned out to explore. "Yet I heard her tell Aubrey Wagner that her lilies were decimated by the rabbits. And then the rabbits were apparently chased off by her sister's terrier. Maybe they were too smart to take the risk again."

"Rabbits aren't known for their brain power, so they'd have come back," Edna said. "Maybe Rosalie had other defenses."

Gertie used her rifle to point to the high fence at the rear of the yard. "We're on the cusp of the back country trails, where there's plenty of space for an exploding rabbit population."

"Why don't they just explode out there?" I asked. "Where it's safe and people don't plot against them."

"Out there, predators plot against them," Edna said. "They're safer in yards or the cemetery, where the food is gourmet."

She was wearing her usual fatigues, accessorized with binoculars and what looked like a sheathed dagger under her jacket. Gertie was also in her standard uniform of a baggy brown poncho, and she'd topped her gray, waist-length braid with a wide-brimmed and battered leather hat. Minnie, her rifle, was in full view today because my friends had come along as security.

"I assume Chief McSnobalot knows you're here?" Edna said, as we walked down the patio stairs and onto the flagstone path that undulated through the garden.

"Not exactly. That's why I suggested coming early. He'll need time at the cemetery before moving on to this place and the flower store. I figured we could just give the place the once-over."

"On behalf of the rabbits?" Gertie asked. "Or Rosalie? Do you think the two situations are linked?"

I shrugged. "Hard to say. She had plenty of enemies, right Edna?" I snapped photos of the closest flower bed. "I can't help thinking that the toxic plants in her mouth came from an irate gardener, and yet she was on their side."

"Roz was on Roz's side," Edna said. "She had a huge ego and no scruples. The type who'd survive like a cockroach in the end times without any help from me."

"I hate to say it but I'm always relieved to hear a victim of violence wasn't a sweetheart," I said. "All lives matter, but the weight feels a little lighter when the person had cockroach traits."

"Don't get me wrong," Edna said, walking ahead of us. "I have nothing but admiration for cockroaches under the right circumstances. But when you've elected to be part of polite society, as we have for the time being, you need to work for the collective good. Not drive your competition out of town with salacious lies, like Roz did Kevelyn Welsh and Joyce Hustings."

"I heard about that," I said, bending to take closeups of some pretty fall flowers I couldn't identify. "Anyone else she stabbed in the back?"

"Plenty," Gertie answered. "I heard she tried to get Lita Peeble booted from the garden club by spreading rumors she was using illegal fertilizers and pesticides in her yard. Said it gave Lita an unfair edge in the annual garden showcase."

"Like doping in competitive sports," I said. "What was the prize for winning best garden in town?"

"There was some sort of trophy," Gertie said. "But it was more about bragging rights. There was a feature in the newspaper with photos of the winner. Before the Tattler died."

"It's being resuscitated by Justine Schalow," I said.

"Another cockroach," Edna called back to us. She was examining the perimeter of the yard now. "Some of the stories she's published in past years seem sketchy. Little better than sensational speculation. She's moved around a lot."

I stared up at her. "You investigated the new reporter?"

Edna got a foothold and hoisted herself to look over the fence. "Due diligence. I caught her joyriding out here a few days ago. Said she got herself turned around, but I wouldn't put it past her to sniff out my compound."

"It's a compound now?" Last time I was in Bunkertown, it consisted of a single shipping container, a firepit and a few locked metal bins.

"Let's stick to the matter at hand," Edna said, jumping off the fence. "You're still Chief Hotstuff's girlfriend and I don't care for him to know about my state of preparedness. May I ask what you're doing down there?"

I'd knelt on one knee to breathe in the fragrance of a rust-colored flower. "Just taking time to smell the— Whoa!"

I sat back hard on my butt. Something had lunged out of the soil and punched me in the cheek below my eye. It let off a raucous screech. My heart pounded and I flailed for Keats, whose shoulder arrived under my fingertips.

Edna and Gertie closed ranks on either side. Keats, on the other hand, was giving a pant-laugh to tell me I was in no peril.

The earth where I'd set my hand had scattered when a clown-faced plastic head on a spring forced its way out. Now, the leering face bounced in the sunlight, taunting me. Percy picked his way through the soil and swatted it.

"It's like a jack-in-the-box," I said, as Percy kept it bobbing. "Must have triggered when I touched the soil. I've never liked clowns."

"A rabbit repellent, I bet," Gertie said. "Like a mechanized scarecrow."

I touched my cheek. "That's going to leave a welt. Poor rabbits, if they get whacked."

Edna planted a boot in the garden and a black bird burst out. This time there was a loud cawing noise, like a crow.

"Okay, this is fun." She started to tiptoe over tulip bulbs and detonate jack-in-the-boxes. There were bears, wolves, hawks and other, more ghoulish, creatures. Each one gave off a different sound. Percy followed, spanking each in turn with a ginger paw. He enjoyed the game, too, whereas Keats couldn't be bothered.

"It's absolute genius," Gertie said, laughing at Edna's antics. "Must have cost Roz a bomb."

"Edna, stop," I said. "Kellan gave us a bit of license but it doesn't mean tromping all over everything. How do we know there isn't a clue here?"

"Keats," Edna said, continuing her game of exploding hopscotch. "He's not fussing, is he?"

"Well, get out of there anyway." Standing, I brushed the dirt from my knees and derrière. "Kellan might have different ideas."

I was glad I was upright when the next explosion struck.

CHAPTER NINE

K eats shot off like a black-and-white missile when water started firing from all over the yard. Gertie, Percy and I followed him up the stairs to the patio and huddled under an awning. Edna had triggered a high-powered sprinkler system with dozens of outlets. All of us were drenched, but she certainly got the worst of it.

"Dagnabit," she said, splashing back to us through the muddy garden. "I should have seen that coming. This place is a minefield."

Gertie frowned as she searched for a dry spot on her poncho and then used the fabric to wipe down Minnie. "I could have done without that, my friend."

"Sorry," Edna said, grinning like the clown bobbing merrily in the ongoing deluge behind her. "Not sorry." She bent over and shook her head, sending a shower of droplets off her curls. "The one day I don't bring a hat. It's a good reminder. You never know when a little rain might fall."

Keats grumbled something insulting at Edna and glared at her. My bold and brave dog would rather take on a savage killer than a sprinkler.

"Oh, lighten up," Edna told him. "This is the most fun I've had in ages. Rosalie has gone way up in my estimation, albeit posthumously. It took creativity and a lot of hard work to rig this place. I'll be looking into similar strategies for both my homes."

"Bunkertown has achieved 'home' status?" I asked, twisting my hair to wring out some of the water. Percy sat at my feet doing an intensive groom.

"Home is where the heart is," she said. "And freedom. I feel my trucst self there."

"Maybe you should move your recliner. It doesn't get much use these days."

Edna scanned the yard. "Don't think it hasn't occurred to me. But it defeats the purpose. Preparedness isn't supposed to be comfortable. I'm toughening myself, one day at a time."

"What about you, Gertie?" I asked. "I haven't seen as much of you lately and wondered if you were bunkering up, too."

She slipped the rifle under the folds of her poncho. "I'm covered for emergencies, but Fleecy keeps me home. I spent so much time afraid when the treasure hunters were ravaging my land that I don't want to give up my creature comforts now. In my view, there's a compromise."

"Actually, I agree," Edna said. "I'm glad you and Fleecy have peace now. All I ever want is for people to plan for the worst and then enjoy the best."

"I admire your spirit, even if it gets me into deep water," I said. "We should head home and dry off. I don't want to go inside before Kellan's collected his evidence."

"We didn't learn much," Edna said.

"Look at that." The flower I'd sniffed earlier had floated free from the soil in the torrents of water that still coursed out of the sprinklers. "We learned Roz was willing to risk her plants to keep the rabbits from getting to them."

"She never did like to lose," Edna said, going back down the stairs for one more look. "It was a point of pride. We had to kick her out of the Bridge Buddies for being too competitive."

"That's saying something, because it was already cutthroat," I said. "What are you doing now?"

Edna stepped off the flagstone path onto the lawn. "Just want to check one more thing."

Suddenly, classical music boomed out from hidden speakers. This time it was an aural assault that must have been painful for the rabbits, with their sensitive hearing.

"Bach," Edna shouted over the music.

"Toccata and Fugue in D minor, if I'm not mistaken," Gertie shouted back.

Edna grinned at my expression. "Don't look so surprised. Preppers have culture, too."

I shook my head. "We can't leave the place like this. People will call in noise complaints. Plus there's a risk of flooding the neighbor's yard."

There was no way to stop any of it unless we could get inside to access the controls. By the time the police got here, there would be nothing left of the garden, and I couldn't help feeling that was disrespectful to the deceased. Regardless of the trouble Rosalie Rourke caused during her life, she had also contributed much beauty for others to enjoy. This was her private playground and potentially her lab for creating gardens that would thrive throughout town. We needed to save what we could.

Keats was already sniffing around for a key when someone shouted, "May I help you?"

Turning, I saw Aubrey Wagner peering over his fence. The genial expression I saw in Rosalie's store yesterday had been replaced by deep concern that creased his forehead and drew his lips into a frown. Knowing a neighbor and friend had been murdered was enough to make anyone anxious.

"Hey, Mr. Wagner," I called, with what I hoped was a reassuring smile. "We're just—"

"Nosing around," he said. "I guess you got a little more than you bargained for."

I ran down a second set of stairs on the side of the patio and gingerly made my way to the fence, worried with every step that I'd set off another booby trap. The next one might injure the pets. "I sure did. This place was fortified. Was that all about the rabbits?"

"That's what Roz said, but I figured it was to keep human intruders away, too," he said. "We were friends, but I wasn't welcome in her yard in case I stole her trade secrets of gardening."

"We had no idea any of this would happen and I feel terrible about the damage done to the garden. It's part of Rosalie's legacy."

He pointed to a gate I hadn't noticed. "If you flip that lock I can come in and help. I do know a thing or two about gardens and fortifications."

Within a few minutes, he'd dismantled the sprinkler and the sound system. Then he gently replaced the dozen or so plants that had been flooded out of their spots. He knew exactly where they belonged, I noticed. Being barred from visiting hadn't stopped him from taking inventory.

Edna shadowed him every step of the way to learn all she could. At the end, she said, "Well done, young man. You were always the quiet but studious kind, who took a shot in the arm like a soldier."

His smile returned. "Thanks, Miss Evans. Would you ladies like to come over to my place to dry off over a cup of tea?"

"It's a kind offer, but we can't," Edna said.

Keats offered a dissenting mumble. We could and should, he told me. "I'd love a cup of tea and a towel to dry off my pets," I said. "Edna, if you and Gertie want to head home, I think we've caused enough trouble for one day."

I deliberately dropped my hand to Keats' ears so she'd notice he was in a point directed at the back fence. The canine commander wanted us to divide and conquer.

"Gertie, how about you and I stretch our legs and hunt for rabbits?" Edna said.

"Hunt?" Aubrey said. "You can't shoot rabbits here, Mrs. Rhodes. I mean, people do, but this is a sensitive time."

"Don't worry, Aubrey," Gertie said. "We'll stick to Edna's binoculars."

"Good," he said. "Because as irritating as these pests are, they don't deserve to die that way. They're proliferating because people were either careless about containing them, or deliberately set them free. I assume that's why town council ignored the problem so long."

"Council knew about the rabbits?" I asked.

"I'd have to assume," he said. "Roz was one to speak up, and the garden club was well regarded."

Edna beckoned Gertie and they clomped over the wet flagstones in their boots. "No one ever believes how quickly trouble multiplies if it's not nipped in the bud," Edna said.

She stooped and offered laced fingers to Gertie, who stepped into them and hoisted herself over the fence. The rifle stuck at the top for a perilous moment and then broke free. After she was gone, Edna backed up, took a run at the fence and swung over with ease.

"Wow," Aubrey said, after they were gone. "I just turned sixty and I can't do that."

"They train hard for it. I want to be just like them when I get to eighty." He lifted his eyebrows and I added, "Without the camo. And the rifle."

Before we went inside, he took me on a tour of his own garden. There were several empty beds, and a large patch of vegetables screened on all sides with heavy-gauge wire.

"A poor crop this year," he said. "Keeping the rabbits out also kept me out. It was so hard to get inside for maintenance that insects got everything the flopper family left."

"Flopper family?" I asked.

Aubrey pointed to short green shrubs in the back corner. Several brown-and-white patchwork rabbits with long floppy ears sat staring at us. "Meet the Floppers. Your dog and cat won't hurt them, will they?"

I shook my head. "It sounds like you have more sympathy for the rabbits than you let on in the flower store yesterday."

"Mixed feelings, I suppose," he said, gesturing to the empty beds. "I was sorry to lose gardens I spent a decade getting just right. But the Floppers need to make a living, too." He shrugged and smiled. "That's not a popular opinion among my gardening friends, so I kept it to myself."

"Were you in the garden club?" I asked, following him to the house.

He shook his head. "I don't like politics, and any kind of club like that ends up breeding trouble fast, like Miss Evans says. My life out here has been relatively peaceful, and if rabbits are my biggest problem, I can live with that."

"It sounds like you managed to stay friends with Rosalie," I said.

Stooping to flick a few colorful leaves off the path, he said, "Yeah. We spent a lot of time together. I was at The Tipsy Grape when I heard the news. Had one too many grapes after that, if I'm honest."

"Seemed like she rubbed a few people the wrong way, though," I said.

He turned at the bottom of the stairs. "You've heard the expression that good fences make good neighbors? Roz did me a favor locking me out. We were always civil." His brown eyes lost focus for a second. "Except for that one time. When I did a maroon theme." He flicked his fingers to the largest of the empty beds. "I introduced a few new lilies and other flowering plants in maroon."

Keats nudged my fingertips and I prompted. "Then what happened?"

"Roz was doing maroon that year. She accused me of competing for the garden tour award, which was ridiculous. There's no way you can place in that competition with a huge vegetable garden dominating your yard." He glanced at a ladder he'd set up against Rosalie's side of the yard earlier to catch us trespassing. "She added another two feet to the fence and I withdrew from the garden tour. Permanently. Peace was restored."

"Edna said she was competitive. That certainly proves it."

"Passionate, is how I saw it," he said, starting up the stairs. "I was protective about my plants, too, at first. Did nearly everything she did to fend off the Floppers. Ultimately, I let it go for my mental health. Roz was obsessed with keeping them out, as you saw, and successful, too. She had money to dump into custom solutions."

"Like the jack-in-the-boxes," I said. "So clever. Nearly scared the life out of me, and I'm sure the rabbits felt the same."

He showed me through his family room, which had what Jilly called bachelor décor, with dark leather furniture and wood paneling on one wall.

"It was the fencing that cost the most," he said. "She brought in pest specialists from Dorset Hills and they dug down ten feet on three sides. That's deeper than most rabbits will burrow."

"Is there a warren nearby?" I asked, as we walked into a bright, neat kitchen that was far more upscale than the family room. "I don't know much about rabbits, but I assume the Floppers have a home, possibly with other escapees."

"Not that I've been able to find. I spent a lot of time wandering the fields before giving up and resigning myself to a barren landscape." He turned on the faucet to fill the kettle. "Roz did me a favor in scaring me off flowers. There was less to lose."

"It *has* been a big loss for you. I'm sorry."

He waved the apology away. "I'll get some old towels."

"Thank you." I looked down at the floor. "I'm so sorry about the muddy footprints and pawprints."

"Don't worry about it," he said, with that genial smile. "A little dirt never fazed a gardener. Or a former gardener."

Keats had gone into a point, and when Aubrey left the room, I looked in the direction the dog indicated.

"Oh yeah, look at that, buddy," I said, admiring a state-of-the-art mixer that took up a third of the available counter space. "Jilly would love that. And the fancy espresso machine, too. Maybe coffee's the better way to go, here."

I snapped a few photos and dropped my phone into the damp pocket of my overalls.

Aubrey tossed me a couple of towels when he got back and while I dried the pets, he poured hot water over teabags in a couple of mugs, and then handed me one. I wanted to ask for espresso instead, but it felt presumptuous.

"Do you know if Rosalie had ill-dealings with anyone?" I asked, accepting a shot of milk from the carton he offered.

While I sipped, he knelt and got to work wiping the floor. "I already spoke to your boyfriend. Although I hung up hard on the nosy reporter."

"Justine Schalow is on the story?" I asked, frowning.

"Of course. She was so excited about the rabbit scandal and now the plot thickens. In fact, those were her exact words. She was toying with cemetery plot puns for a headline."

"That's disrespectful. Hopefully someone will put her in her place." I sighed. "She is the publisher, though. Calls the shots."

"Roz would have found a way, if she'd lived that long. She didn't tolerate much. Even less after the rabbits."

"There was trouble in the garden club," I said.

"Always. Infighting and backstabbing. Someone was always making a run for the lead, because it brought a lot of profile. Everyone had a business to run, even Tizzy with her tasteless cupcakes." He stood and guilt flooded his cheeks with heat. "I mean, flavorless. I consider myself a baker, too. I guess I'm not blameless when it comes to competition."

He went over to touch the huge mixer with obvious pride.

"That's quite a machine," I said. "I was thinking of buying something like it for Jilly as a wedding present."

"It does everything but go shopping for ingredients," he said, laughing. "But it nearly cost as much as the house. If I'd known you were coming, I'd have baked a cake. I guess that wouldn't be right for the occasion."

"Probably not," I said, finishing my tea with a couple of gulps. "Anyway, I do apologize for the intrusion and the mud."

"It's nice to have a visitor," he said. "What happened to Roz has everyone on edge, especially my friends in the gardening community."

Keats nudged me from behind toward a staircase that led to another door.

"How about I leave this way and avoid tracking more mud through your family room?" I said.

"Be my guest."

On the landing beside the door, I stooped to tie my bootlace and glanced into the basement. The glow of fluorescent lights showed a large dog crate in a corner.

"You have a dog?" I asked.

He shook his head. "Tried out a rescue last spring and we weren't a good fit. I'm too set in my ways. I guess I'll just stick with the Floppers until they move on. I sincerely hope that's before our next planting season."

I opened the side door and let the pets out. "I'll do what I can, I promise. Maybe next year you could go all maroon again."

That made him smile. "It's a nice idea, but I don't want to think about what happened to Roz every time I look out the window. We were good neighbors, after all."

Stepping outside, I noticed a gray rabbit hopping toward me

along the side of the house. There was a nick in its right ear. "Hey there," I said.

"Is it Miss Evans?"

"Nope," I said. "Just another hungry hopper."

I shut the door and followed the rabbit up the lane and back to my truck.

Keats mumbled a warning to the rabbit before jumping into the back seat, where Gertie was already waiting.

"Don't scare that rabbit," I told him. "She's trying to tell us something and it's up to us to tune up our ears and listen."

"With what's left of our hearing," Edna said. "I enjoy a little Bach now and then but I've never been attacked by it before."

"Just another weapon for our arsenal," Gertie said, as we drove off. "It's good to have options."

CHAPTER TEN

W e were still damp and bedraggled when we walked into Chez Belle boutique half an hour later. Gertie had decided to come along with us for the final dress fitting before the wedding.

Belle Tremblay flinched and backed against the counter when she saw us. I don't know what horrified her more: Gertie's poncho or the rifle peeking out from the folds.

"Would you mind leaving that in the truck?" Belle said.

At first, I thought she was gesturing at the gun but then realized she meant Keats, whose white chest and paws were filthy, through no fault of his own. Percy had run right past Belle to find Jilly in the change room, so she hadn't noticed him.

"I can't leave my emotional support dog in the truck, Belle," I said. "Being in a designer boutique with my family is stressful, as you can imagine."

She scanned me from my stringy wet hair to my muddy boots. "My talents are wasted in this town."

"Belle, darling," Mom called from one of the two large change rooms. "Don't say that. I value your skills very highly."

Mom and Belle had nearly come to blows on a previous visit because of their drastically different style sense. Belle favored chiffon, tulle and pastel colors, whereas Mom was all about reconstructing secondhand garments, mostly in shades of red. Agreeing to forfeit scarlet for the wedding was a huge compromise for her, but she didn't want to clash with the rest of us.

More accurately, she wanted to compete with the rest of us... and win. She couldn't reach that goal in scarlet this time.

"You and you alone," Belle said, drooping a little. "The local homesteaders simply don't recognize the value of looking their best." She stared at my bibbed overalls and then closed her eyes. "It's breaking my heart."

"That's why you're starting over... with me," Mom called. She opened the change room door, stuck her head out, and then gave a dramatic scream. "Ivy Rose Galloway. Are you kidding me?"

Keats trotted over to greet her, tail wagging, and she shut the door in his face.

"Sorry, Mom. And you, too, Belle. We had a run-in with a sprinkler earlier and didn't have time to change."

"Let's get this over with," Edna said. "Where's my dress, Belle?"

Belle actually clutched her throat as she took in Edna's fatigues. Since my friend had taken the worst hit from the water cannons, she didn't look fit to try on a nice dress.

"You'll need to clean up in the restroom first," Belle said. "You can't touch dupioni silk with dirty hands. It will stain the fabric *and* my reputation."

Edna went ahead of me, and I moved to the window with Keats. "What are you and my mother plotting together, Belle?" I held up my hand. "No, wait. If you're in her class, I don't want to know."

Mom burst out of the change room to stickhandle the conversation. "I've suspended SurvivalDate indefinitely, Ivy. Out of respect to Chief Harper."

That was a crock, and I knew it. "Did business dry up already?" I said, sitting on the ledge with Keats between my knees. "I thought rotational dating was the hottest thing in Clover Grove since organic farming."

"*Too* popular." Mom stepped onto a little platform in front of a three-way mirror. She was wearing a sleek, shimmering silver dress that would be hard to miss, even in the orchard at night. "I underestimated the demands my students would place on my time. They were so needy! No one could decide how to respond to a simple text from a man without consulting me. I was on call day and night, and it was affecting my art."

Mom really did consider her sewing to be art and I respected the care and effort she put into it, even if I didn't always appreciate the end product. She was as flashy as I was low key.

"I respect how you repurpose garments, Dahlia," Belle said. "So much of fashion is sheer waste. Dresses are worn once and then no one wants to be seen in them again—or for anyone else to be seen in them either. They're abandoned like, well—"

"Pets," I finished for her, stroking Keats' dirty flank. "That's what I like most about Mom's work. She rescues clothing and gives it a new home. Are you doing the same, Belle?"

The designer gave a slight shudder. "No. At least, not yet. I'm offering Dahlia retail space for her products."

"It's a win-win," Mom said. "I can't run another full business on top of the salon, but I'd like to find good homes for the outfits I make."

I couldn't help smiling as Mom did a turn and examined her reflection over her shoulder. She had an incredible zest for life these days. Before I came home a year ago, she had become withdrawn, even depressed. Something had changed and she was exploding with creative energy like Rosalie's water cannons.

"You look good," I said. "Did you make the dress?"

"This is Belle's," she said. "Since you're all wearing her designs, I decided to go with the flow."

Gertie slung Minnie over her back and started flicking through the dresses hanging on a rack. "I was going to wear the dress Saul bought me for our fiftieth wedding anniversary, but maybe I should branch out, too."

"It's too late, Mrs. Rhodes," Belle said. "I couldn't possibly alter something in time. The entire Galloway gang is back there, in addition to the bride."

"Never fear, Belle," Gertie said, pulling out a royal blue silk dress. "This will fit me like a glove."

"But it's sleeveless," Belle said, clutching her throat again.

Gertie flicked her long braid over her shoulder and glared at Belle. "Surely you don't buy into the belief that women of a certain age should button themselves up tight? Because I could out-fence anyone in town except Edna and I'm in better shape than most women half my age."

"She's not lying," Edna said, coming out of the back looking marginally cleaner. "Gertie and I like to dress down on purpose and then pop out and surprise people." She winked at me. "Like a jack-in-the-box."

Gertie carried the dress toward the change room. "Tell you what, Belle. If you don't like what you see, I'll top it with a poncho and tell people you asked me to layer up."

"No ponchos over my designs, thank you." Belle wagged a finger at Edna. "And no cardigans."

My sisters filed out of the change room one by one wearing dresses of various styles in complementary colors.

They did a full turn and I applauded. "Awesome," I said, as Belle started to pinch at Daisy, and stick pins into gaps no one else would notice. "The wedding photos are going to look amazing."

"If there is a wedding," Daisy muttered, low enough that Jilly couldn't hear.

"Don't go there, Daisy," Mom said, reluctantly yielding the platform to Poppy, whose halter dress was quite sultry. Like our mother, she wasn't afraid to show off. "This florist situation is a dreadful inconvenience."

"Especially for Rosalie Roarke," I pointed out.

"Yes, of course," Mom said. "Did you know Asher invited her to the wedding, even after she threatened to hold the flowers hostage? I don't know what gets into that boy."

"He has a big heart," I said. "And he wants Jilly to be happy."

"You've been inviting people right, left and center, Mom," Daisy said. "It's got to stop. As the inn's manager, I'm telling you we cannot handle one more guest."

"In fact, you need to uninvite one guest," I said. "Justine Schalow. The reporter."

Color rose in Mom's cheeks. "I can't uninvite her. That would be rude."

"It was rude to the bride and groom to invite a reporter without their permission," I said. "We're looking for less press, not more. So you'll need to figure out a way."

Mom nudged Poppy away from the mirror. "Fine. The vacant seat means we can invite Belle."

Belle spoke around a mouthful of pins. "Asher already did. I think he was worried I'd slack off on Jilly's gown."

"He'll be too busy with the investigation to hand out more invites," I said. "Hopefully. We need his full attention on this case, along with everyone else's. Or the vows might take place in our living room with no guests at all."

"That would be tragic," Belle said. "These dresses are made to be seen. And photographed." She moved on to adjust Violet's simple sheath. Of all the Galloway Girls, Violet was the most understated. Her participation in Edna's survival training had shocked me, and made me realize we never truly know anyone, even our family.

"I'm sure it's one of the garden club grouches," Mom said. "I picked a tulip in town square last spring and Roz gave me a fierce tongue-lashing. She's lucky I even agreed to wear her corsage. Especially with those silly doodads she sticks in them. I threatened to—"

"Mom, never use the word 'threatened' in the middle of a murder investigation," I interrupted. "You know how that goes."

Belle pulled the last pins out of her mouth and beckoned Iris. "We're all friends here, Ivy. I happen to agree with your mother that it was probably one of Rosalie's so-called garden friends. Or perhaps the wronged wife I heard about."

"Wronged wife?" I asked.

The designer gave a delicate shrug. "There were rumors of an affair."

"In the garden club?" I asked. "No one's even mentioned a man's name."

Belle shrugged again. "I'm only passing along what little I heard. In case it helps the investigation."

Gertie came out of the change room wearing the royal blue dress. There was a stretch of bare white leg over her unlaced work boots, but she wasn't wrong about the perfect fit. This time, Daisy started the applause.

"Wait," Gertie said, heading back inside. She came out with Minnie slung over the dress. "The must-have accessory of the stylish senior."

We all laughed and the mood in the small shop lifted.

"Ivy, go clean up and try on your dress," Mom said. "You're the maid of honor, after all."

I decided I was more damp than dirty and ignored her first order. Instead, I knocked on the door to Jilly's change room and cracked it open. "You okay? What's taking so long?"

"Fine," she said, as I stepped inside. "Shut the door."

She was standing in front of another three-way mirror and I could tell she wasn't fine at all. In fact, she'd been crying.

I pulled a pack of tissues out of my pocket and offered them to her, and she patted the mascara under her eyes.

"What's wrong, my friend? Are you upset about the murder?"

"No," she said. "Well, yes. Naturally I'm upset about the murder. But it's not that."

After studying her for a moment, I said, "It's about Bridie. You're upset your grandmother can't come." Bridie still couldn't leave her gated community at will. There were safety issues that hadn't been resolved since our visit a few months ago.

She nodded. "And upset my mother *is* coming. I haven't seen her in years, and I won't lie, I hoped she'd decline." Her eyes filled again. "She still might. And that would be even worse."

"I know, and I get it," I said, hugging her gingerly. "I'm so sorry, Jilly."

"Don't crush the dress!"

The shout rang out from Belle and Mom in the same moment, and we jumped apart.

"Is there a peephole?" Jilly asked, smoothing the dress. It was the most beautiful wedding gown I had ever seen, probably because my best friend had pretty much designed it herself. It was strapless and devoid of the traditional frills. Yet the rich fabric and small train made it look distinctive and feminine.

"Seamstress intuition," I said, twisting Jilly's hair into a knot and sticking a pen through it. "They don't want me anywhere near all that white."

Jilly laughed and my throat loosened a bit at the sound. Occasions like this brought up all kinds of emotions and I felt plenty of turmoil myself. At least I knew ahead of time that my mother, father and grandparents would all be there. I could prepare for any shenanigans among my dysfunctional family. In fact, it was a dress rehearsal for my own big day.

At least I hoped so.

The door cracked open and Belle stuck my dress inside. I quickly slipped off my boots, overalls and T-shirt and let Jilly zip me into the cranberry dress.

She turned me to the mirror and grinned over my shoulder. "You look stunning. And Janelle will, too. Belle shipped her dress to Wyldwood Springs and she'll have it tailored there."

By the time I emerged, Edna had also come out, wearing a simple cranberry dress with short sleeves.

"Belle, I'll need a jacket to match," she said. "It's late October in hill country. What were you thinking?"

"I don't have time to make a jacket," Belle said. "There are so many dresses to alter within a few days, and more people are coming in because of last-minute invitations."

Jilly emerged from the change room and let me help her up onto the platform for all of us to oooh and aaah over her beauty.

All of us except Gertie, that is. "I'll take a jacket, too, Belle," she said. "This dress is nice but there's no place to conceal a weapon."

"Exactly," Edna said. "I was being circumspect about the problem only because I'm in the wedding party."

"I'll deal with the alterations while Belle makes the jackets," Mom said. "Although I'm sure there won't be a need for weapons by then."

"It pays to be armed at all times around here," Edna said, glancing out into the street. "See? There's a situation right now and I need to defer to Gertie, who's properly armed."

We all turned and saw Justine Schalow standing in front of the window at Chez Belle busily snapping off photos of us.

"Stop her!" Mom's voice was shrill. "The groom can't see the dress before the wedding day. It's bad luck."

Gertie stomped toward the door, flipping Minnie over her shoulder along with her braid. "I'll take care of this, pronto."

Justine walked away, without much hustle in her bustle. That changed when she looked back and saw Gertie in pursuit. The reporter started to run, but despite unlaced boots, Gertie caught up to her easily.

She nabbed Justine in the middle of Main Street on a green light.

There was screeching of brakes and shouting, most of it coming from Justine.

Gertie held onto Justine's collar and brandished Minnie at the delivery truck behind them. The driver put his vehicle into reverse, and others laid on their horns. Soon there was a cacophony and both women appeared to keep yelling.

"Help her, Edna," Jilly said.

"Gertie doesn't need help from me or anyone else," Edna said. "She'd be insulted if I joined her in this getup."

"Pardon me?" Belle said. "That's a designer dress."

Edna held up her palm to silence Belle. Then she walked to the door in time to open it with a flourish for Gertie, who promptly surrendered the camera to me. "Take that to the chief to destroy photos shot without permission," she said. "I told Justine that the wedding would be ruined with her paparazzi exploits. She had the nerve to say it was already ruined by murder."

"As if a murder could stop this couple," Edna said, with a snort. "The apocalypse itself couldn't stop them."

Jilly gathered her train and walked over to Edna and Gertie and pulled them both into a hug over the shrill protests of the designer. "I'm so happy to have you as my family," she said. "Both of you."

"Don't you dare cry," Edna told Gertie.

"Why not?" Gertie said. "You are."

The two older women pushed Jilly back in the same moment and blinked at each other.

"Should we go and do some target practice?" Edna asked. "I think I need to shoot something."

"Absolutely," Gertie said. "Minnie's feeling frisky. Your place or mine?"

CHAPTER ELEVEN

Fallbrook barely qualified as a town but I'd always admired its can-do spirit. It didn't have the charm of Dorset Hills, or even the reflected glory of Clover Grove, yet it held its own on the string of beads that made up the greater hill country community. Every town was known for something, and Fallbrook was all about honey. Instead of centralizing production, they supported independent beekeepers who created and branded their own lines.

At first, I fell into the trap of thinking honey was honey. After Kellan took me to a taste test on one of our more romantic dates, however, I started noticing the subtle differences in flavor. The local flora offered different pollen that the bees brought back to their honey factories.

"Wedding favors," I said, as we drove past the roadside stands. "Little pots of lavender honey at every place setting would be the perfect gift, don't you think?"

Keats gave what qualified as a canine snort of derision. There was little he cared about less than party favors for my imaginary wedding. He wanted Kellan to join us officially, I knew, because as much as the dog enjoyed teasing my boyfriend, he always herded the two of us back together in the end. One day we might make the power pack Keats desired, but he didn't care about the "how."

"Yeah, I know," I said, cruising slowly down Fallbrook's main strip. "Focus on the matters at hand. My head feels like it's full of bubbles, like the iridescent clusters kids blow. As soon as I touch one, it explodes."

He put a paw on my leg to ground me, and mumbled. One bubble at a time. That's all we could chase right now. My future wedding wasn't among them.

My head swiveled and Keats' muzzle did the same. Then he stuck his nose to the gap in the window and drew in the nuances of this particular town.

Fallbrook's main drag was similar to Clover Grove's, only shabbier. They didn't have the tax base of the homesteaders to boost their economy. Yet. As my town had benefited from the spillover from Dorset Hills, Fallbrook would eventually benefit from ours. Homesteaders were being priced out of the Clover Grove market and would move out this way to make honey of the situation.

"Hopefully people will stop breeding rabbits," I said. "There's enough around for a decade of Easters. That's how long rabbits can live in captivity, you know. We just need to capture the colony and neuter them."

Keats' mumble was dismissive of that, too. The murder problem had taken precedence over the rabbit problem in his mind. I supposed that was as it should be. Murder trumped everything, especially when a wedding hung in the balance.

"Where to?" I asked. "We're looking for a florist."

As usual, his nose beat my eyes, and he pointed in the direction of Fallbrook Flowers. What the name lacked in imagination, the window made up for and more. Unlike Rose to the Occasion, this store was quaint and picturesque, with a dozen old blue milk cans filled with tall blooms. There were also pots of tulips and daffodils that made me want to skip right over winter.

We pulled into a parking spot right out front beside a white van with the store's name and logo on the side.

"Alrighty, boys," I said. "Keep me on track, please. If we have half an hour afterward, I could visit the kitchenware store we just passed and buy the wedding present. I've left it too late to order online now. As maid of honor, the least I can do is get a gift on time. I'm thinking of going with the high-end espresso machine now. Jilly likes her coffee as much as I do."

Keats grumbled another lecture about priorities as he climbed over me and out of the truck.

"No one likes a finger-wagger," I told him, jumping down. "Good thing you don't have fingers." I scooped up Percy and set him on my shoulder. With strangers, it often went more smoothly if my feline was somewhat contained on arrival. It surprised me that even in small towns, many were dubious about cats, at least as pets. "I've often thought that if you boys had prehensile thumbs you'd fire me. You'd drive yourselves around hill country putting things right."

Keats gave a pant-laugh that wasn't particularly reassuring, but Percy roared a soothing purr in my ear. Today the cat was the diplomat.

I took a moment to collect my thoughts while admiring the window display. Kevelyn Welsh may not have the flash of Rosalie Roarke, but the two arrangements on offer were simple and sweet. Homespun, like the honey for which the town was known. There was apparently no need for pinwheels and parasols here.

When we went inside, a woman was behind a long counter sticking stems into green foam. Her silvery blonde hair was in a topknot that made her look younger than she was, at least until she looked up. The lines bracketing her blue eyes and her mouth said she'd been around the flower bed a time or two.

"Good afternoon," she said, with a smile. "I wondered when you'd look me up."

It was disappointing. The press over our previous exploits made it nearly impossible to gain the element of surprise anymore. My arrival put most people on guard immediately, even when they had nothing to hide.

Most people did have something to hide, it seemed, and my HR skills made me good at drawing those things out. Prehensile thumbs for my pets couldn't replace that, I supposed.

Keats pant-laughed again at my side, which suggested from the get-go that Kevelyn Welsh wasn't guilty of murder. That would have been far too easy. Still, she might have valuable information about the hill country flora community.

I offered my hand and introduced myself, as well as Keats and Percy.

"I looked you up because Mandy McCain recommended your services," I said. "It sounds like you've heard that my best friend, Jilly, is down a florist for her wedding this weekend."

"I heard about Roz," she said. "There are florists far closer to you than Fallbrook."

"Like I said, Mandy sang your praises. I was hoping you could squeeze us in and wanted to press our case in person."

"I don't think so, Ivy," she said. "Because I doubt that wedding will even happen now. I've heard the police put the kibosh on it till they find out who killed Roz. There's no need to waste my time and your money on bouquets that won't get used."

I picked up a carnation from the counter. It was a pale pink, and completely natural, unlike the crazy colors Rosalie had dyed hers. "People undervalue carnations," I said, sniffing the one in my hand. "They're hardy and to me, they smell like home."

That brought the first smile to Kevelyn's face. "They're the work-horse of the average florist. I believe in giving them pride of place in most arrangements. We're not in a big city and there's no need to get too fancy. Let's embrace who we are. Small-town folk."

"Exactly. That's who Jilly is now. My brother, the groom, always was."

"Yet Rose to the Occasion was your first choice," she said, blue eyes narrowing.

I nodded. "For business reasons. I own an inn, as you probably know, and wherever possible, I support the local economy. But now there's a vacancy." I put the carnation in her outstretched hand. "You could consider coming back to Clover Grove."

She shoved the carnation into the green foam so hard she broke the stem.

"Never," she said, although the flower had said it first. "I got chased out of my hometown by slander and gossip from someone who was a transplant. Rosalie Roarke was an invasive toxic weed that spread so far and so fast that the local flora withered and died."

"A toxic weed?" Lifting Percy off my shoulder, I set him on the floor. "That's quite an image."

"People don't think," she said, snipping the carnation's stem and trying again to jam it into the foam. "You can't unleash an aggressive plant into an existing ecosystem and expect anything else to thrive."

"Goes for animals, too," I said. "Like the Burmese pythons that have taken over the Everglades."

Her eyes widened and she recoiled, clutching the battered carnation to her chest. "How dreadful. Roz was a snake, too."

"I don't suppose you kept in touch?" I asked.

"Not by choice." She went back to working on her arrangement and I noticed her hands shook slightly. "We both wanted a spot on the executive of the Hill Country Horticultural Society. That meant we sometimes ended up in the same room, garden or greenhouse. I kept my distance, but even there she tried to undermine me."

"Why? You were no threat to her anymore."

Giving up on the carnations, she crossed her arms. "That's where you're wrong. Some old-school horticulture buffs preferred my classic style to her nouveau approach to floral design. I always admired her creativity, if not her personality. But many were skeptical about her aesthetic. Some of them came to me."

"For weddings and events?" I asked.

"That and more. I have private garden design clients that chose me over Roz, especially in Dorset Hills, where they have money to spend on luxuries like that."

I started walking around the small store, breathing in the overpowering scent of hyacinth. "Then she didn't succeed in driving you out of the region, Kevelyn. Here you are thriving despite the so-called toxic weed."

"Oh, Roz wasn't done with me yet," Kevelyn said. "There was a spot coming up on the executive of the horticultural society. Existing members need to put your name forward and they take a vote, but the president makes the final decision."

I straightened and turned to look at her. "That sounds like trouble."

"Oh my, yes." The original carnation only had enough stem left for a boutonniere, so she set it down with a pucker of disapproval. "I'm not one for politics, but that's what happens in clubs like these. Roz was turning the screws on anyone with clout."

"Especially the president?"

She plucked a new carnation from a bucket. "Edwin Masters was in her smock pocket. I stood no chance at all because of that, so I withdrew my name. It was too stressful."

"That's the president? Is he the one she was having an affair with?"

"An affair? Rosalie?" Kevelyn shook her head hard enough to loosen her topknot and it drooped over one ear. "Not that I knew about." Taking a deep breath, she gently poked the carnation into the sponge. This time it worked. "I mean, I wouldn't put it past her, but bribery was more her style."

I came back to the counter and leaned my elbows on the far end. "Money, or other perks of gardening?" I asked.

"Probably both." One flower followed another into the arrangement as her confidence came back. Obviously she'd been eager to share this story. "Roz had money and influence and she would have used both."

"The spot on the executive was that valuable?"

She finished with a cheery fuchsia gerbera daisy and then used her damp hands to straighten her topknot. "Ivy, there are five seats and they pretty much only open when a member dies. Someone was about to move into a long-term care home and retire from the club. The vote was to happen this week."

"The stakes were pretty high," I said.

"It's the absolute pinnacle of our passion in this region. The indisputable statement that we've made it."

"So Roz was throwing everything she had at the cause."

"Everything. I had nothing going for me in comparison. If only I'd known earlier about the rabbits."

I straightened. "The rabbits? How do they come into it?"

"The executive takes your entire career into account—your contributions to the community, your business and private clients, any media coverage you've had, and of course, personal references. The formal vetting had just begun when the rabbit problem ramped up in Clover Grove. All of Rosalie's garden assets were under siege."

"Oh wow. Now I totally understand why she was so upset when we were there the other day. She could have lost the spot to the rabbits."

"Exactly. I couldn't help but wonder if that was someone's plan all along." She selected a rose from a bucket and winced as a thorn pierced her thumb. "The machinations start well in advance and it was obvious the departing member wasn't going to hold his place forever."

"Seriously? You think someone would concoct a plot like that for a seat on the horticultural executive? Those rabbits were pets. I bet dozens upon dozens have died already."

"I'm just musing aloud," she said. "Like most gardeners, I'm no fan of rabbits. But I wish them no ill. It's not their fault if they were pawns in a dirty game."

I spun in a little circle. "This sounds unfathomable to me, Kevelyn."

She pulled a thorn off the rose and dropped it on the counter. "I'm sure it does, and I wanted you to understand the scope. I know you and Chief Harper will do your due diligence."

Keats gave a mumble beside me and I looked down to see him pointing. On a display case sat a few dozen small jars of honey.

I picked one up and smiled. "Lavender honey. Do you keep hives?"

"Not me. Too dangerous for my tastes. But I like to help out the local economy, like you said."

"Bees fascinate me," I said.

"Me too." Finally her smile was genuine. "It's a natural extension of gardening. Their communities are highly complex, too."

"I'll buy this one," I said. "Lavender reminds me of the inn. My sister pipes it into the air."

"Just take it," Kevelyn said. "You and your pets have done great work for hill country." She came around the counter with the broken off carnation and looked down at Keats. "Would he agree to a boutonniere?"

"I doubt it. He's a hardcore working dog with no patience for appearances. Baths are all drama at our place."

Keats mumbled something sassy just to take back his pride.

"I believe that was a yes," Kevelyn said, bending to stick the carnation through the buckle on his collar. "Very handsome. And a valuable dress rehearsal for the wedding. Now, do you want to order the flowers, or is the bride coming down herself?"

"Let me get the specs and shoot them to you when I get home," I said, slipping the jar of honey into my side pocket. "I want everything to be just right for Jilly. And thank you."

"No problem," she called after me as I walked to the door. "Be careful, Ivy. As you've already seen, the garden mafia can be deadly."

Keats herded me briskly to the truck and I sensed that shopping was off the table. "Garden mafia," I said. "That's a good one."

Percy landed mid-back with 20 claws splayed. Then he climbed onto my shoulder and gave my earlobe a little love bite.

"You're like a rose, Percy," I said. "The perfect mix of beauty and thorns."

Keats gave a ha-ha-ha as he hopped into the passenger seat and then stopped with an urgent mumble.

Getting behind the wheel, I followed his sightline and groaned. "What is *she* doing here?"

CHAPTER TWELVE

K eats' commentary as we pulled out into the late afternoon traffic was halfway between a mumble and a growl. He turned and watched through the back window, where Percy was already in position, tail lashing.

I wasn't the only one who didn't like Justine Schalow.

"I don't need to know her to dislike her," I said. "Normally I try to keep an open mind, but she lost her chance with that rabbit exposé. If she'll put animals at risk just to get a story, we don't want to know her."

Keats offered some advice that sounded a little more evenhanded.

"You're right. I don't want to know her but I do want to know what she's doing. We'll circle back. Fallbrook isn't somewhere you go for an afternoon unless you're in the market for honey. Justine doesn't seem that sweet to me."

Taking the next right off Fallbrook's main drag, I turned again twice. By the time I stopped at the light near the flower store, however, Keats had raised his paw while still staring out the back.

"She's following me? Are you kidding?"

He wasn't kidding.

The new Clover Grove scandalmonger was tailing me in her beat-up grey sedan. I expected her to show interest in our interventions for the rabbits, but chasing me down to Fallbrook likely meant she was prioritizing Rosalie's murder.

"Kellan won't like that, boys," I said. "He won't like that at all. So I feel fully justified in what I'm about to do."

Keats panted an eager "do it do it do it."

I laughed. "You don't always enjoy this. It's rough going, especially when I'm at the wheel."

He repeated the exhortation, clearly willing to take a few bumps for the cause. No sheepdog of his caliber wanted a reporter scooping his story. Or preventing a quick resolution by getting in the way. The more Justine knew, the more she could hamper our work. We were going to have to nip her in the bud.

Keats gave a happy pant. He liked that idea.

"Nip her in the bud, not butt," I said. "She might deserve it, but having my emotional support dog slapped with a muzzle order won't do much for my nerves or yours."

I took a series of fast turns designed to shake the reporter, but she clung like a burr. This wasn't her first tail, that much was clear.

"All right, rabbit hater, you'd better hold on to your poison pen because we're going into the abyss."

The back country trails still felt like an abyss to me, especially when I got too far away from the farm. I could make my way to Dorset Hills pretty easily, and thanks to my father's recent efforts to get me situated, I had some other common routes marked. More importantly, he'd marked the routes to avoid, like the one near Potter's Bog, the Bermuda Triangle of hill country.

"Should I take her there, boys? Let her sedan sink without a trace?"

Keats' mumble became the voice of reason.

"Right. We could slip in, too, and the truck is heavier than the sedan. I don't want to take any of the police away from the investigation. Distractions put the wedding more in peril."

Keats pounded white paws on the dashboard, urging me on.

"Can you get me to Dad's orange route?" I asked, taking a back lane on the edge of town. There had to be half a dozen entry points out here. On the fringes of any local town, the barrier between civilization and the wilderness became porous.

The dog gave a yip and I saw a gap between hedges. It was barely wide enough for the truck and obviously one of the lesser used entry points, but it did the trick.

"Get us home, buddy. Not the hardest way, but hard enough to shake Justine."

At first, I was as nervous as usual. Every trail looked much the same, with obstacles in the form of trees, boulders, creeks, marshes and small cliffs. Keats stuck his muzzle out the window to sniff for molecules of Clover Grove and periodically redirected me with pokes in the arm and taps on the dashboard. I caught a few glimpses of the sedan in the mirrors but they got fewer and fewer. Justine was falling behind.

Eventually, Keats offered a point and I looked up. Splotches of orange paint on trees above our normal sightline told me we'd found Dad's trail. All I had to do was stay the course now.

Knowing I was close to home meant I could pick up speed, at least as much as the truck and the pets could handle. My teeth clacked together when I took one hill too fast and my hip hit the console hard coming down.

The smell of honey quickly filled the car.

"That's going to be hard to clean," I said, as Percy retreated to the footwell in the back. I suspected he had a trace of motion sickness and even my stomach was getting queasy.

"Whew." I let up on the gas as we cruised down the lane to the farm. "It's good to be home."

That relief turned to guilt when I saw Kellan's SUV parked

beside the barn. Outrunning a reporter on the back country trails wouldn't qualify as being careful to him.

"Don't tell him," I said, pulling in beside his vehicle. "Omission isn't the same as lying."

Keats' mumble suggested Kellan might not agree with my loose interpretation of the truth.

"Fine, but he's been known to skip a few details with me, too, remember. Do we know what he got in that envelope from Vernie Cobbler's safe? No, we do not."

The dog walked over to me and yipped to have the door opened. It was a "let the games continue" sort of sound.

Kellan was so focused he didn't initially notice us when I walked through the barn and out the other side. He was wearing jeans and a leather jacket, and my breath caught in my throat when I realized anew how handsome he was. It took me by surprise every time.

Today he was even more so because he was up on top of my manure pile driving a spade into the muck. The spade was shiny and still had the price tag on the side.

"Hey," I said. "You bought your own spade? What was wrong with mine?"

"Old and clunky." He drove the spade in hard and left it there. Then he walked down the "stairs" that were bigger than I'd left them. He'd carved them out more to accommodate his bigger boots. "You deserve the very finest in farm implements. Consider it a gift to both of us."

"You certainly know the way to my heart, Chief. I'll think of you whenever I use it."

"I want my own line of fertilizer," he said, kissing my cheek. "Let's call it the Bold and Blue special."

I laughed. "We'll need a recipe. I suppose you'll want to feature high notes from Elaine, the emu, since she's named after your aunt. But it's all about balance and the fit with our local ecosystem."

He stepped back and rested his hands on my shoulders. "Why are you flushed? Your ears are bright red."

I touched one ear and found it hot. It was annoying to have such a visible "tell." "I'm still annoyed at Justine Schalow. She followed me today."

His brow furrowed. "Followed you where?"

"Down to Fallbrook. I wanted to see if I could line up bouquets and such for the wedding."

"At Fallbrook Flowers? Where Kevelyn Welsh works?" He took another step back and his hands dropped from my shoulders. "The florist Rosalie Roarke reputedly drove out of Clover Grove."

"That's the one." I tried to meet his eyes and failed. "Mandy said she did good work and we're in a bit of a bind with only a few days to go. I wanted to make our case in person and see her work firsthand."

"Uh-huh." He crossed his arms. "I don't suppose you mentioned Rosalie at all."

I shrugged. "She came up in passing. Kevelyn is still bitter about what happened and I don't blame her. It seems like the garden community really bites."

"You can tell me all about it on our drive," he said.

"Our drive? Are we going to Clover Grove Gardens?"

I didn't feel excited about the prospect and his grim expression suggested he didn't, either.

He shook his head. "I don't feel right about enjoying our special place when Asher and Jilly have been driven out of theirs. The cemetery is crawling with officers. We had to set up a tent around some of the monuments. Some of my staff are uncomfortable being inside with the remains of Earl Spratt."

"Earl Spratt! What's he doing there?"

"He was buried on his former property and the town couldn't rightly put him back there. So now he's rubbing shoulders, as it were, with the Bingham family."

"Hazel's father would have been outraged."

Kellan sighed. "The umbrage of the deceased is outside my purview, thank goodness."

"You know who I haven't checked out yet?" I asked. "Lita Peebles and Joyce Hustings. Both women were caught up in garden club politics."

"Alibis," he said. "My team made good headway, today."

He led me out of the barn and opened the back door of his SUV. Keats jumped right in, but Percy backed away.

"Percy, come on," I said, trying to catch him. "Whatever Kellan has planned, I'm sure you'll enjoy it."

"What's with him?" Kellan said, as the cat repeatedly dodged me. "Never known him to turn down an adventure."

"I think he's been getting motion sickness," I said. "Just lately."

Keats gave a ha-ha-ha.

When I straightened, Kellan was staring at me. "Your ears are even redder. And I keep noticing the smell of honey. What are you hiding?"

"I told you about Fallbrook already," I said, looking down at the sticky stain on my overalls.

He turned to check out the truck with the keen eye of the professional investigator. "Fresh mud splatter. You took the trails home and at some speed, too. What on earth were you doing, Ivy?"

Keats urged me to spill it with a mumble.

"Outrunning Justine Schalow," I said. "She was loitering outside the flower store, so I assume she followed me there. I decided to take her on a tour of the back country. You know, like our town's version of a housewarming party."

He shook his head but his lips twitched, too. "You could have caused damage to your truck, yourself and your pets. Not to mention Justine. Where is she now?"

"No idea. I lost her even before we found Dad's orange trail markers. His system is genius, Kellan. As long as I stick with his map, I'll always make it home."

He pulled out his phone and texted someone. After a second he looked up. "No calls at the station from the reporter. You'd better hope she doesn't fall into Potter's Bog. It'll be on you, Ivy."

"I can live with that."

"Well, I can't live with police resources being diverted to rescue," he said. "Any delay is on you, too."

"Justine will be fine. Edna says she's one of the cockroach people. The ones that will not only survive but thrive after the apocalypse."

"Listen, you're not getting honey all over my car. Nor am I sitting in the driver's seat you just left sticky."

I couldn't blame him for that. "I've got spare overalls in the barn. Let Percy stay home if he wants."

Instead, Kellan knelt to press Percy again. "Come on, my fluffy friend. I promise you a smoother ride. And I need you."

I stopped in the barn doorway. "Sounds like we're investigating instead of romancing."

"We can do both," he said. "Probably. My wooing game might be off till I get your brother married this week. I'm feeling more pressure because of that."

"Yeah, me too. Postponing will devastate Asher."

"Not Jilly?" Kellan asked, with a quizzical look.

"She's more about the marriage than the party," I said. "It's gotten too big and showy for her. Asher's invited half the town out of sheer joy and Mom's invited the other half to show off."

"I see Jilly's point," he said. "We'll definitely want to take a different approach."

My ears got hot again at the mention of our future nuptials, but before I could open a dialogue, he lured the cat into the SUV and closed the door. Then he looked at me again and said, "Go."

His expression had switched from boyfriend to cop. It was like a mask he slipped on and off without effort.

When I came out in older, rattier overalls, he held the passenger door open for me.

"I know we agreed to team up more on this case for the good of the wedding," he said, "but it's going to be hard to focus knowing you're ripping around the back country in a completely unnecessary race." Keats mumbled something sassy and Kellan continued, "Yes, I had plenty of unnecessary races back in the day, but it wasn't while there was a killer at large and an investigation underway."

I took a moment and then spoke. "Justine Schalow shouldn't be chasing this investigation, either. She doesn't have my experience, or more importantly, my team."

Taking that as an invitation, Keats climbed through the seats and into my lap.

"I'll speak to her when I return the camera you dropped off," Kellan said. "I don't want her tailing anyone or writing about it, either. She could jeopardize her safety and the case."

"We managed just fine without a newspaper for months. There are bigger towns she could have chosen. Why Clover Grove?"

He checked my pants to make sure they were clean before patting my knee. "Could it be because we currently have the highest rate of serious crime throughout all of hill country? That's a journalist's dream come true."

"Then why work the rabbit angle? She could be looking into rising crime and figuring out why you've staffed up."

He cracked a smile as he drove down the lane. "I think it's pretty obvious why I staffed up."

"Don't make me wait for the next news cycle to find out."

"Simple. Edna finally convinced me about the end times. I'm staffing for the apocalypse."

"Very funny." I picked up his hand and put it back on his own knee. "You don't trust me with important information."

"Important policing information that hasn't been fully verified," he said. "When I can tell you I will tell you." He raised his palm before I could ask. "Asher doesn't know, either. Only my superiors."

"Fine," I said. "I'll wait to hear it from the rumor mill."

"They're too busy to take your call right now," he said. "The town's abuzz over the videos of Edna detonating Rosalie Roarke's garden."

I looked at him quickly. "You released a security feed?"

"Of course not. A neighbor filmed it. Aubrey Wagner."

"Aubrey? Why would he share that? He and Roz were friends."

"It wasn't intentional. He was trying to send the footage to me and it went to Tizzy Cousins by mistake. At any rate, it's making the rounds."

I rubbed my forehead. "That's not good."

"Really not good," he said. "Not only was I prevented from gathering possible evidence, but—"

"It looks like we were utterly disrespectful of a woman who's barely cold."

"Precisely. Edna sure had fun."

I grabbed his hand and put it back on my leg. "I'm sorry. I asked her not to, but there was something about the buried landmines that brought out the worst in her."

He left his hand on my knee. "Or the best, depending on how you look at it. When I'm off duty, I admire her zest for life. I can only hope we're like that at her age." He paused and added quickly, "Not quite like that."

"Back country races still on your menu?" I asked.

"As long as my old bones can take it." He squeezed my hand. "After all, that's how I won permission to date you."

"Speaking of dates," I said. "Where exactly are we going this evening?"

"It's a surprise," he said. "But you're going to love the vibe. Garnet Point has nothing on this place."

He turned the car into a parking lot, and I said, "Oh, no."

CHAPTER THIRTEEN

"This isn't exactly what I had in mind, Kellan," I said, staring up at the tall twin gates of Clover Grove Cemetery. "As much as I love a mystery, sometimes a division between work and fun is a good thing."

"I keep trying to tell you that but you like to blur the lines," he said, pulling out a big key chain and finding the right one to unlock the doors.

I glared at him. "We'll be surrounded by the earthly remains of too many people I knew. Once their case is closed, I'd just as soon leave them to their eternal rest. Visiting only reminds me about what happened. They call it PTSD for a reason. The trauma's real."

He let the pets through the gates and then ushered me inside. After locking the gates, he took my hand. "I'm right here with you. We'll avoid any past victims of violence."

"Well, if you're thinking this can be our new meetup place, maybe dig a little deeper." I looked over and saw a tarp covering an empty grave. It wasn't there the day before. Were they preparing for Rosalie, or had someone else passed that I didn't know about? They were probably in a hurry because the ground would freeze before long, delaying interment till spring.

Kellan pulled me along quickly past the new grave. "This definitely isn't on my list as a replacement. We can reclaim the garden again. It's been our place for decades. Plus we have Garnet Point."

"Garnet Point is a good contender," I said. "But harder in winter."

"Let's worry about that later. We've got another pressing matter." He swept his hand around. "Them."

We had a long-eared audience. Dozens of rabbits sat on the grass among the tombstones. The gray one with the scarred ear was back and parked beside Vernie's marker.

"If we're going to catch some of them, we're poorly equipped," I said. "Want to stuff a couple in your jacket?"

My boyfriend tried to repress a shudder and failed. "I don't care to stuff my best leather jacket full of rodents."

"They're not rodents," I said. "They're lagomorphs."

He released my hand and zipped his jacket to his chin. "I don't care to have them hopping loose in my car, either. Especially with Keats and Percy along for the ride. That kind of mayhem isn't good for road safety. As Chief of Police, I need to set an example."

"Especially now that Justine's revived the Tattler. A story like that would increase subscriptions."

"Not going to happen," he said. "When the investigation is complete, you and the Mafia can do whatever's needed to extract these rabbits. For now, I just want to find their headquarters. I've sent my people all through the cemetery with no success. It was time to call in special officers Keats and Percy."

"Ah. I see. Once again my pets are the main event and I'm the side dish." I smiled, though. When Kellan consulted with Keats and Percy, it warmed my heart. To my mind, it said he saw and accepted me as I was, with all my eccentricities. Sometimes I wished he had more eccentricities himself. He was probably the most balanced and stable person I knew—even more than Jilly—and it made me feel a little outclassed. At the same time, I was profoundly grateful that he had those qualities.

Keats mumbled something and circled back to poke at my fingers with his nose, which was damp from the dew forming on the grass as the sun sank behind the trees and high walls. As always, the dog sensed when I needed a little canine reassurance, and he put his excitement over the rabbits on the back burner to fulfill his primary duty. His next mumble advised me in no uncertain terms that Kellan was getting a good deal, too. As far as the dog was concerned, the better deal, in fact. That made me smile again.

"What's that about?" Kellan asked. "You two are having a private conversation."

I turned the smile on him. "I wish I could communicate as effectively with the rabbits." I pointed at the bunny on Vernie's grave. "That one is trying."

"Which one?" he asked, peering around. "They all look the same to me."

"The same? They're snowflakes! Every single one is different."

Keats gave a pant-laugh to let me know my boyfriend was teasing me. Sometimes I got too invested in animals to see the humor. Especially in inhospitable surroundings, like a cemetery where people were supposed to arrive already dead, unlike Rosalie Roarke.

I reached for Kellan's hand, and as his fingers laced through mine, romance insinuated itself up my arm and into my heart. We really did have interesting dates. I was a lucky gal.

The gray rabbit hopped ahead of us, with Keats and Percy following as closely as I'd allow. The boys' tails were up, and the white tip of the dog's tail made him easy to follow in the gloom that quickly deepened as we entered the old part of the cemetery.

"Why are you so keen on finding rabbit headquarters?" I asked. "I didn't expect that to be high on your priority list."

"It's high on other people's priority list," he said. "Thanks to the news, people are constantly encroaching on my crime scene. I've had officers on patrol around the clock in a wider radius than usual. Families show up with nets, claiming they want to find their lost pet. Or take in a new one. Their hearts are probably in the right place."

"I wish others had been so kindhearted when they set their rabbits free. But I suppose no one realized the implications."

"At least if we can find the colony I can cordon it off and deploy staff efficiently. If they're constantly redirecting spectators, they're not helping solve the murder."

"Keats and Percy will find the warren," I said. "Cori and crew have been looking but your staff turned them away, too."

"Trust me, I know. One day I'll haul Cori Hogan in for harassment by text."

"She's worried the rabbits will go to careless owners. Cori always puts animals first."

He waved his free hand. "Can we leave Cori out of date night? She steals my buzz."

We were passing the police tents and yellow tape now. I tried to push the image of Rosalie out of my mind. Not to mention Earl Spratt, a truly horrible man.

"If you're getting any kind of buzz from this date, you really are perfect for me," I said.

"Was there room for doubt? I thought I was done proving myself."

Weaving through the headstones, I towed him after me. "Are we ever done proving ourselves to the people we love? I consider it a daily practice. Like gathering eggs and—"

"Please don't compare our relationship to mucking out stalls," he said. "What we've got here isn't a chore, is it?"

"You're looking at it all wrong. I think of chores as rituals that give structure to my day and remind me to be grateful for everything I have." I gave his hand a squeeze. "Which is a lot."

He came up beside me after we passed a decaying stone that

bore the surname of one of the founding families. We were among the town's so-called elite now.

"Ivy, only you could compare me to feeding a pig and lift my heart at the same time." He released my hand and dropped his arm around my shoulders. "And the town elders all witnessed it."

I winced at the thought. "I don't like to think they're still hanging around. Hopefully they've long since moved on to whatever awaits us beyond."

He squeezed me tighter. "What awaits us is probably a far different fate. There was corruption in these parts even before townships formed."

"Step lightly, then," I said. "We don't want to annoy anyone."

"I think we're safe enough here. It's their descendants I worry about."

I turned quickly to stare up at his profile, still clear in the last of the light. "Whose descendants? Is this about what you found in Vernie's safe?"

"Look," he said. "Keats has found something."

At first, I thought he was throwing me off the trail. He probably was, but it was also true. Keats had lifted one paw in a point.

"Is he looking at the wall?" I asked, before noticing the dog's muzzle dip down. "Ah. Holes. Two, three, even more. All about a foot in diameter. He's found the rabbit underpass." Stepping back, I looked up. "Does that mean we need to use the overpass?"

Kellan laughed. "Happily, no. I mean, we could, if you're looking to add some spice to our routine. But I'd hate to rip my favorite jacket on those barbs."

"What then? Do we go back and walk around outside?"

He took a key ring from his pocket and jangled them. "Boys, show us the door."

"Another door? Sweet!"

Two tails rose like flags as they led us along the rear wall of the cemetery to the corner.

"Did Rosalie have a key?" I asked.

Kellan nodded. "As head of the garden club, she had access to the cemetery and public gardens. We haven't been able to find the key, which means the killer may have it."

"I was afraid you'd say that."

The heavy wooden door was the same color as the wall and was shielded by overgrown shrubs. Keats went into another point and Kellan switched on a high-powered flashlight to show me where the soil had been disturbed.

"There were footprints," he said. "One of them clear. It was bigger than Rosalie's but could have belonged to either a man or a woman."

"Anything distinctive about it?" I asked.

He shook his head. "Same rubber boots worn by the majority of homesteaders and gardeners in our region."

Keats took a good sniff around but came up empty, judging by his noncommittal mumble. Percy, meanwhile, started to scale the brick wall by digging his claws into the gaps in the mortar. I plucked him off and tucked him under my arm. "Let's stick closer together, boys. The terrain is likely far tougher out there."

I was right about that. Keats took the lead and Kellan followed, shining the powerful flashlight and moving branches to break trail for us. Percy eventually squirmed his way out of my grip and ran ahead to join Keats. He didn't like being coddled during an expedition.

There was a big reveal coming, I suspected, because Keats was offering a running commentary. He was far enough ahead that I could barely make out his tone but it sounded like he was practically burbling.

A snippy yip sailed back to me. This dog *never* burbled. He was just enjoying his work, as a sheepdog should.

Kellan turned back and directed the light offside so it didn't blind me. "Are you okay? I expected more complaining about our date destination."

"Not at all. I mean, I'd prefer to show up for the wedding photos without a missing eye, but working to help animals is my calling."

"Crime-solving is just your side hustle? Seems like you've been gearing up to go pro lately."

"My vote goes to the animals every time," I said. "But maybe when you retire we can hang our PI shingle together."

He flashed his teeth in a grin and turned back when Keats issued a command to get a move on it. "Yes, sir!"

The woods opened to a clearing that was about twice the diameter of my barn. It looked like any other clearing until a pair of white ears popped out of a grassy mound in the middle.

Keats started to raise his paw, realized it was unnecessary and settled for a mumble of triumph.

"It doesn't look like much," I said. "I guess I was expecting something grand from a word like 'colony.'"

"Business on top and a party underneath," Kellan said. "We might be standing on a nursery way over here. Their doubling rate is insane. There are plenty of foxes and hawks around here, but they can't keep up."

"That's partly because people started dumping after word got around," I said. "Cori's asked around and there are reports of people commuting up the range to set their rabbits free. It doesn't seem to occur to them that they were bred for captivity and don't have the wherewithal to survive out here."

"Except that they have," he said. "I don't know if they could handle our winter, but they've done well so far."

Ears were popping up all over, and as they decided we came in peace, a few dozen rabbits emerged.

"I didn't even know they came in so many flavors," Kellan said. Before I could protest, he added, "Poor choice of words. I'm just shocked by the array of coats, colors and sizes."

"They're so beautiful. It hurts my heart that people want to kill them. Do you think the town will step in?"

"I don't know, Ivy. The tax base is primarily homesteaders and farmers. This crew represents a lot of damage to crops and gardens. There won't be much canning this year."

"You'll let us get them out, then, right? Now that we've found headquarters, we can do the extraction."

He shone the light around the clearing. "It won't be easy, even with Cori's expertise. The rabbits chose this place for its shelter and multiple escape routes."

"The Mafia will figure it out. They always do." I took his hand again. "But we'll need to move fast. It's a lot easier and faster to exterminate than extract a hundred rabbits."

"Possibly more," he said. "Say goodnight to the lagomorphs and let me look into it. For now, I have a murder to solve and a long night ahead."

As my furry tour guides led us around the outside wall to the cemetery parking lot, I asked, "Do you think Rosalie's death had anything to do with the rabbit problem?"

This time he did let the light hit my face and I squinted. "There are plenty of suspects, as you know. Possibly too many to process before our desired deadline. What I can tell you, in the spirit of teamwork, is that she was definitely poisoned. We just don't have confirmation of the type, yet."

"It looked like yew," I said.

"Pardon me?"

"In her mouth," I said, over Keats' pant-laugh. "Yew berries. That's what happened with Felix Milloy, remember?"

"There was yew," he confirmed. "Also castor bean, oleander and something called rosary pea. The killer was leaving nothing to chance."

"Then we need to look in the gardens of everyone in the club," I said. "Keats will be able to sniff that stuff out."

The dog mumbled a confident affirmative.

"Let us verify the toxin, first," Kellan said. "And remember, if it looks too obvious, it usually is."

"That's the problem," I said. "Our local killers are too smart. I expected them to be as stupid as Skint, the guy who owned Keats. It wasn't that hard to figure out his game."

"I think you've hit on something there," he said. "We've got some wily killers and historical underpinnings here that make things interesting."

We walked along the cemetery wall and turned the corner. The parking lot seemed bright after the bush, but Kellan kept his flashlight on.

Just as I noticed a sedan tucked into the woods on the other side of the parking lot, Keats went into a point.

"Now that *is* interesting," I said, gesturing to a spot at the top of the wall. "There may not be much canning this year, but someone's in a real pickle."

CHAPTER FOURTEEN

Kellan could look and sound very imposing when he was riled, and he unleashed the full force of that power now, along with the strong beam of his flashlight.

"Ms. Schalow, get down here at once. Do you think yellow hazard tape doesn't apply to you?"

"I have a press pass," Justine said, shielding her eyes with one hand. There was a trace of a smirk on her face and I had to give her points for courage under pressure.

She was straddling the top of the wall between two long iron spikes. Few could have fit into that tight spot without puncturing an organ or two. It must have been dreadfully uncomfortable.

"Press passes work at a film premiere, not a crime scene," Kellan said. "I'm not sure where you practiced journalism before."

"We don't have a movie theater," I said. "Do we?"

Kellan flicked his eyes at me with a silent warning not to undermine him. I decided to comply, or at least give it a good try, which was more than could be said for the sheepdog who was pant-laughing at my side.

"I was just stopping by to feed the bunnies, Chief Harper,"

Justine said, kicking a white sneaker as she tried to readjust her seating. "I broke their story. I feel a responsibility to help."

"Help?" The word slipped out before I could stop it, and Kellan closed one hand around my forearm to keep me quiet.

"Yes, help," she said. "I know all about you, Ivy Galloway, and you're not the only one around here who cares about animal welfare."

Kellan's fingers were like a vise but I still had to bite the inside of my cheek to stop the flow of caustic words that wanted to gush out. They would probably only splash back in my face. That's how angry words usually worked.

I dropped my free hand and Keats offered his ears to calm me. Kellan must have felt my inner energy shift because he released my arm and crossed his own.

"Get down, Ms. Schalow. Now." His tone was even. Calm. Implacable.

"At the risk of stating the obvious, Chief, I would if I could." She tossed her scraggly ponytail defiantly but there was an undercurrent of something else in her voice. "I'm in a bit of a—"

"Pickle?" I asked.

"Something like that," she said. "My shirt hooked through a spike and I'm stuck."

Wearing baggy clothes was never a good idea on a mission like this, as I knew too well. My overalls were a hindrance going up, over and under. I wore stretchy black pants when I had a plan in advance and paid the price when I didn't.

"Chief, could you just pop inside and pick up my ladder? Otherwise, I'm coming down the hard way, and you'll have to catch me."

"I could call the fire department," he said, pulling out his phone. "They'd be here in ten minutes or so. If they're not dealing with a real emergency."

"Humpty Dumpty sat on a wall," I said. "Humpty Dumpty had a—"

"Ivy," Kellan interrupted, as he turned and walked away. "Can you stay out here while I get the ladder? I need you to—"

"Play nice, Ivy," Justine said, with a bigger smirk. "We can get to know each other while the chief keeps me from having that great fall you're rhyming about. Mind you, it's only eight feet. Hardly terminal."

"Depends on whether you crack your head open," Kellan called back. "Remember, all the king's horses..."

"A sense of humor," Justine said, as his voice faded. "Rare in a cop."

I kept my fingertips on Keats. "A head injury is nothing to joke about, Justine."

She stared down at me with eyes that looked hazel, like mine. I hoped that's where the resemblance ended.

"You would know," she said. "Heard you got clobbered saving your dog."

Her comment would probably have stung had it not been for my close contact with said dog. Thinking about my battle with Skint—my first true battle with anyone—could bring on crippling PTSD flashbacks. But not with Keats present and on duty.

He mumbled something that was simultaneously encouraging and chiding. It sounded like a reminder not to fall for the bait people like Justine casually tossed from above. I'd evaded plenty of manipulative reporters before, not to mention sociopaths.

"Best day of my life," I said, tipping my head back and directing a smile at her. It was my very best HR smile. The one designed to take back the upper hand. Each time I dug into my tool chest and found it there, I felt a whoosh of relief. As much as I loathed my old corporate life, there was no question that it had given me strength and skills. "So far."

"That's saying something," she said. "Because you've had a lot of big days. So far."

I shrugged. "I do what I can to help the community."

"Me too. That's what a good journalist does. And I could see this community needed help more than any other in hill country. Your poor boyfriend can't stay on top of crime. It's all anyone talks about at every coffee shop and gas station on the way up the range. His name comes up at every dinner table. So does yours."

Keats gave another warning mumble. The bait was getting harder to resist. I could taste blood from biting my cheek so hard.

"That's interesting." I made sure my tone was flat. Another gift HR gave me was the ability to strip emotion out of my voice at will. "Do you mind if I ask how you came upon the rabbit story, Justine? Did you get a hot tip?"

Her ponytail made a swishing sound over the waterproof fabric of her black jacket. "No hot tips. I just did what I usually do when I arrive in a new town. Took a tour. The cemetery is always a good place to start, because you learn family names, and see recent additions, if you catch my drift. Verna Rae Cobbler had fresh grass and plenty of flowers, and as a result, plenty of long-eared visitors. At first I couldn't make head nor tail out of the abundance of bunnies. But a trip to town hall enlightened me."

"They talked to you about the rabbits?" My HR neutrality slipped and showed my surprise.

"Oh, Ivy. Poor naïve Ivy. Don't tell me you trusted politicians to be open about a problem. Or put animals first."

"Our mayor has done just that many times," I said.

Justine had a smug smile on her face that I wanted to slap off. Keats' grumble said the same. Lucky for her she had the height advantage. Otherwise, she'd have felt sheepdog teeth in her calf.

"She's done the opposite as many times. You just don't know about it." Her smug smile grew. "I hope you didn't think you were friends, Ivy. Politicians really aren't capable. When you've been in my position, you learn all about that."

There was no question I had plenty of weaknesses, but naïveté wasn't among them. If anything, I was too cynical. So, for the moment, I'd give Mayor Martingale the benefit of the doubt.

"I wouldn't actually want to be in your position, Justine," I said. "It looks mighty uncomfortable."

There was a clatter of metal on the other side. Kellan had found the ladder. I expected him to set it up inside, but he decided to leave Justine stranded a little longer. It was better to bring her down outside, where she couldn't pull any funny business.

Disappointment flickered across her face as she watched the flashlight bob away on the other side. "You get yourself into some tight spots too, right, Ivy?"

"Anything to help animals," I said.

"Same." She shifted a little and her grip on the spike tightened till her knuckles showed white.

"Did you really think your exposé was helping the rabbits?" I asked. "Because from where I stand, it put a target on their sides. They didn't ask to be set free. The fact that they've managed to thrive in the wild is remarkable."

"But they've done a lot of damage," she said. "And now some-one's died because of them."

"You don't know that's true." I tipped my head to one side. "But if it is, maybe it wouldn't have happened if you'd left it with the politicians. Has that occurred to you?"

She mirrored my head tilt. "Are you suggesting Rosalie Roarke's murder is my fault?"

"Of course not. You didn't stab her, I'm sure."

Now she tipped her head the other way. Stuck as she was, her moves were limited. "Nice try, Ivy. I know she was poisoned, and with what."

"Really? Then your connections are better than mine. And I thought mine were good."

"You don't survive in journalism without making connections." Her smug smile came back. "It pays to be nice, you see."

All I could see in that moment was an orange cat climbing up the vines. He was making good headway and intervening in this situation was more likely to hurt than help.

"It's not nice to take photos of people trying on clothes," I said. "Yet there you were outside Chez Belle today."

"People want a society column," she said. "Gossip sells papers."

I took out my phone and took a photo of her. "Snap for snap."

Finally, her face scrunched in annoyance. "You can delete that, just like I'm sure the chief deleted my photos. Anyway, I'm just doing my job. Keeping people informed."

Percy was on top of the wall and assessing the best way to maneuver around the ironwork. His green eyes met mine and I shook my head slightly. As detestable as I found Justine, I didn't want her to fall on the pavement. I preferred to defeat her the hard way, by giving her enough rope to hang herself.

"I think you did the rabbits an ill turn," I said. "Don't be surprised if that comes around to bite you in the butt. Did you know their teeth never stop growing?"

She tried to shrug without losing her grip. "Not that interested in rabbits, to be honest. But I'd love to hear about how you've single-handedly sent the crime rate spiraling out of control in Clover Grove."

Out came my HR smile again. "Is that what they're saying at the gas pumps? And over casseroles at dinner tables? Because it's giving me way too much credit."

"Exactly what I said. You're just a pawn, Ivy, and I'm going to prove it."

"A pawn? How so?"

She adjusted her seating again and I had a sneaking admiration that she could play her games from a perch like that. Unfortunately, it meant she was a worthy adversary.

"It can't be a coincidence so many people have died since you came back," she said. "Even you must wonder."

Many a night I lay awake wondering about that very thing, but my smile still held. "Sometimes it really is a coincidence. At least, so the chief tells me. He would know."

"There you go again, being naïve," she said. "Chief Harper doesn't know any more than you do. You're both pawns and I intend to blow the top off this story."

Percy had other plans for her, at least in the short term. He picked his way around the spikes with feline grace and dogged determination.

"That's a really bad idea, Justine," I said. "You don't know how things work around here."

"And you do? Seems like you're the one nearly getting herself killed on a constant loop."

I couldn't help laughing. "You're not wrong. But now you're the one stranded, and you know why? Because I have something you don't."

There was another flip of her impudent ponytail. "Do enlighten me about your magic shield, Wonder Woman."

"There's no magic," I said. "Just community. Friends and family, furry and otherwise. Give yourself time to develop that foundation before you tempt fate like this again."

Holding the spike with both hands, she leaned perilously over the edge. "I don't need advice from you."

"I hate unsolicited advice, too," I said. "But there's something you really should know. Right now."

"Yeah? What's that?"

I pointed to the fluffy orange menace. "Percy, stop please. Let Justine stand or fall on her own."

Her gaze followed mine and she frowned. "I've never really liked pets. Reporters can't afford to be tied down."

"I can't afford *not* to be tied down. That's what I was trying to tell you about community."

"Shoo," she said to Percy. "You'll make me—"

A sneeze cut her off. Followed by another.

"Percy, back away," I said. "She'll fall and I can't catch her."

The cat held his position, tail curling around a spike.

"Go," Justine said, chafing at her eyes with her Gore-Tex sleeve. "I'll throw you off this wall, cat."

Keats mumbled a warning, either to Justine or Percy.

Neither one listened and the reporter leaned forward to swat at the cat. If he hadn't seen it coming, it might very well have knocked him off the wall. Instead, he hooked his paw around the spot where the iron connected to brick.

"Don't you dare hit my cat," I said, moving under the wall with arms outstretched. "Percy, come down. Try not to gouge my face before the wedding."

"Your brother's wedding is doomed," Justine said. "In fact, the marriage is doomed. It's obvious."

That sent a rush of rage through me. She could say what she liked about me, but not Jilly and my brother. They were innocent victims of her news story and whatever else she was trying to stir up here.

I was about to tell her so when I noticed that Percy had stopped his advance. He was making scraping motions on the top of the brick wall. The spikes prevented the full sweep of his litterbox move, but he was still making a strong pronouncement. Normally, that move signified someone's departure from the planet, but Justine was very much alive.

"Don't say that, Percy. Please." There was a note of panic in my voice. I didn't want Justine dead, and certainly not this week, or she'd be correct that the wedding was doomed.

"So, you really do talk to your animals," she said. "You're as crazy as people say."

She leaned over to take another swing at Percy, triggering exactly what the cat had predicted.

The movement made her lose her grip and her balance. Her arms flailed.

Then came the sounds of tearing fabric, a clatter of metal and a scream.

CHAPTER FIFTEEN

K ellan turned to me with Justine in his arms. "That was close."
A canine grumble beside me suggested, "Not close
enough."

"Put me down," she said. "And tell that dog to shut up."

The fact that she could understand Keats' tone notched her up
in my estimation. Only slightly.

"He thinks you're rude," I said. "You didn't even thank the chief.
You could have broken a limb. Or one of his."

Justine squirmed in Kellan's arms but he had no trouble
restraining her. She reminded me of Elaine, my emu. Layers of
clothing concealed a slight, gangly body.

Maybe the same thought occurred to Kellan because he set her
on her sneakers so abruptly that she nearly lost her balance again.

Keats started to go in for a nip but I snapped my fingers to hold
him back. There was a jangle of handcuffs and I liked the direction
this was going.

With a few easy moves, Kellan pushed her against the wall and
pulled her hands behind her. He cuffed one wrist, walked her backward and then pulled her arms around a maple tree aflame with
orange leaves. Then he snapped the other cuff closed.

Justine thrashed against the tree. "You can't cuff me. What are the charges?"

He pulled out his phone and walked away.

"Trespassing?" I suggested. "Being a public menace? Animal abuse? A night in the slammer might enlighten you." I couldn't help smiling for real this time. "You did say you liked to be enlightened."

"I'm sure you've warmed the cell up for me," she said. "You've done worse."

Keats didn't hold back this time, and seeing her jump was almost as satisfying as hearing her squeal when his teeth connected. I knew how much that little pinch hurt. Sometimes it left a bruise.

"Ow! Tell him to stop that. And tell the cat to stop looking at me, too."

Percy was still on top of the wall, with his tail wrapped neatly around his paws. He looked quite pleased about his role in apprehending a pest.

I signaled for the cat to come down and circled back to the conversation.

"I've trespassed, too," I admitted. "In the interests of protecting the public and especially animals. So far, I've evaded a cell."

"I've survived worse. And it won't stop me from pursuing my story."

"The rabbit story is under control. Leave it alone, Justine."

"That's not the story anymore, obviously," she said, still pulling against the maple tree. "I intend to figure out who killed Rosalie Roarke and why. And then how it all ties in with you."

"That'll keep you busy," I said, "because it has nothing to do with me."

Kellan put the phone back in his pocket. "Thanks for giving me more reason to detain you, Ms. Schalow. If you're intending to impede my investigation, you'd be safer in lockup."

"I have a lawyer, Chief. You've got nothing on me."

"We'll see about that," he said. "Pretty sure I've got a couple of ladders with your prints on them. That's a good start."

My brain did the math. "She was here the night of the murder?"

"I never went in," she said. "Ivy and her posse arrived first. So I just sat in my car in the bushes down there till I heard sirens."

"Do we believe that?" I asked Kellan. "A reporter normally runs toward trouble, not away from it."

"I'll wait for my lawyer," she said.

A police SUV pulled up and my brother hopped out. "I'll take her in, Chief. It beats the rabbit security detail."

Kellan shook his head and tossed his key to Asher. "I want to have a private chat with Ms. Schalow. Just put her in the back of your car and use mine to drive Ivy home."

Asher looked disappointed. I could imagine that standing for hours in the darkness protecting rabbits wasn't exactly fascinating. It probably gave him too much time to think, and my brother was a man of action.

"Chief, you're off duty," Asher said.

"Technically, I'm never off duty," Kellan said. "Especially when there's a killer at large."

"Which is pretty much always," Justine said. "This town is the wild west of hill country."

"Justine tells me they're talking about us at every gas pump all the way up the range," I said. "You in particular, Kellan, but I'm a hit at the dinner table."

Asher stared at Justine and then turned to his boss. "What if she tripped on the way to the car? Got a little road rash?"

Kellan pressed his lips together. "I know you're joking, Officer Galloway, and so does this reporter. But she wouldn't hesitate to use that comment."

"Correct," Justine said. "In a story of small-town police brutality."

"I misspoke," Asher said. "Let me carry you to the car if you prefer. You look distraught."

"I'm not distraught," she snapped. "Except over being unfairly cuffed."

"After a fall like that you'll be in shock," I said. "Not sound of mind."

"Speak for yourself." She kicked wildly with one sneaker, trying to connect with Keats. "As for your savage dog, he's going to pay for this."

Kellan intervened before I could respond. "Officer Galloway. Please help this traumatized woman to the car now, before her threats get her into even more trouble."

My brother did as he was asked, handling Justine Schalow like precious cargo as she thrashed all the way to the police SUV. Once she was locked inside he turned and shook his head. "Feisty one. Sure you want to handle her alone, Chief?"

"Yeah, I don't want to take anyone else off site. So as soon as you drop Ivy and the pets home, go back to your post." He squeezed my shoulder. "Do me a favor and stay there, Ivy. I'm going to be tied up for a while."

I nodded. "I've had enough for one day. That reporter stole my spark."

Walking to the police car, he said, "You'll find it on the farm. Do a little dance with Alvina."

"Good idea," I called, as Keats guided Asher, Percy and me to Kellan's SUV. "I like the way you think."

My brother waited till Kellan's taillights faded in the distance before driving out of the parking lot. He signaled a turn toward the farm and I touched his arm. "Asher, would you mind if we run a little errand in town first?"

"Yes, I mind. You heard the chief. He wants you to go home and stay home."

"I know, but this isn't about the murder or the rabbits. It's about the wedding," I said. "Kellan wouldn't mind a wedding errand, would he?"

My brother's brow furrowed as he turned to shoot blue eyes at me. He'd inherited those eyes and fair hair from our father, whereas all five Galloway Girls took after Mom, with dark hair and hazel eyes. In the light from the dashboard, however, I noticed for the first time that he had the same determined set of Dahlia's jaw.

"I think the chief would mind, yeah," he said, heading for the farm.

There was a hint of doubt in his voice. I'd hit my brother in his weak spot: Jilly.

"You're probably right. Hopefully I can find a moment to do this tomorrow. It's such a busy time."

"What errand could you possibly do at this time of night?" he asked.

If he was fishing, he was weakening.

"It's something that I feel as maid of honor will make a real difference on the big day," I said. "But you're right. It's late and Jilly won't mind if things aren't perfect. She'll be grateful to have a wedding at all now."

My brother glanced in the rearview and side mirrors and made a skillful U-turn. Keats gave a pant-laugh from my lap, and then set his paws on the dashboard. I had lied to Kellan about having enough for one day. The boys and I had a little juice left and we were going to use it.

"What exactly are you planning to do?" Asher said, when we were about to enter the town.

"Something I couldn't do without you," I said. "At least not easily. Can you turn right here and park? We'll walk back."

He did as I asked and we all got out.

"You're bringing Keats and Percy?" he asked. "Isn't that going to attract attention?"

"Maybe," I said. "The fact that you're in uniform is going to attract more. People are used to me roaming around with my pets."

"You've got a point." He reached into the back seat and grabbed Kellan's second-best leather jacket. It didn't help as much as he hoped, but I let him enjoy feeling disguised. "This had better not get us into trouble, Ivy."

"It's about your wedding. That still needs to be a priority, right?"

"I don't hold out much hope of that happening. At least, not like we planned." He raked one hand over his head as we walked back to Main Street. "Everything was going to be perfect, right down to the last detail. Just like Jilly deserves."

I patted his arm as he churned up his hair. "It's okay, brother. Jilly may deserve perfection but she doesn't expect or need it. I've known her a lot longer than you have, and I know what really matters to her."

"A woman deserves the wedding of her dreams," he said.

The set of his jaw—Mom's jaw—told me he was going to cling to this belief, but that didn't stop me from trying to talk some sense into him.

"Asher, I'm serious. I've known Jilly since college. We were roommates for years and now she's more of a sister to me than my own. Do you think we haven't talked about weddings before?"

He grudgingly turned and there was pain in his blue eyes. "I want this for her. Jilly's life hasn't always been easy."

"I know that. And yours hasn't been easy, either, which is why you're so hung up on the perfect wedding."

"That's not true," he said, speeding up. "I have a great life."

"*Now*. That wasn't the case when you were running around Huckleberry Marsh like a feral child. It wasn't the case when you got suspended half a dozen times in high school and hung on by charm alone. You and Kellan are both lucky the principal didn't press charges over what you did to his car. Maybe you wouldn't be cops right now."

He stopped suddenly. "Kellan told you that?"

"Yeah. And he told me you bartered for me in a back country drag race. Like I was yours to give away."

Asher churned his hair harder. "It wasn't like that. Half a dozen guys at school wanted to date you and someone had to play gatekeeper."

"Me. That's who gets to play gatekeeper in my life, brother. Does it seem like I need a bodyguard?"

Sighing, he met my eyes. "Back then, I thought so and Daisy did, too. She tried to keep you from dating at all. You were the baby of the family."

"Yet old beyond my years in some ways," I said.

"You were always lost in your own world. Hanging out at the library. Trying to win awards at school. The least likely of our family to take down killers." Finally the famous Asher Galloway grin shone out under the streetlights. "I've been proven wrong, but at the time I guess we were trying to protect you so you could get what you wanted out of life. Which was to kick the dust of this town off your shoes and run."

"It sure was. I could not wait to leave Clover Grove behind."

"See? And my thinking was that any of my half-feral friends would hold you back." He beamed at me and the warmth of his good heart filled my own. "Kellan convinced me he'd respect whatever you wanted. So I let him win that race."

"Let him! That's not how he tells it."

"Well, who are you going to trust? Him or your own family?"

"Both," I said, laughing. "You've grown into good men. There's nothing feral about you now."

He shrugged his broad shoulders. "Wouldn't be so sure about that, sis. Being a cop means walking a fine line sometimes. I'd argue none of us Galloways would be where we are if we hadn't run loose and—"

"Raised ourselves?" I interrupted.

"I guess. Mom wasn't cut out to do that job alone. We're lucky we had Daisy."

"On that I agree fully," I said. "And we've come full circle to my original point, which is that you seem to be putting too much pressure on yourself to create the perfect wedding when all Jilly wants is to be married. To you. The half-feral swamp boy."

"Don't tell her that," he said, catching my arm.

"She knew that long before she met you, brother. That's what I'm trying to say. She fell for you as you are, not as you'd like to be. You need to ease up on yourself. I have full confidence that you're going to make a wonderful husband and father."

His jaw was still set in a stubborn pout. "Wedding traditions have meaning for me."

"Why is that? It's not like we saw many growing up. And a good marriage was never modeled well for us."

"Look at our grandparents. They're devoted to each other."

"We didn't know them till six months ago, Ash. I still feel like you've gotten hung up on the movie version of romance."

There was a long pause. "Maybe. I suppose it's an antidote to what I see as a cop. The accidents, the deliberate crimes, the inhumanity. Is it wrong to want something simple and perfect?"

"Not wrong, just unrealistic. Especially with our history. Stop putting so much pressure on yourself. Just trust me that Jilly doesn't want an old-school wedding or marriage."

"She's marrying me to take care of her. That's the vow."

I huffed in frustration. "Brother, that's such a dated interpretation of the vow, and Jilly is a modern woman. Marriage is about the power of equals caring for each other." He started to argue again and I raised my hand. "I'll leave that to her to explain. Regardless, the details of the wedding itself are nearly irrelevant."

We were nearing Main Street and he slowed. "Then why are we running this errand to make something irrelevant special? Aren't you mixing your messages?"

Keats gave a pant-laugh and mumbled that my brother had a point. I'd taken my argument one step too far.

"I'm the maid of honor. Her best friend of nearly seventeen years. It's different."

"Ivy." Asher caught my arm and I kept walking, towing him along. "It occurs to me that Rose to the Occasion is on the corner."

"Is it?" I threw him an innocent look. "How about that."

"No way. I'm not taking you in there. Kellan would have my head."

"You can just remind him of the famous road race that won my hand," I said. "He owes you one."

"This has nothing to do with the wedding, does it? You duped me."

"It has everything to do with the wedding. Jilly left detailed specs for the flowers with Rosalie the day she died. I want to collect them for the new florist. Easy peasy, right?"

"Except for that yellow hazard tape that bars entry. Even if I had a key I wouldn't take you in."

"Don't worry." I turned into the alley behind the store and gestured for Keats and Percy to fan out. "Leave it to the boys."

"Leave *what* to the boys?" My brother's voice had notched up a level. I hadn't heard him squeak like that since puberty.

"You'll see." It was 50:50 who would find a spare key first. Usually it was about access. Keats was the victor up to about waist level, with Percy taking the wins at higher altitudes. This time, the cat quickly gave a triumphant meow from the ledge of a dumpster. The key was in a notch in the wall created by a missing brick.

Standing on tiptoe, I collected the key and dodged around my brother as he tried to block the door.

Keats aided me there with a well-timed nip that made Asher squeak again. "Ow!"

By the time he could focus, I'd stuck the key in the lock and pulled the door open.

"Just tell Kellan I tricked you into it," I said, turning on my phone light. "He'll believe you."

"You did trick me into it," my brother grumbled, following me inside. "Are the flowers even a thing or was this all a ruse to let you poke around?"

"The flowers are a thing," I said. "I wanted to surprise Jilly, so I didn't go back to her for specs. Now we can get it just right."

"If we can find the order. The computer's already gone."

"It was on paper," I said, "and I know exactly where Roz put it."

Asher pulled something out of his pocket and handed it to me. "Gloves. At the very least, leave the evidence alone."

"Good point. I'll just take photos. That's a good compromise, right?"

"There's no compromise here," he said.

I scanned the store and found nearly everything was gone, except for the counter itself, and buckets of flowers in the cooler that were starting to droop.

Circling the counter, I crossed my gloved fingers, hoping the police hadn't emptied the drawer under the cash register.

I pulled it open, feeling Asher's breath on my ear.

Empty.

"A bust," he said. "You made me cross a line for nothing."

"Garlic for dinner?" I glared at him and nudged him away. Keats and Percy needed room to move around. Their posture told me our work here wasn't done.

Asher blew right in my face. "I like to live a little when I'm not seeing my girl."

"See, there you go again, Mr. Romance. Jilly goes through garlic like you wouldn't believe, yet you're sparing her delicate sensibilities."

"Can we just go before someone sees the light and Kellan comes after my badge?"

Keats mumbled something and my brother backed away slightly

without knowing he'd been told to do just that. The dog offered a half-point. It was the best he could do with my brother crowding him with big boots.

At the bottom of the counter was a long board that didn't look like a drawer, but there was a little notch just big enough for a gloved finger.

Percy got between my feet and pawed at it.

"Understood," I said. "Back up, boys. All three of you."

The long, shallow drawer was full to the brim. On top of the pile sat Jilly's floral wish list, which Rosalie had shown every sign of ignoring.

"Found it! See?" I snapped a photo and then moved the list aside.

"I see that you're still poking around," my brother said.

"That's because Keats and Percy aren't done."

The dog was still in a point and Percy used an orange paw to flick at things inside the drawer.

"Is this how you three work?" Asher said. His tone was a mixture of frustration and wonder.

"Yep. And before you comment, be aware that Kellan deploys the boys' skills on the regular."

"Then let him hire them to find whatever needs finding."

Keats mumbled something and I interpreted. "There's no payment involved. They work for love, and tonight, that's literal. If they can figure out who killed Roz, your wedding can still go on. Your ring bearers are on the case."

"I don't see any hot clues," Asher said, garlicky breath enveloping me as he bent over.

Keats turned his blue eye on my brother and barked a warning.

Asher backed off instantly, no interpretation required.

Percy flipped a photograph to the top of the pile and I snapped another picture.

Then the cat backed away, with a flashy sweep of his paw.

"Isn't that his litterbox maneuver?" Asher asked. "Not that I believe in any of that crap, but don't you claim it means someone is going to..."

His voice drifted off and I picked up for him. "Die? Usually, but maybe not always. We can't take the gesture too literally." Keats and I both laughed. "Get it?"

"I get that you're weird. Totally." He nudged the drawer closed with his boot and beckoned.

"Yeah? Well, so is your fiancée," I said, following him. "We listen when these animals communicate."

"And then you get yourselves into all kinds of trouble. If I have anything to say about it, that's going to stop."

All the sibling camaraderie fizzled out in my heart. "That's for Jilly to decide."

"Ivy, we both want to have kids," he said, holding the back door open. "It's not safe with the things you do."

We were outside in the alley now and I locked the door and replaced the key. "So it's safe for you to be a cop and have kids?"

"That's my job. But I guess my point is that we can't both be taking the same risks and raise a family." He caught my arm. "I want my kids to have more than we had. I want them to grow up feeling safe."

I stared up at him and most of the anger in my heart evaporated.

A mumble at my knees told me Asher had a point.

"See? Even Keats agrees," he said.

We walked back to the car in silence with Keats mumbling a little pep talk along the way.

"It really is up to Jilly," I said. "But I promise you I won't ever pressure her to help me. Especially after you have kids."

He nodded and gave me a brotherly shove. "Thanks. You still have Miss Evans, the fiercest warrior in hill country. And Mrs. Rhodes and her rifle."

Keats gave an indignant yip that made my brother hastily add, "Plus the pets, of course. Don't bite me again, dog."

"I was telling Justine Schalow earlier that my strength comes from community," I said, as Asher opened the passenger door for me. "Friends and family. Furred and feathered companions."

"Get in, weirdo," he said. "I should have let Wilmer win you."

"Wilmer! The guy who runs the car wash?"

"He's a straight-up dude. Old-fashioned values. You'd have half a dozen kids by now and a nice garden for canning."

"There's nothing to can this year," I said, sliding in and patting my lap for the pets.

He shut the door and walked around to the driver's side.

"I'm going to be in so much trouble," he said, getting in.

"I know, brother, I know. And it's only going to get worse. Now, you've got to prove whether your drag race braggadocio was just garlicky wind."

"What do you mean?"

I pointed to Keats, who was pointing at a sedan pulling out from a spot across the road. The driver didn't put their lights on. "I mean we've been watched. And they're getting away."

"I don't think so," my brother said. "I wasn't named eight-time champ in the back country derby for getting outrun by a sedan." He turned the key in the ignition. "Game on."

CHAPTER SIXTEEN

"I feel bad for him," I told Keats and Percy as we drove down the lane the next morning. "What a terrible blow to his pride, practically on the eve of his wedding."

Keats gave a pant-laugh and propped his paws on the dashboard. My brother's battered ego wasn't something to worry about in this sheepdog's opinion.

"You don't understand," I said. "Asher's sense of identity is all wrapped up in his driving prowess. Kellan's too, if I'm honest. That's how it starts for teenage boys around here. At least it used to, and judging by my nephews' affection for cars, it probably still does."

I turned onto the highway and the truck gave a little stutter as I geared up. It didn't do that often anymore, but I'd had very little sleep. After Byron gave his two a.m. report to Keats, only Percy went back to sleep. By four, I was down in the barn doing chores so that we could get an early start on the day. There was a lot to be done before closing out the day with Jilly's bachelorette party. No one had put the kibosh on that since it was being held at The Tipsy Grape. That's about all I knew, because my sisters had organized it, leaving me to worry about the bigger question of whether or not the wedding could take place at all.

"I wish the back country derby was a rite of passage for girls, too," I said. "My first year here would have been so much easier if I were a confident driver who knew how to navigate those trails. As if learning the ins and outs of hobby farming and inn-keeping weren't enough."

Keats mumbled something vaguely complimentary. Normally he didn't indulge me, but he threw me a bone now and then when life was extra challenging.

"Thank you, buddy." I gave his sleek side a pat. "I tend to think I got most of the brains in the family, too. Even Mom says so. But that comes with a downside."

His next mumble opined that there was no such thing as being too bright. As one of the top-rated breeds for intelligence, he was biased.

"The flip side of being a little brighter than the average human is that I worry," I said. "Unlike you, I ruminate constantly and imagine all the worst-case scenarios."

Percy fell over on his side rather dramatically and kneaded the air with his paws. Then he let out a purr that drowned out the motor. It was a clear message to relax and take life in stride.

"I hear you, Percy, but that's not really possible for the humans you love. At least, not this week. Jilly's at home working as if the wedding is a go, while dozens of guests from out of town are on standby, including her mother and cousin, and my grandparents. It looked like we had a lead with the mysterious car last night, but it fizzled."

Technically, it was Kellan's SUV that had fizzled. When my brother turned the key, it made a strange chugging sound and died. Twenty minutes later, a police mechanic arrived to confirm sabotage and a tow truck carted the car away.

Kellan was too busy at the station with Justine Schalow to come in person, but my brother's expression—and the distance he held the phone from his ear—told me the discussion had not gone well. I called Gertie to pick me up and was gone before the tow truck left.

"I hope the photos I took will help ID the driver. But Asher ran the plates and said it was a rental. Bottom line, someone followed us to the florist and wanted us to know about it. A bold move."

Keats mumbled, ending on a positive note. Asher and I had come up empty but that didn't mean the dog did. He may have sniffed or heard something that would come in handy later.

Ten pricks in my thigh brought clarity to my under-caffeinated brain. When kinder techniques failed, Percy often dragged me back to the present by force.

Disengaging his claws one by one from my denim overalls, I tickled his belly. For all his attention-seeking, he didn't particularly enjoy that and batted my hand away with a newly freed paw.

"What was going on with you and Justine last night, Percy? It looked like you were announcing her time of death. Should she be worried?"

He sat up and stared at me, unblinking. Justine should certainly be worried, I gathered.

Keats added a look with his blue eye and a shiver ran down my back.

"Boys, no. Another murder would certainly pound the last nail in the coffin of Jilly's wedding."

Percy collapsed again and folded his tail over his nose. I read that as meaning Justine would still be a thorn in our side for some time to come. The cat was persistent to the point of obnoxiousness when the threat was imminent.

His fluffy tail lifted so that he could blink at me and then the orange curtain dropped again.

He didn't get much of a rest before Keats pounded on the dash to tell me it was time to turn in.

"Turn in to what, exactly?" I asked, staring at what looked like an impenetrable wall of trees on the side of the highway. "There's nothing here."

Keats' mumble begged to differ. Just because I couldn't see it didn't mean it wasn't there.

"Honestly. I'm all for discretion, but the idea of bushwhacking at this hour has zero appeal. It's barely light out here, let alone in there."

The dog was insistent, so I sighed and then rolled over the gravel and down the gentle slope to the edge of the forest. That's when the high beams revealed two ruts leading into the bush. It couldn't be called a trail, much less a road, but it was something.

The white paws did a little dance on the dash as the truck forced its way through unforgiving branches.

"This truck used to gleam when I moved here," I said. "The poor thing has had a rough go under my care. I hope my animals fare better."

Percy sat up as the ride got bumpy and let out a soulful meow.

"I do my best, Percy, but this is no magic carpet."

Eventually, the tracks ended and we had no choice but to get out and forge on by foot and paw.

I grabbed a heavy backpack from the bed of the truck and slipped my arms through the straps. For once, I'd come prepared.

"All right, boys. Take it from here."

I expected the worst and was pleasantly surprised when we arrived at the rabbit colony after about 20 minutes of breaking trail. There was an easier route but Keats ignored it for the very good reason that we were bypassing the cops stationed nearby.

It was worrisome how easily we gained access, but no one else would have a navigation system like mine. Most nosy nellies would park in the cemetery lot and give up in rough conditions like these.

I expected to find the warren quiet, as it was when Kellan and I visited last night. Today, however, it was bustling with activity. Two dozen rabbits in a dazzling array of colors sat on top of their little mound with its many exits. Another few raced around the clearing, once, twice, three times.

"Are they playing?" I asked. "Do rabbits actually play?"

Keats gave a noncommittal rumble. Neither of us knew much about rabbits, but that's what I was here to remedy.

Setting down the backpack on a little hill that offered an unobstructed view, I pulled out a blanket with waterproof backing, binoculars, a tall thermos, and a tablet computer. My phone screen was too small for the research I wanted to do today.

Once the boys and I got settled in, I studied the rabbits through the binoculars as they went about their morning routine. Eventually I set the binoculars down, poured myself a steaming cup of coffee, and propped the tablet on my knees.

"Harlequin," I said, pointing from the colony to the tablet. "Havana. Californian. Rex. Lop and mini lop. Lionhead. Rex. Jersey wooly. Rex. Rex. Rex and Rex again."

I scrolled through the photos of domesticated rabbits, getting excited with every discovery. It was like a game that kept you going with frequent dopamine hits.

"I had no idea there were so many breeds. But the Rex is clearly predominating here. There's just about every color going. Black, blue, lilac, otter, sable and red. They're bigger than most of the others and seem calmer, too. Look, a couple of them are hopping this way. Promise me you won't startle them, boys."

I expected backtalk but both pets settled down on the blanket.

After tipping the rest of the coffee down my throat, I screwed the lid on the thermos to give our visitors my full attention.

It probably should have surprised me that the gray rabbit with the chink out of its ear was among the first to arrive, but after what happened with Picasso, the painted bunting, my mind had cracked wide open.

"In a good way," I said, feeling Keats' warm brown eye upon me. "That head injury rattled something loose, buddy. Now I see patterns I couldn't before. Doesn't mean they weren't there, but until we rescued each other, I was oblivious."

He mumbled a reminder to focus. The rabbit ambassadors had stopped about a yard from my blanket. Six out of eight of them appeared to be Rexes, and thanks to the handy rabbit guide, I could tell that my pretty gray friend was very likely an opal Rex.

"I think it's a girl, because some of her friends are a little bigger. So let's keep it simple and call her Opal." I smiled at her. "How does that sit with you, my new friend? I wish you could tell me what happened to your ear."

We stayed still for ages and there was a lot of nose twitching on their side. Keats and Percy did a lot of sniffing of their own. All I could smell was damp moss and soil.

Finally, the rest of the ambassadors moved off, leaving Opal behind. She hopped tentatively to the edge of the blanket, as far from my pets as she could get.

I took that as an invitation to reach out very tentatively to touch her side. When she froze, I pulled my hand back. After a few minutes, I tried again. This time I could feel her relaxing under my fingertips.

"What gorgeous fur you have, Opal," I said, daring to run my hand along her back. "I read that Rex fur is the softest of all. No guard hairs."

She seemed indifferent to my compliments, and eventually hopped away to rejoin the others. Just before she reached the warren, she dashed at her friends and they scattered. There was a flurry of fur, long ears and big feet, and then all settled again. It seemed that they were just burning off steam. Or trying to generate a little warmth on a chilly morning.

"We definitely need to get them out of here before the first frost," I said. "That's probably only a few weeks, max."

Opal tossed something into the air that jingled, and then chased it. Grabbing the binoculars, I stared as she did it again. She tossed a red object into the air and ran after it. A black Rex did the same thing with another jingling toy and soon little bells were ringing all over the clearing.

"What on earth?" I said, getting to my feet. "Stay, boys." I walked over slowly, and all the rabbits except Opal retreated into holes or hopped away to the trees at the edge of the clearing. "Are those cat toys?"

They were cat toys. And bird toys. And small dog toys, probably meant for tiny breeds.

I wasn't the only one visiting the colony, apparently. Others had come bearing gifts, including hay, by the looks of it.

"How strange," I said, kneeling to take a photo of Opal as she nibbled on a cardboard box. There were little bits of aluminum on the ground around her that glittered in the rays of sunlight that managed to pierce the trees. "I'm glad you have other friends who know how to treat a bunny right, Opal. But I'm your ticket to safety and warmth, so don't get too comfortable here."

She angled sideways to look at me and for a second, it seemed like she understood.

Then she dropped the cardboard and zipped into the woods with her friends, and a uniformed police officer walked into the clearing.

CHAPTER SEVENTEEN

"You didn't need to nip him," I said, after we were on the road again. "The guy was just doing his job."

Keats gave an insolent mumble to suggest he was doing the same.

"Your job is not to bite cops. I worry you like the flavor of uniforms."

He pawed at the window to get me to open it.

"Not until we've had this discussion, Keats. You're already dismissing me without the distraction of fresh air."

I had never heard a dog sigh before meeting this sheepdog. At least, that's how I interpreted the gust of wind he sent my way. Then he collapsed theatrically in the passenger seat.

"I know it was just a nip, and the common language of herding dogs, but that recruit did not. When he screamed, that was your sign to back off, not double down."

He covered his muzzle with his paws, possibly to suppress a pant-laugh.

"I mean it, Keats. It's one thing to bite our boyfriend, who has a sense of humor, and another to terrorize a newbie who's trying to make a good impression on his boss' girlfriend. He was embarrassed enough over our slipping past him. You didn't need to add insult to injury."

His next mumble asserted it was exactly what he needed to do. The recruit was likely to be more attentive from now on, and most certainly wouldn't underestimate Keats.

Or Percy, who had hit him square in the back and tried to crawl onto the guy's shoulder.

"We'll need to pay for his dry cleaning and repairing the pants," I said. "Honestly."

Keats got up again and this time I rolled down the window. The lecture was really a formality and he knew it. I had expected to get put through the wringer when the cop found me there but by the time the boys were finished with him, he was happy to see me go.

"I'm glad we managed to get around the cops but I do worry about the rabbits. Obviously they have at least one fan who's visited with toys, but there could be other sneaks like us who don't feel as kindly toward Opal and her crew. In fact, I'm sure there are."

Keats stuck his nose out the window and drew in deep gusts of fall air.

"I'm determined to get that wedding present today," I said. "But there's something I want to check out first."

He turned and shot me a look with his blue eye. The time for games had apparently ended, or so his mumble told me.

"You think we need Edna? It's just a friendly visit."

Now he did pant-laugh. So many of our friendly visits went the wrong way.

"All right. Better safe than sorry."

I was doubly safe by the time we drove down Finch Pefferlaw's lane. Edna had been shooting tin cans at Gertie's house nearby and I was able to get a two-for-one deal on protective services.

"I love visiting Finch," Edna said, from the passenger seat. "It's a great exercise."

"Exercise in what?" I asked, glancing at her. As usual, she was in fatigues. Gertie, in the back seat, wore her usual poncho over jeans.

"In enduring hostility," Edna said. "We won't survive what's coming if we're too nice."

I laughed. "No one could ever accuse you ladies of being too nice. You're known far and wide as fierce warriors."

"Oh, you'd be surprised," Gertie said, arranging her braid and her rifle in her lap in the back seat. "People persist in seeing us as... well, old ladies."

"Don't let that worry your pretty head, Gertie," Edna said. "Their ignorance works in our favor. Lots of people think you're too incapacitated to hit a target with that rifle. Meanwhile, you're the second-best marksman in town."

"Harvey Dunbar can still outshoot me," Gertie said, with a sly laugh.

"As can I, my friend," Edna said. "And lately I've been beating the pants off Harvey in fencing, as well."

"What an interesting turn of phrase," I said, "considering he's your date for the wedding."

She stared at the side of my head. "We covered this already. Asher invited Harvey and I'm glad he did. He's quite a dancer and you know I like to cut a rug. Preparing for the future just means I can enjoy the present more."

"Exactly," Gertie said. "Since Fleecy came to stay, I've taken great joy in life's simple pleasures."

The catnapping of Fleecy had led us to the Pefferlaw place before, and I'd visited a couple of times recently about an antique birdcage that had been in Finch's family for years. Ultimately, he donated it to be sold at auction to benefit animal rescue. That's how I knew there was a good guy under that rough veneer. He was just a reclusive homesteader who mostly lived off the grid and preferred to be left alone.

Jaws let us know nothing had changed in that regard. The huge mastiff came down from the porch and put his paws on the passenger door to show Edna his tonsils in the deepest bark I had ever heard.

Keats barked back in a foolhardy display of bravado. His killer ear-hold slowed many a human but I sensed it wouldn't faze Jaws one bit.

"Outmanned and outclassed," Edna said, moving Keats away from the window. "Knowing that is the better part of valor. No way am I sticking a limb outside this truck."

"Me either," Gertie said. "I wouldn't have the heart to shoot a dog even if he attacked. So the bell would toll for me."

"As long as you'll shoot zombies, Edna will give you a pass," I said, as Finch came out of the barn and walked over to my window. I rolled it down a crack and said, "Can you call off the dog, Finch?"

He shook his head. "No need to get out. You can say whatever needs to be said from in there. And it had better need to be said, because I have things to do."

Edna leaned over to stare at him through my window. "I used to be a loner like you, young man. Then I realized it's easier to get picked off that way. One day, you might need an army."

"Jaws is an army unto himself." Finch's dark brows furrowed but I could swear his lip twitched. "We'll be fine."

"I'd love to pop inside and get some of your wife's delicious homemade preserves," Edna said. "She's a lovely lady."

"You can see her on Saturday at the farmer's market in town," he said.

"We can't make it next Saturday," Edna said. "There's a wedding."

"I know. I declined my invitation." Now he did smile at my expression. "Things to do, like I said."

"Asher?" I asked.

Finch nodded. "I went down to the police station to report a trespasser and left with a wedding invite. Shame we're already booked at the market. Can't disappoint our jam fans."

"It would have been nice to see you at the farm, Finch," I said. "I know you could give me some tips on livestock management."

"I probably could, but I wouldn't. It's not my business to help your business."

"My animals aren't my business. They're my pleasure. It's a hobby farm." I rolled down the window a little more. "Do you raise animals for meat, Finch?"

The smile evaporated instantly. "Did you really come here to ask me that?"

I shook my head. "Just curious. I'm going to take a guess and say you can't eat your furred and feathered friends."

"This farm is fully capable of sustaining my family. That's all I need to say about the subject."

"Admirable," Edna said. "Everyone should be able to say the same."

Finch whistled to Jaws, who left Edna's door to come around and sit beside him. "Stay," he said. To Edna, not the dog evidently, as he wagged a finger in her direction.

"Do you mind if I ask you a question, Finch?" I asked, inching the window down a bit more. I wanted to see his eyes, but not leave enough room for Keats to taunt Jaws.

"I've made it clear that I do," he said.

"You've made it clear that you enjoy a robust hostility practice," Gertie called from the backseat. "Just as we do. And for your information, I see you at the butcher shop all the time. You don't eat your critters."

"But I could," he said. "That's the point. I don't need to do it to know it. If my family's welfare was at stake in the way you ladies suggest, maybe I'd have to think again."

"Here's my question," I said, before he could reactivate his canine weapon. "Do you know who raises Rex rabbits?"

There was a slight pause before he shook his head. A telling pause. "Nope. But if you're looking for a rabbit, I hear the cemetery is overrun with them. Had to put that reporter off my property for asking even nosier questions than you."

I couldn't help grinning down at the dog. "Ah Jaws, thank you for that. There's no love lost between Justine and me."

"But you've got nosy in common," Finch said. "It could be the start of a great friendship."

I ignored his red herring. "So, which one of your neighbors raises Rex rabbits? You could save me from going door to door to ask."

"If you've got time for that, knock yourself out," he said. "Hours better spent with your livestock. There's my advice."

I turned the key in the ignition. "Okay. I'll tell them you sent me. Maybe you'll get more visitors."

"Then I won't need to feed Jaws for weeks. Good to whet his appetite for the end times."

"Young man, I like you," Edna said. "I didn't think I would, but you're growing on me. Like fungus, but a symbiotic relationship is still a relationship."

Finch closed his small dark eyes for a second. "Just go. Please?"

"Sure," I said. "But let me run a theory by you. I'm guessing one of your fellow homesteaders was raising Rex rabbits and set them free. They outnumber the rest by a wide margin. It had to be a large number."

"You know what they say about rabbits," Finch said, shrugging.

"I think that's how this whole problem started," I said. "Someone released their fluffle and it got out of hand."

"Fluffle?" He raised a palm. "Never mind. Ivy, I don't know anyone who's raising Rex rabbits right now."

Keats' paw rose in a point over the qualifier.

"Not right now? How about earlier this year?"

Finch took a step back from the truck, but his eyes flicked in the same direction Keats was now pointing. "I'm not nosy like you. Also,

I value peace with my neighbors. Hostility takes energy and I'm off the grid."

I laughed. "All right, we'll leave you in peace, Finch. You told us nothing and whatever I find will not reflect on you. I promise."

"I really didn't tell you anything," he said, eyebrows gathering like crows again.

"Not intentionally, but I still know exactly where to look."

He blinked and his mouth worked for a second, as if dealing with competing and uncomfortable emotions. "Try looking the other way for once, Ivy. It would be a lot safer. Maybe for all of us."

We stared at each other in silence as I pondered. "What happened about that trespasser you reported?"

"Nothing. All I had was footprints from someone crossing my land a few times. I've put up a camera, but never caught anyone in the act. I shared a photo of the prints with the police."

"Recently?" I asked.

"Off and on. If there's a pattern, I couldn't make it out."

Now *my* eyebrows came together. I didn't like hearing about patterns that couldn't be figured out.

Finch must have read my mind. "It's not what you think, Ivy. And thinking makes things complicated."

I put the truck in reverse, waved and started to roll away.

Edna wound down her window and stuck her head out. "Exactly how zombies operate, young man. If you refuse to think, I withdraw my invitation to my army."

"I withdraw your right to buy jam from our stand," he called back.

She lobbed a cackle onto the wind. "Fine. I'm plenty sweet enough."

CHAPTER EIGHTEEN

K eats navigated down the road half a dozen farms and directed me to turn into an unmarked lane.

"Must we?" Gertie said. "I've never trusted the MacBride family and the feeling is mutual."

"This is where Zander holes up?" Edna asked. "Another eccentric recluse." She cackled again, more quietly. "You'd think there'd be strength in numbers but there's no faith among oddballs."

"There seem to be a lot of eccentrics in Clover Grove," I said. "Speaking as one of them, naturally. Why do you think that is?"

"History," Gertie said. "Generations of lawlessness threw the door open for oddballs and villains. A culture grew around them and of course they bred like rabbits."

"That's what brought my parents here," Edna said. "Back then, nobody dared look at you the wrong way for fear of getting shot. The police of the time were either completely ineffective, complicit or both. When my sister burned down our house they barely investigated, which ultimately suited me fine. Turned me into what I am today." The next cackle was barely audible. "For good and for ill."

I reached over and patted her camouflage knee. "For good. Definitely."

She flicked my hand away but then patted my arm to soften the blow. "You're not eccentric. Not by a long shot."

"Tell that to my mother," I said. "Anyone with over sixty head of rescue animals isn't exactly mainstream."

"Dahlia isn't mainstream either," Edna said. "Nor is Calvin, obviously. Which is why all of you Galloways have a spark of rebellion."

"All of us? My sisters are pretty tame. Except Poppy. And more recently Violet, when she joined your survival class."

I stopped there, remembering how Daisy, the most conservative of us, had perhaps done the boldest thing of all in taking up with an unsavory man. The brief dalliance had significant consequences.

Edna stared out the window as we drove down a twisty lane that doubled back on itself twice. "You never really know your family. Take my word for it."

Easing off the gas, I turned. "Is there anything else I should know? Before it blindsides me?"

"Let me comb through my mental archives," she said. "For the moment, I suggest we give our full attention to Zander MacBride."

"I second that," Gertie said. "If we want to sit down during the wedding dinner, it would help not to get shot in the butt. On the bright side, that's probably the worst he would do. He's a gentleman, by a certain code."

"All right, then. Let's turn on the charm, ladies," I said. "Between the three of us, we can almost equal Jilly."

"I *was* charming before Saul stole my heart," Gertie said. "And treasure hunters trampled on it."

"I never was charming," Edna said. "Seemed like a waste of energy to me."

"You stole one heart," I reminded her, as we emerged into the open space beside a classic red brick hill country farmhouse. "There must have been some stardust on you then."

"Used it all up in one go," Edna said. "Although I must admit, I've felt the occasional twinkle lately."

I glanced at her again, eyes widening. "Directed at anyone in particular?"

She shook her head before patting tight curls. "At life in general. I'm finally coming into my own and it seems to create a certain..."

"Frisson?" Gertie suggested.

Edna turned to grin at her. "I didn't expect a fancy word like that from you, old friend. But it does suit the situation. I have a new passion for life, even as I contemplate the end of life, at least as we know it."

"We need to enjoy what we have while it lasts," Gertie said, smoothing flyaway tendrils of hair and running her fingers down her braid. Then she arranged her poncho to conceal Minnie. "It's nice to have a good second inning."

"Oh, come on. Third inning at least," Edna said, and they laughed in unison. It was more than a cackle. A true belly laugh of satisfaction that made me smile, too. I could only hope to have third and fourth innings like them.

The reason for hair patting among my colleagues soon became obvious. If Zander MacBride was the man coming down the front stairs, he was a six-foot, broad-shouldered silver fox. He was probably 80 but looked far younger in his red-checkered shirt and fitted jeans. Maybe he had a nice smile, but for the moment there was a scowl that rivaled Finch Pefferlaw's on his face.

"Good morning, Mr. MacBride," I said. "I'm—"

"I know who you are, and you know you're not welcome," he said.

"I do?" I was simultaneously relieved and dismayed that the oddball contingent didn't bother with pleasantries. "Why would I know that?"

"Because if I wanted to meet you, I would have already," Zander said. "You're not hard to find." He peered into the truck. "Ladies. You're not welcome either, but I won't shoot you if you leave now."

"Oh, Zander," Gertie said. "No need to get your lumberjack shirt in a knot. We come in peace."

"Why come at all, Gertie?" he said. "You value your privacy as much as I do. I wouldn't drop by your place unless it was life or death. Same for you, Edna."

Edna shrugged. "Maybe it is. Ivy wanted to visit and she usually has her reasons."

"I do." Opening the door, I jumped out before he could stop me. My main goal was to release the pets, who were probably more likely to get a look around than I was. "It won't take long, Mr. MacBride, I promise."

"No promises needed," he said, and now he flashed a Hollywood smile with a lot of teeth that were too bright to be natural. "I'm armed, just so you know."

I shook my head. "I'm starting to see nearly everyone is around here except me."

My weapons were deploying to the barn on eight paws, however. Zander MacBride didn't seem to notice that. Perhaps the charm offensive from Gertie and Edna, who'd joined us at the front of the truck, had worked a little magic. Gertie moved her braid from one shoulder to the other in a move that looked decidedly flirtatious. Meanwhile, Edna wore a smile I hadn't seen before that wasn't exactly coy, but was far from hostile. She also positioned herself so that Zander had to turn away from the barn to look at her.

The look in his sharp blue eyes turned to confusion and bewilderment. "What exactly is going on?"

"Just being neighborly," Gertie said. "We dropped in on Finch Pefferlaw first and are making our way down the road."

"Should have brought cookies," Edna said. "Or cupcakes from that new place in town."

"Don't like cupcakes," Zander said. "Can't imagine Finch does, either. I'm surprised you left in one piece."

I laughed. "I'm always relieved to leave the Pefferlaws' in one piece. Especially since Jaws arrived."

"Remind me to get a mastiff," Zander said. "When you're leaving. I'll give you exactly one minute to get to the life and death part of your visit."

"Rabbits," I said, without further ado. "I'm looking to add a few to my fur family and I heard you raise Rexes. I'd like a red, a blue, a black and an opal. Maybe more."

His eyes narrowed to blue sparks. "Finch told you I'm selling rabbits?"

All of us shook our heads at once. "Word reached me in town," I said. "You know what the grapevine's like around here. Everyone knows what everyone else is raising. People are always trying to buy my emu and she's not for sale. But I heard you had more rabbits than you could handle."

The spark of blue turned into a cagey stare. "You heard wrong, and I think your dog will say so when he's finished his rounds."

Keats stepped into the open doorway of the barn and mumbled confirmation. And a little more.

"But you did, at one time," I said. "Or so my dog thinks."

Zander stared at Keats and shrugged. "Too much trouble. Always fighting."

"Fighting!" After what I'd seen at the colony, that surprised me.

"Sure. The bucks tear each other up and the does aren't much better. I didn't do enough research before giving them a try. It was a sad waste of beautiful fur."

"Waste of—? Oh. You weren't raising them as pets."

"I was farming them, Ivy," he said. "You're a hobby farmer, whereas I'm the real thing. The rabbits were an experiment that didn't work out."

"So, you set them free," I said, as dog and cat returned to us. "To live their best lives."

His laugh was a sudden, raw bark and he turned to Edna and Gertie. "What do you make of these new age hen huggers? Emu huggers, now."

Edna shook her head. "They haven't known hard times, as we have, Zander. We didn't have the luxury of hugging our dinner."

"Saul gave me a rabbit coat for our fifth anniversary and upgraded to chinchilla on our tenth," Gertie said. "Nothing beats fur for a hill country winter."

He glanced at me. "You could learn from your friends, youngster."

"I learn from them every single day, Mr. MacBride." I summoned Keats and Percy with a gesture. "And these two, as well."

Percy scaled my back and sat on my shoulder, offering a purring sound that tickled my ear. Keats sat beside Zander, taking the man's measure.

"There isn't a single Rex left, so you can be on your way," he said.

Staring up at him earnestly, I asked, "Are you the one who started the wild colony?"

"You think I'd tell you?" His next laugh was derisive. "At least you had the decency to speak to me directly. I sent that news reporter running with a rocket under her sneakers."

A prickle of annoyance in my belly became a flare of heat in my cheeks. The fact that Justine was a step ahead of me irked me more than I cared to admit. But she had been chased off with nothing and according to Keats' fixated blue eye, there was still more information here.

"Maybe you want to set the record straight," I said. "With the police, if not Justine Schalow. A man who values his privacy so much wouldn't want it said that he started a huge problem for Clover Grove."

"Your rabbits have multiplied and are behaving like locusts," Edna said. "They're decimating the local flora."

Gertie tossed her braid again. "I'm sure Zander didn't think through all the implications when he set them free. Did you, Zander?"

His lips sealed off that Hollywood smile and he stared at the barn.

Keats gave a mumble that made me nod. "Ah. Mr. MacBride, you didn't set them free at all, did you?"

His expression didn't change but both hands clenched into fists. "Like I said, it was a farming experiment that didn't work out." His mumble was not dissimilar to Keats' and ended with a mild curse and the words "bunny huggers."

"Trespassers?" Gertie said. "I've had my share."

"It was a deliberate hit," Zander said, at last. "They tried a few times. I found footprints and bolt cutters. My dog put them off." He looked me square in the eyes. "So they took the dog."

I gasped. "They stole your dog?"

He flapped a dismissive hand in my direction. "It was a farm dog, Ivy. A tool, like a tractor. I don't waste emotion on animals. But that dismantled my only security system at the time. A few days later, they came back for the rabbits. Every last one of them gone."

"How many?" I asked.

"I lost track at forty. Every color you could imagine."

"I've seen them," I said. "Were there other breeds, as well?"

"Just Rexes," he said. "I think other people were hit, too."

"And no one reported it?" I asked.

Edna gave a heavy sigh. "I suppose no one wanted to be known for raising rabbits for fur or food. That's the culture we live in these days. Soft."

"You calling me soft, soldier?" Zander asked.

Now Edna laughed. "Hardly. Although I think you might have foreseen what could happen. You used to be a sharp man, Zander."

He kicked at the soil sheepishly. "I underestimated the sentimentality of these people."

"And the brazen disrespect for property," Gertie said.

After a pause, he met my eyes directly again. "I'll also admit I didn't expect the rabbits to survive, let alone thrive. I'd have spoken up if I'd known they'd hijack the cemetery and get someone killed." The Hollywood smile struggled to escape the clouds of guilt. "If someone had to go down, Rosalie Roarke wasn't a bad choice, though. Hard woman to like."

Edna and Gertie murmured agreement, and Keats nudged me toward the truck. We'd clearly learned all there was to know here.

"Thanks for your candor, Mr. MacBride," I said, climbing behind the wheel.

"I'm a nice guy." He delivered a full-on smile that my octogenarian friends mirrored. "Otherwise, your brother wouldn't have invited me to his wedding."

"Do you still know how to dance?" Edna asked, walking around to the passenger seat.

"Guess we'll see," he said. "Wear your combat boots."

"How I wish," Edna said. "I'm a bridesmaid."

His next smile was authentic. "The bride's lucky to have you, and I guess you'll dance me into the ground."

"Whatever happened to Mrs. MacBride?" Edna asked, as she got into the truck. "She was a lovely young blonde."

"Hair today, gone tomorrow," he said. "They make 'em flighty these days." He stared at me with eyes that didn't have the warmth of his smile. "That goes for you, too, girly. Back in my day, women—"

"I'm going to stop you there," Gertie interrupted, pointing from me to Edna. "Because these women could kick your behind from here to eternity."

"Sounds like more fun than raising rabbits," he said, closing the back door once Gertie was inside. "A man needs a security camera nowadays."

"One of the blessings of modern times," Edna said. "I've seen *your* face plenty of places it shouldn't be, Zander MacBride."

He looked shocked. "What are you talking about?"

"Lumberjack shirts stand out like a sore thumb." Edna gave her cackle a little more exercise. "I hope you'll leave it at home for the wedding."

"Hit it, Ivy," Gertie said. "It's always nice to leave on a high note."

CHAPTER NINETEEN

It wasn't easy to surprise Meryl Martingale, partly because she was a politician, trained in masking her feelings, and partly because she'd had a little work done to keep her face from giving away her emotions.

Today, when she stepped inside the mayor's suite and found the three of us seated in the waiting room, she startled visibly. I'm sure the sight of one woman in camouflage and another in a ratty poncho and long braid took her aback. It couldn't have been me, in my overalls with a cat parked on my shoulder. I was the most normal of our cast of oddballs.

Probably.

"My staff told me there were people in costume," she said. "They thought you were a theater troupe."

"That's what we told them at reception," Edna said, sticking out her hand. "She's obviously new in town and I couldn't resist."

The mayor had met both of my friends at parties at the inn, so when she cased out Gertie I knew what she was expecting. "I assume you left Mildred at home?"

"Mildred. I like the sound of that," Gertie said, neither

confirming nor denying. The rifle was in the truck but that probably wasn't the type of news to share in town hall, either.

"I was just hoping for a quick word with you, Mayor," I said, looking around at the eager faces of staff who weren't even trying to conceal their curiosity. "In private."

"Just you," she said, crooking her index finger and walking into her office.

"We're taxpayers, too," Edna called after us. "Don't play favorites."

"Ivy's a prominent local businesswoman," Meryl said, with a bland, inauthentic smile that probably resembled my HR mask. "And a mentor to my niece."

"I'm so glad Bronwyn's coming to the wedding," I said, when the oak door closed behind us. Meryl sat down and gestured to the cushy leather chair across from hers. Keats circled her with the white tip of his tail swaying gently. His approval rating was proof that Meryl was less false than many in her line of work. "When does she arrive?"

Meryl's finely penciled eyebrows lifted just a bit. "Ivy. You must know the wedding is basically on hold. Unless there's been an arrest in the last hour that Chief Harper neglected to mention."

"We'll find the killer," I said. "It's all hands and paws on deck, Mayor. We're proceeding as if all will go off as planned, so don't stop rehearsing."

She laughed. "I think I can manage to get Jilly and Asher married as long as the community is safe."

"It *is* the entire community, apparently," I said. "Between Asher and my mom, nearly everyone's invited. That's partly why I'm here. To make a plea to let the show go on. The police force has pledged full security and I think the event will go a long way to raise the town's spirits. One of Clover Grove's finest is marrying a talented chef. They're as close to royalty as we can get around here."

She crossed her legs and smoothed the wool skirt of her smart suit. "You know what would raise their spirits more, Ivy? Being alive."

"With all due respect, you're overstating the threat, Mayor."

Percy got down from my shoulder, walked along the arm of the leather seat and jumped into Meryl's lap. It did her credit that she didn't shoo him off. On the contrary, she let him settle and then scratched him lightly under the chin. His purr boomed out and he flexed in bliss.

"Don't deploy your cat to do your dirty work," she said, running a hand over his back and then shaking a clump of hair in my direction. "You know I like and appreciate you, Ivy, but when I was elected, I pledged to put the community before my personal preferences."

"But—"

She gave an imperious sweep of manicured fingertips. "I'll be ready at a moment's notice as soon as the person responsible for killing Rosalie Roarke is behind bars. Until then, you're spending valuable time here when you three could be, well... doing your thing." The "three" in this case included the cat in her lap as well as the dog beside her sky-high pumps.

"About that," I said. "I also wanted to speak to you about the rabbit problem."

The mayor's sigh was slightly exasperated. "I thought we were talking about the murder problem."

"I can't help thinking there could be some overlap there," I said. "Although my team is still in the intelligence-gathering stage. What I know is that someone—or several someones— released rabbits raised for fur. Or food. Or both. Those rabbits formed a voracious colony, and got on the wrong side of regional gardeners, represented by Rosalie Roarke."

Elegant fingertips passed over the cat from ears to tail again. "Are you suggesting that Roz was plotting against the rabbits?"

"Not suggesting. She told Jilly and me so when we were at her

store ordering flowers. I just didn't understand the scope of the problem, then."

"And you think animal rights activists went after Rosalie in
retaliation?"

"It's one theory," I said. "Not my only one."

"Probably a stretch," she said. "Behind these walls, I can admit
that Roz had detractors who probably had more plausible motives. I
hope you're not getting too caught up in the rabbit storyline to see
that."

As a semi-professional sleuth, I wanted to protest, but I knew my
weaknesses. I would likely always be easily sidetracked by animals. I
didn't need to be so easily sidetracked by a politician.

"Mayor, it would be so much easier to focus on the murder
problem if you assured me you're looking into the rabbit problem."

"Of course I am," she said. Her hand slowed ever so slightly. I
didn't need Keats' blue gaze to tell me she was hiding something.
"We have the very best minds working on it."

"Thank goodness," I said. "You've formally enlisted the Rescue
Mafia?"

"Rescue Mafia?" Her eyes shifted to my temple. "Oh, yes—"

"That's a relief," I said. "I'm sure your counterpart in Dorset
Hills is backing them to handle this situation. Isla McInnis is definitely one of the great minds needed to help."

"It's a significant problem, Ivy. Unprecedented. If they were
regular rabbits, the state wildlife service could deal with it. If they
were pets, our own Animal Services department would step in.
Instead, we have something in between."

"That's where the Mafia thrives," I said. "The space in
between."

"I don't always like the way your friends handle issues." She slid
Percy off her lap and he landed on the gleaming hardwood floor with
a little grunt of disgust. "They're cavalier about the law."

Keats directed his blue eye at her. It must have been uncomfortable because she angled herself away. I waited until she looked back at me and said, "I'm a little cavalier about the law myself, sometimes. You've encouraged that."

"Encouraged is the wrong word." She glanced around the office as if we might be overheard. "And that's different, because it's about people."

I caught her eye and tried to hold her gaze. "Mayor. These rabbits are people to me."

"Oh, Ivy, they're not. They're rodents. Pests."

"They're domesticated animals meant to be house pets, even if some people were raising them for fur. I'm surprised you'd want our town to be associated with something like that, anyway. Most homesteaders are gentle and kind to their animals."

She leaned forward, cheeks reddening, and then flung herself back in her seat. "It's not easy pleasing everyone, you know. No one ever tells you political life is like walking a tightrope. In stilettos."

"Better you than me." I stuck out one work boot, which dropped flecks of mud from my morning trudge through the forest. "I would put animals before taxpayers every time."

"Then you wouldn't have the budget to keep the lights on," she said. "I'm doing my best to balance competing priorities. I hope you know that."

I looked down at Keats and he turned his warm brown eye on me, and then the mayor. She *was* trying, that much was clear. Whether she was succeeding or not was a different matter.

"All I'm asking is that you let the Mafia handle this humanely. I made a commitment to the rabbits. They're *my* constituents."

The mayor closed her eyes, and then pressed her lips together. She was trying to hold back frustration, laughter or both.

"The rabbits are not your constituents. It's a vermin problem in our town cemetery."

Percy jumped into my lap and I hugged him. "Think what you

will, Mayor, but the head rabbit came to me at Runaway Farm and asked for help."

Her sigh was blustery enough to flutter Percy's tail. "That is ridiculous. There is no 'head rabbit.'"

I grinned at her. "That's where you're wrong. She's an opal Rex who's had to fight for her role, judging by her battle scars. She's like you in many ways."

This time the laugh escaped her. "Please don't compare me to the mayor of rabbits. Although there is no such thing, of course."

"I suppose not, but I still made a commitment to help them and I'll see it through." Reaching out, I touched Keats' ears. "Justine Schalow told me you'd throw me under a bus."

"The reporter?" the mayor said. She crossed her legs neatly, and then recrossed them.

"That's right. When we caught her breaking into the cemetery last night she said I was naïve for trusting you to have my back."

"I have your back," she said, crossing her legs yet again. "But there are too many rabbits for me to back all of them, too."

"I told her she was wrong. After my efforts to serve Clover Grove, I'm sure you'll do all you can."

Her stiletto bobbed anxiously. "I am. It makes it more challenging to have a reporter around. Especially one as persistent as Justine."

"Tell me about it. Seems like she just wants to stir things up for the sake of a story. Some of us are working for the greater good."

"Including me," the mayor said. "Generally speaking, I have nothing against the media. I think they keep politicians more accountable. I wouldn't be much of a leader if I didn't stand behind my decisions and answer the hard questions. That said, this job isn't always black and white. There's a lot of nuance."

"I prefer my job, then. There's no nuance when a pig's running you down. Or a murderer's coming at you with an ax. I guess I can only do my best for the rabbits."

"Ivy. Don't you have enough to worry about with the other problem? And the threat hanging over the wedding?"

Hoisting Percy onto my shoulder, I got to my feet. "I always have enough to worry about. For example, I still don't have a wedding gift."

"Just focus on that. And help the chief where you can." She got up, too. "I hope he's looking into the garden club. My guess is there's a bad seed there. No pun intended."

I walked ahead of her to the door of the suite. "Why is it that every club in this town is full of in-fighting?"

"It's not just this town. We're no worse than any other town. And no better."

"We are better," I insisted, turning at the door. "What sets us apart, as well as Dorset Hills, is the way we prioritize animals. That's why we have the patronage of people like Hannah Pemberton. And that's why we get such generous donations from people like Verna Rae Cobbler. The town coffers don't need to cover this situation, you know."

She looked up at me, and I knew I'd hit the mark at last. "You have a point," she said.

"It's a shame it comes down to money," I said. "But whatever works. On behalf of my long-eared constituents, I thank you for considering their plight in a new light. With that load off my mind, I can move on with my investigation."

"You do that. We still have a couple of days to save the wedding. I really do hope Jilly and Asher get to tie the knot in style."

"Would you like to meet her?" I asked. "I could set up some face time so you can explore mutual topics of concern."

"Jilly?" she asked. "I speak to her often."

"Opal," I said. "The mayor of rabbits."

Reaching around me, she opened the door. "Get going. And in case you didn't know, Asher set up a gift registry at a couple of stores in town. Nearly everything's checked off already."

"My gift can't come from a registry," I said, signaling Gertie and Edna to join me. "It needs to be unique. Meaningful."

"No pressure," Edna said. "I'm getting them his and hers survival kits."

"You don't want to know what I'm getting," Gertie said.

The mayor walked us to the outer door herself. "That's correct, Mrs. Rhodes. I don't."

"Jealous," Gertie said, walking out ahead of us. "I have the treasure to spend on good people and I'm going to use it."

"As long as it's legal," Meryl called after us as we walked down the hall toward the exit.

"Better to be memorable," Gertie called back. "On their fiftieth anniversary, they won't care about a teapot someone chose from a registry."

Meryl's face fell, suggesting she'd chosen that exact item. It was just a lucky guess on Gertie's end, but my senior friends had great intuition when it came to landing a shot like that.

"If they put it on the registry they want it," I said. "Jilly will be thrilled with anything, Meryl." Now that we were outside her office, I felt comfortable using her first name.

"You can't use a china teapot in a bunker," Edna said, as we walked into the parking lot. "That's likely where we'll be when they reach their fiftieth anniversary."

I couldn't help smiling as Keats circled to herd us to the truck. "You'll be one hundred and thirty-something by then, Edna. You'll have earned a spot of tea."

There was a tussle at the passenger door as the two women competed for the front seat. Edna surrendered sooner than I expected.

"You know what I've learned, Ivy?" she said. "Tea made in a tin can over a bonfire is the best. With the stars shining overhead, it tastes like freedom."

Gertie climbed into the passenger seat, reaching back to touch

Minnie, who was lounging under a blanket in the rear footwell. "If we make it to that age, I suppose we'll be happy to drink tea any way we can find it."

I hopped in on my side. "If anyone can last that long, ladies, it'll be you two."

"It's never too late to embrace our healthy lifestyle, Ivy," Edna said. "Simplicity and stress reduction improve survival rates."

Keats gave a ha-ha-ha. No one with a barn full of high maintenance rescues had a simple, stress-free life.

"I'll settle for a hundred as long as I can take my coffee out of a mug. With pie," I said, driving away.

"Bush league," Edna said. "But we still have time to change your mind."

CHAPTER TWENTY

After dropping Gertie and Edna to resume their target practice, I drove back to the farm to collect Jilly. I'd given up on my hope of gift shopping in favor of having my friend's company on the next mission. It would benefit greatly from her specialized finesse.

I was surprised to find her wearing a pretty dress and full makeup.

"I haven't even told you where we're going," I said, as she got into the truck.

She gave me a strange look. "Have you forgotten the party tonight?"

"Of course not," I said, although I most definitely had. "How could I forget the bachelorette party? I've never been to one and I can't wait to see how it works."

Jilly welcomed Percy into her lap. As with the mayor earlier, the way her fingertips moved over the cat's fur told me how she was feeling. Revealing moods was one of his superpowers.

"I'm worried about what Poppy may have cooked up," she said, as we pulled out of the lane and headed toward Dorset Hills. "Leaving a bachelorette party in your sisters' hands is risky business."

"Daisy is at the helm," I said, soothingly. "Half a dozen seniors will be there. And it's at The Tipsy Grape. How wild could it be?"

"Everyone gets a little nutty around weddings," she said, but her fingers slowed.

"Daisy will keep a lid on it. Please try to enjoy yourself, Jilly. With all that's going on, you need to seize those little moments where you can."

"I never thought of myself as someone who craved routine, but I miss it," she said. "Another day of chaos and I might head out to your manure pile for some fertilizer therapy."

I laughed. "Expect total transformation, my friend. Kellan enjoys it so much that he brought his own spade."

"Nothing says commitment like his and hers shovels," Jilly said. "You're practically engaged."

My laugh switched to a sigh. "Not quite. I honestly thought he was going to ask a month ago at Garnet Point but the winds shifted and that was the end of it."

Jilly's fingers picked up speed again. "I hope what's happened recently doesn't faze him. It's just a coincidence that things went haywire right before my wedding. I mean, who could have foreseen an exploding rabbit population and a dead florist?"

I geared up on the highway and the needle leapt so fast that Jilly shifted her hand to my arm, depositing a clump of orange fur on my sleeve.

Settling back in the seat, I eased up on the gas. "No one. It's freakish. And I'm sure you miss visiting the cemetery with Asher."

She gave me a grin. "Hope you don't mind, but we're borrowing your place on his dinner hour today. He wants to see me before the party."

"Just in case you get lured astray by any of Clover Grove's eligible men, I suppose. He won't be happy until the next ring's on your finger." I grinned back at her. "No one in this town expected my brother, the player, to fall with such a thud."

A little color rose in her cheeks and made her prettier than ever. "I hope the wedding gets to happen as planned," she said. "You know I never cared too much about such things, but once you planted the idea for the orchard wedding, it seized my imagination. Now it feels like the only way it can happen and still feel right."

"I tried to pressure the mayor today but didn't get very far. All she did was pressure me back to solve the murder."

Keats gave a reassuring mumble and tried to push Percy out of the prime position. The cat gave a growl and raised a paw to swat the dog. That was unusual. No matter how much posturing went on between them, Percy's claws didn't show with Keats. "Boys, settle," I said. "We're all on edge but that's when we double down as a team, remember?"

There were a couple of grumpy grumbles and two bodies jostled in Jilly's lap. By the time they finally settled, we were in Dorset Hills and driving past Bellington Square, with its huge bronze German shepherd sculpture. Even from the road, we could see the gorgeous fall floral arrangements throughout the square. Unlike Rosalie Roarke's original work, these were classic, with orange, yellow and maroon chrysanthemums. There probably wasn't a pinwheel or parasol to be found.

Edwin Masters, the architect of those arrangements, was standing at the counter when we walked into Twig Master, the florist on a side street near the center of town. It was situated close to the hospital, which was no doubt good for business.

He glanced up as he finished wrapping a bouquet for a gentleman and I sensed any introductions would be a formality. The Twig Master knew who we were, and probably why we were there. What's more, he was uneasy about the visit. If I had any doubt, Keats didn't. His fur ruffled around his neck, and Percy puffed, too. Their former squabbling was replaced by shoulder-to-shoulder solidarity.

Jilly and I rubbed shoulders, too, as we inspected deep pails containing irises, peonies and cheery sunflowers.

"It's him," I whispered. "The guy Roz was hugging in the photo I found in her store."

"Let's see if we can get him to admit to a torrid affair," Jilly whispered back. "Maybe it was a crime of passion."

The heady floral scents that appealed to me a few days ago made me slightly queasy now. I doubted I would ever appreciate flowers the same way after what had happened.

"Rabbit food," I muttered.

Jilly let out a little snort and then squeezed my forearm. "Stop it," she said. "Square breathing. Four rounds. Pronto."

We walked to the front window, counting our breaths and holds, and when we were done, I said, "Are you going to make me do that before we walk up the aisle?"

"There's never a bad time for square breathing. Maybe especially at the altar."

"Good point. Some people might realize they're making a mistake just in time."

"Half my business would disappear," a man's voice said. Edwin Masters had come up behind us and heard the last words. "So, I can't really endorse meditation at a wedding."

Jilly gave a tinkling laugh designed to disarm him. "We saw your displays in Bellington Square, Mr. Masters. Stunning work."

"Thank you." He pushed round spectacles back up his nose and stared at Jilly with brown eyes that seemed equally round. "I was lucky to get the commission."

"Luck had nothing to do with it," Jilly said. "It's about taste, skill and experience."

He inclined a head of bushy white hair modestly. "Kind words from a lovely lady."

"I would imagine that's how you were named head of the Hill Country Horticultural Society as well," I said.

"That, plus greasing a few palms with peonies." He touched a large fuchsia bloom with one finger. "These postings are political."

"Political peonies?" Jilly said, amping up her smile. "How does that work?"

He beckoned, and we followed him to the counter. "To land a spot like that, it takes a mix of reputation, influence, timing and a bit of luck. Plus a lot of volunteer hours. I tried to get that vote for about twenty years. It nearly cost me my marriage."

Jilly's eyes widened. "Oh no. Why?"

Edwin's chin dropped and he stared at the daisies strewn across his workspace. "The power went to my head, I'm afraid." He looked up again and smiled ruefully. "Flower power will do that as much as any other kind."

Reaching for a daisy, Jilly tilted her head. "Did this have anything to do with Rosalie Roarke, Mr. Masters?"

He matched her posture. "I expect you know it did and that's why you're here. There's no need to pretend this is about your wedding. Flowers are a small world, and I know you've signed with Kevelyn Welsh."

"I have?" Jilly sounded confused.

"You have," I said. "Surprise."

"She'll do a good job for you," Edwin said, eying Jilly's coat. "Maybe better than Roz, given your style."

"You probably know we've heard you had a close relationship with Rosalie, Mr. Masters," I said.

"It was combustible, on every level. Roz was incredibly talented and just as competitive. Our aesthetic was so different that a clash was inevitable."

"She wanted to be admitted into the horticultural society, I presume," I said. "It sounds like the top of the charts as far as flower enthusiasts go."

"Very much so, yes. But Roz wasn't the right fit. A role like that calls for a classic aesthetic, along with people skills. Half my job is managing egos."

"That doesn't sound like the Roz we met," I said. "Although we didn't know her well."

"I'm sure she told the bride exactly what you wanted for the wedding—and that she could take it or leave it," he said, with a smile.

Jilly laughed. "Pretty much, yeah."

"That was the artist talking," he said. "She totally lacked political finesse."

Percy and Keats went behind the counter to do their inspection, but I was beginning to wonder if we'd been misled about Edwin. Maybe the photo was a false lead. "It doesn't sound like there was much love lost between you and Roz, Mr. Masters."

He turned abruptly and pulled a bucket of big orange blooms from the cooler behind him. "She was like these dahlias, you see. Bold. Brilliant. Belligerent. And for a while, she did turn my head, I'm afraid. I didn't realize she was using me to get on the board, although everyone else did. Including my wife."

I avoided meeting Jilly's eyes and tried not to laugh. Had my mother grown into the personality of the flower she was named for?

"Rosalie's ploy didn't work, obviously," I said.

"I lost my heart, not my mind. I take my role on the board seriously." His cheeks flushed a mottled maroon. "More seriously than I take my marriage, according to my wife. But it never went as far as Goldie thought. At worst, it was what our daughter would call micro-cheating. Rosalie and I spent a little too much time driving around hill country critiquing flora and stealing other towns' best ideas. That's all."

My intuition said Edwin was telling the truth, and my canine lie detector, who'd returned to my side, seemed to agree. His mumble prompted me to try a new direction.

"Mr. Masters, do you know who'd want to kill Rosalie?"

He replaced the dahlias in the cooler and pulled out a bucket of red roses. "I know plenty of people who had reason to want her out of the way, although not necessarily dead." Peering at me through his round glasses, he added, "I told your chief as much already, when he was here earlier to talk about poisonous plants."

"Were you able to tell him what plant killed her?" I asked.

"I gave him an exhaustive list of what grows around here. But the toxicology results were inconclusive. Or so he said."

"Not as simple as yew berries?" I asked.

"Too obvious," Edwin said. "Rosalie would have been insulted if someone had been so... basic."

I couldn't help laughing. "I guess gardeners hold themselves to different standards. It's not enough just to get the job done."

"If it were a garden enthusiast, as the way she was found suggested, the killer would likely want to make a statement." His hand shook slightly as he rearranged the roses in the pail. "Roz left a trail of devastation not so different from the rabbits she was fussing about."

"Did she speak to you about plans to do something about the rabbits?" I asked.

"Roz wouldn't speak to me at all after I told her I'd made my decision about the available seat. She was... well, indignant is putting it mildly. She hit me with a pot of impatiens."

He rubbed his temple, where there was still a trace of a bruise.

"That sounds pretty basic, too," I said. "Who did make the cut?"

"Tizzy Cousins. I drove over to tell Roz the day she passed."

"Tizzy, the cupcake baker?" I said. "She didn't seem as knowledgeable or invested as the rest of the garden folks the day we were there. I'm sure that didn't go over well with Rosalie."

"Definitely not. But Tizzy passed every test with flying colors," he said, with a shrug. "And she's well-liked. I felt she could bring unity to the society, instead of division. In the end, that's my most important role as president."

"Flowers are about peace," Jilly said.

"And celebration," I added. "Mr. Masters, I'd like to hand out a flower to twenty guests at a pre-wedding party tonight. What bloom says bachelorette party?"

He laughed for the first time. "Gotta be something swanky for this lady. I think I know just the thing."

When he disappeared into the back room, I followed Keats' direction to investigate behind the counter. I snapped photos of everything in the refrigerator and as much as I could capture from under the counter.

I was back in my spot by the time Edwin returned with his arms full of peach rosebuds with golden centers. Skinny glass vials filled with water encased their stems and clinked and clattered as he handed them to me.

"Love it," I said. "Classy without being stodgy. Just like our bride."

Edwin joined Jilly in laughter again. "With taste like that, we might open a spot for you on the society one day."

"I hear someone has to die first," I said. "So I wouldn't wish that on myself or anyone else. Besides, my aesthetic leans to long ears and big teeth. A bouquet of sweet bunnies would see me up the aisle."

The florist winced. "I'd keep radical sentiments like that to yourself, Ivy. My people will go to great lengths to protect their gardens. It's a huge investment of time and energy."

Jilly ushered me to the door.

"See you at the wedding," he called.

We turned in unison and I beat Jilly to the question. "The wedding?"

"The groom invited me," he said. "He was here with the chief and I think the smell intoxicated him. He invited a regular customer, too."

Jilly managed to smile and sigh at the same time. "It will be lovely to see you, Mr. Masters. If the wedding comes off at all."

"You'll find the killer," he said, with more confidence than I felt.

"Flower people are only experts at plotting gardens. I'm sure you folks will sniff out the rot in no time."

Rot. That's exactly what I'd smelled when we walked in.

Edwin Masters didn't seem to know it, but something was dying in his store.

CHAPTER TWENTY-ONE

K ellan was out behind the barn when I got home. He was expertly wielding his very own spade to turn manure, despite being in uniform.

Descending the "stairs" at a bound, he swept me into a hug and whirled me around. "I just wanted to remind you that you have a boyfriend."

"My memory isn't all it could be, but that's something I never forget," I said, laughing. "The best boyfriend in the world."

He did a fancy sidestep, taking me with him, no doubt as a reaction to sheepdog maneuvers below. I didn't want to ruin the moment by checking.

"I hope you still think so later," he said. "Crazy things happen at bachelorette parties. Even in Clover Grove."

I pushed him away a little so that I could look up. "Seriously? Like what?"

"Don't look at me to give you ideas," he said. "Just don't end up in Justine Schalow's gossip column."

My face puckered before I could stop it. "She's not on the list. I made sure of that."

"You trust your family to keep a list? Look what's happened to the wedding. It's a free-for-all. If it comes off, that is."

He gave a little yelp that suggested I'd be forking over more money for uniform repair. I moved away and shook my finger at Keats. "We deserve a moment, buddy. Especially before the debauchery of the bachelor and bachelorette parties."

"Our party has been postponed," Kellan said. "Over half the guests were cops and I can't spare a single one. Including the groom. Assuming he wants to be a groom on Saturday."

"Poor Asher. Never has a man wanted to be a groom more than my brother, and so many obstacles are being thrown in his path."

"I know. I'm doing my very best to get that guy married off. Jilly's made him a better man. Kids will settle him down even more."

"He's changed so much since I got home." I couldn't help sighing. "Sometimes I miss the fun-loving brat of the family. Even though I know it's for his greater good."

"And the town's greater good, too. The way things are going, he'll make chief one of these days."

I stood on tiptoe and kissed his cheek. "That job's taken."

"It's taken *here*," he said, grabbing my hand. "Plenty of towns in hill country would be lucky to have him. He's better than half the chiefs, now."

My stomach instantly tied itself into a convoluted knot at the thought of Jilly and Asher moving away. I didn't want to admit my selfishness to Kellan, however, so I grabbed my spade and climbed the stairway to comfort.

"Any progress on Rosalie Roarke's case?" I asked.

"Possibly. It looks like she was poisoned with the castor oil plant."

I stuck the spade in and wrapped my arms around the handle. "I thought castor oil was healthy."

"It is, but the beans contain ricin, which is one of the most toxic substances around."

"That certainly suggests someone with gardening knowledge was behind this."

"Especially since that wasn't the only toxin in her system. She'd consumed a deadly cocktail of poisonous plants, most in lower quantities."

"What about the yew berries?" I asked.

"Garnish, apparently. They weren't in her mouth long enough to do any damage."

I came down the pile again, sufficiently distracted from Jilly's impending departure. "This killer was pulling out all the stops."

"And yet, the results aren't conclusive. The report suggests there may not have been enough of any of them in Rosalie's system to get the job done."

"It explains why she was extra cranky and didn't look well on the day she passed, though. She turned down her monogrammed cupcake, which I tried to claim."

"That's my girl," he said, grinning again.

"Never pass up dessert," I said. "Although I don't visit Tizzy's bakeshop, out of loyalty to Mandy, who lost some business when First Frost opened. Unlike Roz, Mandy's the live and let live type." Keats gave a pant laugh and I added, "Poor choice of words."

Kellan and I spent a few minutes chatting about the politics of the garden club and the horticultural society.

Then, leaning against the barn, he crossed his arms and scowled. "Must everything be tainted in this town? Even flowers? I don't know if I can feel the same sense of peace in our favorite place."

"Then we'll find another," I said, gently prying his arms apart and moving into them. "I'm sorry I don't have more intel. The rabbits sidetracked me today."

I thought about filling him in on my visit to Finch Pefferlaw but figured he didn't want to be sidetracked himself. He cared about the rabbits, I had no doubt about that, but his first responsibility was to humans.

Keats took a dive at my pant cuff and mumbled his humble opinion that we should get a move on it. I presumed he was referring to solving the murder rather than pre-wedding celebrations.

Giving me a last squeeze, Kellan released me. "Remember, no crazy antics tonight. The last thing I need is for my officers to get pulled away over a girls gone wild situation."

"Do you know Jilly and me at all?" I asked. "We only agreed to go because my sisters insisted on it. Both of us would rather be here on the farm."

The knot in my stomach twisted again. Soon the kitchen would be empty much of the time. I might even have to learn to cook for myself. That wasn't a skill set I'd needed as the grim reaper of HR, but in Boston there were more options for the culinarily challenged.

"What's wrong?" Kellan asked. "You look like you ate a bad cupcake."

"I'd check into those cupcakes," I said. "They weren't toxic, but they weren't that good, either."

Draping his arm over my shoulders, he walked me back into the barn and out the other side. "Go and have fun. It's just a party."

"I know. But there's something worse coming. And I may not get out of it alive."

CHAPTER TWENTY-TWO

"We're late for this party and it's all because of you," I told Keats as we headed into town later.

He mumbled something sassy back. Defiant, actually.

"Don't you think I have enough trouble without being assaulted in my own bathroom? It was just a bath."

His next mumble was no less cheeky. It sounded like he was telling me to be grateful he'd only scratched my arms and legs, when he could have delivered his patented earlobe-piercing move. To him a bath felt like a life and death situation.

"You wouldn't dare," I said. "Try anything of the sort and I'll hand you over to the herding harpies to change your ways."

Keats shook from head to tail, as if shrugging off bathwater. The ladies of the Clover Grove Herding Club were as toxic as the plants that Rosalie ingested. His next mumble was decidedly more ingratiating, although we both knew I'd never surrender him to anyone under any circumstances. The very thought made me shudder as he had.

Resting his muzzle on my leg, he whined.

"I know. This wedding business is stressful enough without pressure to look good on top of it. Do you think I want to be wearing a dress and heels right now? I hate dressing up unless it's specifically for a date with Kellan. But for the next few days, we need to put on a show for Jilly's sake."

He lifted his head to stare at me with intense eyes and mumbled something like "she loves us as we are."

"She absolutely does, but she's trying to please everyone, especially Asher and Mom. Plus she's anxious about her own mom coming into town, and even Janelle. And she couldn't bring Percy tonight for comfort. So we need to support her as much as we can, and being clean and presentable isn't too much to ask."

Keats continued his back talk and I threw him a rare glare. "Listen. I put up with your dog stank without complaint most of the time, but if you get yourself into a position of needing another bath before the wedding, I'm dropping you at Sudzy Pups in Dorset Hills. Let a professional handle your tantrums."

More backtalk suggested I was equally lucky he put up with my farmyard fresh fragrance.

I raised my hand to cut him off. "Let's stay focused, stay clean and try to get this wedding on track. No bickering."

Bath time was probably the only thing Keats and I did bicker about and I rarely cared to fight for his whites. I needed him with me for the events ahead, however, and a clean dog was a welcome dog.

Usually.

His blue eye zeroed in, followed by a mumble.

"I know you do plenty to support all of us, but yes, I need to add clean to your long list of duties. You can go back to being grubby as soon as they drive off on their honeymoon."

I sighed and he relented, shoving my hand off the gearshift so that he could lend his soft ears to the cause.

"We'll be fine after she's gone. Totally. There will finally be time to take up target practice with Edna and Gertie. Maybe a little swordplay. Expand my self-defense skill set so that I feel more confident in the world. I think I've been outsourcing that to others."

His next mumble was both soothing and rallying. The canine equivalent of "fiddlesticks."

"I'm just rattled, and I think it's a combination of the magnitude of the rabbit problem and the timing of the murder." We were on Main Street now and there wasn't a parking spot to be found. That was odd for a weekday evening, but I preferred parking on side streets anyway. The spots were bigger and the spectators fewer. "And Justine," I added. "She beat us to Zander MacBride. I'm fine with Kellan getting the jump on us, but Justine? She's new to the community and a friend to no one, at least as far as I know. Where is she getting her intel? No one stupid enough to get herself stuck on a cemetery wall can be a legitimately good reporter. Can she?"

Keats' silence spoke volumes. I had gotten myself stuck in many awkward places and liked to consider myself a legitimately good sleuth. In some ways, a reporter was just a sleuth who blabbed about her findings.

"Ugh. Please let those awkward moments be the only thing Justine and I have in common. Because if she really is a good reporter, it's going to cause us a world of inconvenience."

The dog offered another dismissive "fiddlesticks." She might be good, but she was working alone, whereas I had a tremendous team, starting with a clean, handsome dog. My secret weapon.

"Okay, here's the plan," I said. "We mix and mingle with the ladies tonight and see if we can find out anything more about whose naughty list Rosalie was on. Tomorrow we'll come into town as soon as the stores open, buy the espresso machine and then stop by the cupcake store to grill Tizzy."

Keats approved the plan and we walked to Main Street in better spirits. I had the basket of two dozen roses looped over my arm.

Daisy was waiting for us outside The Tipsy Grape. She had dolled up for the occasion in a nice dress but her expression was serious. "Don't freak out," she said.

"Why would I freak out?" I asked, craning around her to look inside. Now I understood why there was no parking. The place was packed with women. More than double the number of roses in my basket. "What on earth? Jilly doesn't know fifty women in this town."

"Closer to seventy," Daisy said. "The owner just capped us because of overcrowding."

"Okay, well, I'll take a pass to keep the body count down," I said.

"Not a chance," Daisy said. "You need to put a lid on Poppy. I arranged for Teri Mason to give us painting lessons and there are easels set up in one corner."

"That sounds fun," I said. "I'd like to try it."

"We can't even hear Teri over the music. Poppy had a party theme of her own and went rogue."

"Uh-oh. What's her theme?"

"Pole dancing. She hired someone from Dorset Hills to install a pole and give lessons. Between painting and pole dancing, which do you think is more popular?"

I closed my eyes. "Jilly must be freaking out."

"She was drinking champagne out of a bottle with a straw."

My eyes popped open. "She barely drinks."

"Exactly. I took the champagne away and tucked her into a corner with Hazel Bingham and Martha Kinkaid. They'll protect her for now."

"I knew I should have brought Percy, regardless of their stupid rules," I said. "Keats, you'll need to transfer your full emotional support to Jilly, got it?"

His tail swished to let me know he had it handled.

"I'm sorry, Ivy." Daisy's eyes, so like my own, fixed on me earnestly. "I used to be able to handle Poppy along with everyone else but it's getting harder. Sometimes it feels like a never-ending school field trip with a dozen overstimulated kids."

I couldn't help laughing at the description. "Sounds about right, sis. And you do a great job in a tough situation. Let's just send the pole dancing instructor home early and we'll play the party games Iris set up."

"Violet arranged a scavenger hunt, too. Everyone wanted to contribute. Jilly is so popular."

"Popular, yes, but obviously no one knows her very well, because this is the exact opposite of what she would have wanted for her bachelorette party. I told Iris and Poppy weeks ago that a small, private dinner at the inn would have been up Jilly's alley."

We walked inside just in time to see two women I didn't recognize push a huge gift-wrapped box out of the back room on a wheeled cart.

"I don't like the looks of that," Daisy said.

"Why not? Jilly deserves a big gift for enduring this."

The top popped off the box and a young man stood up. He was wearing a chintzy looking tuxedo and set a top hat on his head with a flourish.

The loud music changed to something less sultry and more raunchy.

"Oh no, he's not a—"

The man loosened his bow tie, pulled it off, and tossed it into the crowd of women who gathered closer to the box.

He was a stripper, or at least a dancer.

My classy best friend would die a thousand deaths if his clothes came off and bills were tucked into... well, anything.

"Poppy did this?" My voice was a growl. "Where is she?"

"This wasn't Poppy," Daisy said, pointing to my wilder sister, who looked decidedly startled at the turn of events. "I have no idea who hired him."

"Well, I know who's firing him," I said, letting Keats guide me swiftly through the throngs.

He was flamboyantly shrugging off his tailcoat when I reached the gift box and grabbed his arm.

"Hello, I'm the maid of honor," I shouted over the music. "What's your name?"

"Brick House," he said, with an impish grin. "And you can pay me extra to—"

"Keep your clothes on," I said, pulling a stack of bills out of my purse. I'd intended to buy a few rounds but the money was better spent here. "Please put that jacket and tie back on right now. And tell me who hired you."

Brick House did as I asked. "Anonymous payment. Do you want me to go?"

I signaled a waiter to turn the music down, and women started booing. No doubt these were the people who never received an invitation to this event.

Keats nudged me in the shin and I took the hint. "Don't leave, Brick. Stay and enjoy the party. Work the crowd fully clothed. Please avoid the bride, though. She's the blonde cowering behind the seniors in the corner."

"Got it," Brick said. "Do you want me to entertain anyone in particular?"

"Watch out for my signal." Brick and I exchanged smiles. "You seem like a nice guy in the wrong job."

"Just earning college tuition," he said. "I plan to study business."

I pulled a card out of my purse. "The bride and I can give you some advice another time. When you're in plain clothes."

He thanked me and then jumped over the side of the box and melded into the crowd.

"Party pooper," someone said, behind me. I turned to find Edna in full combat gear, grinning. "There's nothing like a dancer to create a cover for your investigation."

"No one could even hear me over the music. Tell me you didn't arrange that, Edna. Jilly's probably mortified."

"She's marrying your brother, so she'll have to get used to feeling mortified. But no, I wouldn't waste a penny on something as frivolous as that. Think about how much Spam it would buy for the bunker."

Gertie came up in time to hear Edna's words. "It wasn't me, either. My money goes to animal causes."

"Same here," Remi Malone said, joining us. "It's going to cost a bomb to get that many rabbits neutered, vaccinated and rehomed."

Cori and Bridget just shook their heads. The Mafia knew how to have fun, but when there was an "open case" in the rescue world, they were all business. Showing up tonight was a testament to how much they liked Jilly.

"Just let it go for now," said Evie Springdale. "It'll all come out in the wash and we probably only have a few minutes to talk bunny before you're called into bridesmaid duty."

Keats mumbled his agreement.

I filled them in on what had transpired earlier in the day in relation to the rabbit colony.

Cori snapped her gloved fingers suddenly and then whirled her hand at Keats. The dog left my side to do her bidding, which would normally annoy me, but in this case was most welcome.

Justine Schalow was hovering right behind Bridget, the tallest of the Rescue Mafia, trying to eavesdrop. Seeing the reporter jump after a well-placed nip gave me great satisfaction, and grins zipped around our circle like wildfire.

"Something needs to be done about that problem," Cori said, as Justine moved away. "My contacts say she's been driven out of several towns."

"I volunteer for pest control," Edna said. "There are dozens of old wells she could fall into by accident. Just say the word."

Cori nodded too quickly. "Heard she's not much of a climber."

I laughed. "We can't dump her down a well. It would take police resources to find her and they're needed. So let's just use evasive maneuvers and focus on the rabbits."

"We've got a plan," Cori said. "Almost. Just a few minor details to work out. Like how to extract them right out from under Chief Hottie's nose. Evie and Remi had to sweet talk some cops when we got caught trying to reach the colony earlier."

I could have told them how to get in but there was no way to extract more than 100 rabbits with so many police on duty.

"We'll need to wait till Kellan is done," I said. "But I'm glad you have ideas because they deserve better than what I fear the mayor is planning. She wasn't at all encouraging today."

Cori looked at Remi, who said, "We'll brief Isla again on the situation. Maybe our mayor can talk your mayor down."

"I hope so, because I'm invested in Opal and her fluffle."

"Opal?" Cori asked. "Don't go getting attached, Ivy. That's why you'll never make a good rescuer."

"Or survive the end times," Edna added. "You'll be lagging behind our army and trying to keep that ark afloat."

"Don't pick on Ivy," Remi said. "We're only handling the rabbits and she's working on the murder and the wedding, too."

That reminded me of my other duties. Leaving my friends, I followed Keats into the crowd. He had a destination in mind, which I assumed was Jilly's corner. Instead, he led me to a quiet spot near the door, where Tizzy Cousins was chatting to a tall, imposing woman a decade or two her senior.

"Greetings," I said, smiling as I offered my hand to the stranger. "I'm Ivy Galloway, maid of honor."

"Goldie Masters," she said, smoothing a silver bob that was as subdued as her husband's hair was unruly. "Your brother invited us to the wedding so I figured I should come out tonight in support of the bride."

"Same," Tizzy said. "Although it's difficult, when we're all heartbroken over Rosalie."

Goldie's pursed lips suggested she was anything but heartbroken over Roz's departure from the world.

I glanced down at Keats, who was no longer in the party mood.

His ruff was up and he looked from one woman to the other with his blue eye. I would have to part them to find out what troubled him.

Signaling Brick, I introduced him to Tizzy, who walked off with him without a backward glance.

"How strange," Goldie said. "And unbecoming of a member of the Hill Country Horticulture Society. We chose Tizzy because of her manners. She's not exactly refined, but miles ahead of that other one."

"You mean Rosalie?" I asked.

She fluttered her fingers. "The departed. I didn't wish her dead, of course, but I won't say I'm sad she's gone. Roz turned my husband's head, as I believe he mentioned to you."

I nodded. "I can imagine how hard that was, especially after you've raised a family together."

"And run a successful business," Goldie said, toying with a pendant that looked as expensive as her watch and bracelet. "But as far as I was concerned, the worst thing was the gardening. Edwin was over at Rosalie's house all the time, helping her with her rabbit problem. He should have been home tending the garden we built together."

"That's a beautiful metaphor, Goldie."

"And completely true. We have extensive gardens built one plant at a time over decades, Ivy. And it's at risk of rabbit incursions, too. It's only a hop, skip and a jump to Dorset Hills." Her lips pursed again and she held out her wrist to show me the bracelet. "Guilt gifts. They mean nothing to me. My heart has always been in flowers and Edwin knows that. It was our love language."

"I'm sorry," I said, glancing down at Keats and finding him still puffed. "I hope time will mend all wounds. And gardens."

Her eyes became cold and unyielding. "Not as long as those varmints are around."

"They'll be gone soon, don't worry. The mayor and the police have the situation well in hand."

"I don't believe you," she said. "You sound as slippery as a politician."

The comment was like a kick to the gut with a sensible shoe. "On the contrary, Goldie. I care about our town's beautiful gardens very much, but I care about animals far more. In this situation, I'm backing the rabbits."

She shook her ritzy bracelet at me. "I'd be very careful if I were you, Ivy. Very careful, indeed. People feel strongly about this."

Keats leaned against my leg and I felt the vibration of his growl.

"Is that a threat, Mrs. Masters?" I asked. "Because if it is, I rescind your invitation to the wedding."

"You can't rescind an invitation made by the groom."

"It's my farm," I said, snapping my fingers for Keats as I left. "Watch me."

CHAPTER TWENTY-THREE

"You didn't need to be so rude," Mom said, following me down the short hall to the restroom.

"Sure, I did," I said. "I'm tired of people turning Jilly's wedding into a circus, and when someone threatens me, they're not welcome."

I passed the restroom and kept walking.

"Where are you going, Ivy? You're one of the party hosts."

"I've left everything in capable hands. Gertie went to get Minnie from her van. If that man so much as undoes a button—"

"Since when did you become so buttoned up?" Mom asked.

I turned quickly so that I could catch her expression. "Did you hire that dancer, Mom?"

"Hardly. Nor did I participate in the pole dancing, as empowering as I believe it can be for women. It's not a good look for the mother of the groom."

Keats' fond tail-fanning told me she was telling the truth.

"Thank goodness," I said, moving forward again. "Maybe you can empower yourself privately with your class."

"I only have a sewing class now, as I told you, and I don't think Brick House is their style."

At the back door, I turned again. "Mom, can you please stick with Jilly? This party is everything she didn't want and she needs support."

"Then stay and give it to her," she said, hazel eyes narrowing. "Whatever you're planning to do can wait."

I shook my head. "The very best thing I can do for Jilly and Asher is make sure their wedding goes off as planned. I have a lead."

"You can't go alone. Where's Edna?"

"Distracting the very people I want out of the way. She's needed here with Gertie."

Mom pushed past me and opened the back door. "Let's go. If we hurry, we can make it back before the scavenger hunt."

"Keats and I can handle this one," I said.

Unfortunately, my dog thought otherwise. He nudged my mother in the calf and sent her out the door in a hurry.

"Don't even think about nipping me," she said, hurrying ahead through the staff parking lot. "I'm coming of my own free will."

"Against *my* will," I muttered.

She glanced over her shoulder, moving twice as fast as I could in heels. "If Keats wants me along for the ride, doesn't that tell you something?"

"Yeah." I caught up to her. "I'm just not sure what it is."

"That I'm an asset, plain and simple," she said, letting him guide her down the street to the truck.

"How can you be an asset in a secret investigation dressed like that? You look like a stop sign. A shiny one, too."

Her outfit was scarlet satin, for the most part, and appeared to have been reconstituted from at least four others.

"I changed twice before leaving the inn," she said. "I had a sneaking suspicion I needed to go with an A-line skirt for freer movement. Although I do hope we won't be climbing fences."

"We'll be climbing fences," I said. "Still time to back out, Mom."

"I recall doing a better job at that than you," she said. "I attribute my fitness partly to belly dancing. You should come along sometime."

I let Keats into the back seat and offered Mom the passenger seat out of respect to her satin. "No thank you."

"You're going to need more hobbies," she said, as I closed the door a little harder than necessary.

After I got behind the wheel, I answered her. "I have over sixty hobbies, feathered and furred. Plus manure. You know how important my fertilizer is to me."

"Oh, darling. Honestly. Do you really need to say those things out loud?"

I pulled away from the curb and did a U-turn. "Actually, yeah. I spent decades of my life not speaking my truth. Or even knowing it. Now it's a priority for me to be authentic." Sticking my hand between the seats, I let Keats give my fingers a poke of approval. "One serious conk on the head got my lips moving."

"Not every thought needs to be shared," she said, tapping red fingernails on the passenger window. "Especially those related to manure. And more especially at such an important time for our family. Your grandmother would be appalled."

I stopped at the corner and took a moment to stare at her. "You're probably right that I share too many thoughts now, but you must realize you do the same. How does your mom feel about that?"

The red nails moved to buff paw prints off the dashboard. "Mother says you and I are cut from the same cloth. Can you believe it?"

Her obvious indignation made me laugh and Keats joined in from behind. My mother was horrified to be in the same category as this farmer.

"I can believe it. Maybe I shouldn't blame the concussion, but your genes." I took another few turns and checked over my shoulder to make sure we weren't being followed. "Cut from the same cloth.

It's a good expression but most people would say I'm more like Calvin."

"It's okay to call him 'Dad' in front of me," she said. "I would imagine you've all been walking on eggshells since he came back, but I've adjusted."

Her fingers twitched and I knew she wanted to touch the old locket hidden under her dress. The small heart had several red stones from Garnet Point my father had given her when they were just teens. Sometimes I thought she still had feelings for him, despite the fact he'd left her to raise six kids largely on her own. Yet her robust dating rotation seemed only slightly diminished. She could be out every night of the week if she wanted. Instead, she was often home sewing or working with Belle Tremblay at Chez Belle.

"We can tell you're okay," I said. "At first I was afraid the wedding would be awkward but you and Dad both seem at peace."

"I wouldn't go that far. How peaceful can I be when my parents are coming? I don't understand why Asher had to invite half the world."

"I don't understand why you had to invite the other half. Jilly wanted an intimate affair and most of the local populace will be there."

"Maybe they should have eloped," Mom said. "Like Calvin and I did. It was about as private as you can get. No pressure at all." She paused for a moment, and then added, "It would have been a disappointment if they had, though."

"They may still need to elope, the way things are going."

"Jilly won't," Mom said, touching my arm lightly. "Because of you."

"Me? Why would you say that?"

"She can't elope and leave you behind. That would be breaking the friendship code."

I shook off her hand. "She should do what she wants to do, and I support her fully. *That's* the friendship code."

"Ivy, I'm not finding fault with you. Really. The bond you have with Jilly is beautiful and something I've never experienced. You've been through so much together."

A lump formed in my throat and Keats leaned through the gap to lick my ear. He didn't splash licks around liberally so I guess I was even more upset than I knew.

"Some might call it a trauma bond," she said. Her voice was unusually gentle. "It's so strong that I worry for Kellan. Maybe he doubts he can compete with Jilly, as well as Keats and Percy."

This time I offered a dry croak. "I'm sure Kellan doesn't think he comes second to Jilly."

"Well, I'm probably wrong. What do I know about love?"

That worried me more than anything else. Mom never admitted she was wrong.

"He does come after Keats and Percy," I said. "But he's okay with that."

"That's different. He wants to be the number one human, I would think. Don't you feel the same way?"

I covered the last few blocks without speaking. Finally, I asked, "If Jilly and I are too attached, why isn't Asher bothered?"

Mom laughed. "My son has many wonderful traits, but intuition isn't one of them. He sees what he wants to see, and I have no idea where he acquired that skill because his parents are not so fortunate. At least, not anymore."

I pulled up under cover of some low-hanging branches. "Mom, I don't want Jilly to feel like she's dragging me around. She deserves to run free and live her life."

She patted my arm again and held on when I tried to pull away. "You'll work things out, Ivy. You always do. I'm very proud of you."

The lump in my throat came back. "Why did you have to choose this moment to get all touchy-feely? We're in the middle of an operation."

"You're always in the middle of something. I'm proud of that, too. Worried, but proud. I love how you're making a difference in the world. I should never have pushed you into business school. That was projecting my own ambitions onto you—ambitions I didn't know I had at the time."

"Well, you're a businesswoman now twice over," I said. "Not counting SurvivalDate, which also did great as a startup."

"I'm happy I've had new opportunities this past year. And it all started when you came home from Boston." She stared around. "I'm even thinking of taking Buttercup off the blocks. If I can run a business, I can drive that car."

"Mom, don't say that to Asher before the wedding. That might be the only thing that's ever really fazed your golden boy. He was the laughingstock of the police force."

She waved jaunty fingertips to silence me. "Whose fence are we scaling this time, darling? I'm ready for action."

"This house belongs to Tizzy Cousins. And our next stop is Goldie Masters' place. Edna is keeping them at the party so that I can do a sweep of their gardens."

"Looking for what? More rabbits?"

"Toxic plants. Rosalie Roarke was poisoned with castor beans, among other things, and they're uncommon around here. Kellan told me the township prohibited them because of injury to livestock and pets."

We got out of the truck and followed Keats back to Tizzy's house. As usual, Mom was twice as fast as I was, and my heels kept getting stuck in the grass. She turned from a silly gadfly into a secret agent whenever I let her join me.

I could tell she was a little disappointed when we got to the back gate and found it unlocked. Tonight wasn't her night to outclimb me.

Unlatching the gate, I let us into the yard. The light from the street was enough to show that the gardens were large. I held Mom back and flicked on my light for a quick scan. Much of the foliage had been devoured by my long-eared friends, it seemed.

"At least there won't likely be booby traps," I whispered. "Tizzy let the rabbits win this round."

"What a shame," Mom said. "I do feel for gardeners who invested so much time in their hobby, only to see it laid to waste."

"It only happened because people set their rabbits free," I said. "They're just making a living the best way they know how."

"I know. And they're so cute. Look at that one."

She redirected my phone light at the back of the yard, where there were dozens of short shrubs.

"Opal," I said, walking toward her.

"You've named the rabbits?" Mom said.

"Only this one. So far."

"And how do you know it's the same one?"

"Her coloring. She's an opal Rex. Plus, there's a nick out of her ear."

Keats hung back to give the rabbit space but it wasn't necessary. She hopped over quite briskly and then turned to make her way to a smaller bed in the opposite corner.

"Is she inviting us to follow her?" Mom said.

"Definitely. There's something she wants us to see."

Keats reached Opal first and went into a point.

"What is it?" Mom asked. "I just see more plants."

"Yes. They're in good shape because the rabbits know better than to eat toxic plants."

I quickly snapped some photos and then got my penknife and a plastic bag out of my purse.

"Ivy, don't touch them," Mom said, sounding alarmed for the first time.

"I came prepared." I pulled out gloves, snipped a few clippings, and dropped them into the bag. Then I peeled the gloves off carefully and added them, as well as the knife, to the clippings. "Anything else we should see, Opal?"

The rabbit hopped much faster across the yard to the gate and turned sideways to look at me. Then she kicked up dirt with her big rear paws and shot under a hole in the fence.

"What was that?" Mom said, following me out of the gate. "It looked like a sign even to me."

"I don't speak rabbit yet. But she was sure in a hurry, and that probably means we should be, too."

Keats thought so. His ruff rose and his tail puffed as he led the way up the side of the house. Opal was ahead of us and she ran a zigzag pattern across the lawn and into the road.

There, she paused under a streetlight.

"Opal," I called, as loudly as I dared. "Get off the road."

The rabbit didn't move.

"She'll move when she needs to," Mom said. "If she's survived in the wild she knows how to escape predators."

"But maybe not cars," I said. "There's one turning onto the street now. Keats, go herd her across, please."

The dog didn't move. What on earth was going on?

I looked down and saw he was pointing in the direction of the car.

"Do you think it's Tizzy?" Mom asked, straightening as she readied for a confrontation.

"Edna would have texted if she left the party." I stared down the road. "Uh-oh. Let's run for it."

CHAPTER TWENTY-FOUR

I was grateful to have parked up the street under heavy trees. It gave us a few moments to get to the truck before the car reached us. All I could do now was avoid getting caught red-handed. Knowing we were onto her would give Tizzy time to come up with better cover stories, or worse, skip town, taking all hopes of our family wedding with her.

"Opal, get out of the way," I called again. "Don't risk yourself to save us."

Mom was ahead of me, covering the grass in leaps and bounds. "You're giving that rabbit too much credit. She's just doing what rabbits do. Freezing in terror."

I was running, too, but when I looked back over my shoulder, Opal wasn't frozen in the headlights of the oncoming car. She was hopping toward it in her zigzag pattern, possibly hoping to be noticed. I guessed she was hoping the driver would see her and stop, buying us some time. It was a brave move, because the vast majority of townspeople wouldn't stop for a rabbit right now. What was one less in the big scheme of things?

Keats gave a yip of warning but I was so busy staring back at Opal that I missed the little ledge between Tizzy's lawn and her neighbor's. My heel turned as it landed and I ended up rolling several yards down an incline. I stared up at the midnight stars for a moment, stunned.

The dog came back and nipped at my hip to get me moving.

"That's not helping," I said. "Mom!"

She was already bending over me, with her hand outstretched. "Oh darling, your dress. But I can repair it for you."

"The dress is the least of my worries," I said, clambering to my feet and picking up the plastic bag.

"Your attire should never be the least of your worries," she said, tugging me forward. "That's what I keep telling you."

"Well, I think I sprained my ankle in these heels," I said, wincing as I walked. "That wouldn't have happened in work boots."

"It wouldn't have happened if you'd been looking ahead instead of behind," she said, urging me on with impatient jerks. "Don't they teach you that in sleuthing 101?"

"I'd pay good money for a class like that," I said. "I'm entirely self-taught, you know."

"Why do you think I worry so much?" she said, taking the key from me and opening the driver's door of the truck.

I thought she was just being kind, but instead of helping me in, she hopped behind the wheel herself.

"Mom, no. Let me drive."

"You just twisted your ankle and this isn't the time to go light on the pedals. Get into the passenger seat, Ivy Rose. That's an order."

"I want to change my middle name," I grumbled, hobbling around the truck. "Rose reminds me too much of Rosalie Roarke."

Once I was seated and Keats was in the back, she turned the key. "I ran out of good flower names when I got to you. Look on the bright side... it could have been Castor."

I couldn't help snickering. "Or Begonia."

"Impatiens would have been perfect," she said, letting the truck roll down the slight slope. "But I didn't know that at the time."

"I think I may have inherited that trait from you, too," I said. "Anyway, letting you drive is a bad idea. It got us in big trouble the last time you did it."

She slid forward in the seat to reach the pedals more easily and geared up smoothly. "Not that big. And I learned from it."

Peering into the side mirror, I saw the sedan was stopped in the middle of the street, and the rabbit was a small blob in the headlights. Opal had somehow managed to hold her ground. That was one brave rabbit. A leporine heroine.

"What did you learn?" I asked.

"Not to underestimate myself, for starters," she said. "I let everyone else's opinion of my driving wear down my memories of impressive skills. My problem was focus, but that's been improving lately, and I won't let my guard down tonight."

"Your focus *has* been improving. It's impressive, Mom."

She was silent for a moment, perhaps examining my comment for secret snark, which was so often there. "Thank you, darling. I appreciate your noticing." Turning the corner, she picked up speed fast. "The other thing I learned is to avoid getting caught. Luckily the police are too busy with the murder case to waste time on minor traffic infractions."

"I wouldn't count on that. Kellan deployed his recruits into the community to make sure there's a visible police presence everywhere. It helps people feel safe."

"No one's really safe in this town," Mom said, taking a hard right without signaling. She hadn't turned the headlights on, either, but it was bright enough to see the road ahead. "Everyone feels it but they don't know how to manage the worry. It stops people from enjoying the simple things. Like taking a ride under a nearly full moon. Let's savor this, Ivy."

"Can I savor after we've dropped the plants at the police station?" I asked. "At which time, I'll be behind the wheel?"

She craned to look in the rearview mirror and made another

sharp turn that threw me into the passenger door. There was a scrabble of claws on the back seat, followed by a grumble.

"Sorry, darlings. I see lights behind us, and we'll need to course correct."

"Meaning what?" I asked.

The answer was yet another turn into what appeared to be a laneway to someone's home. A dead end.

When the lane ended, however, I saw it was another beginning.

Mom giggled as we rolled over a series of intentional speed bumps into the back country trail system. "Oh my, what fun. Roll down your window, Ivy and breathe in freedom."

I did roll down my window because I was feeling lightheaded. "What I smell is terror, Mom. Please slow down."

She sped up instead, and my stomach gave an ominous rumble. It was a good thing Keats' bath made me skip dinner, because it would probably be making a reappearance now. "Mom, I'm going to barf."

"Don't use the bag with the plants," she said. "Digestive enzymes are the enemy of evidence."

I stuck my nose out the window and pulled in a few deep breaths. "I hope you know where you're going."

"Of course I do. This is one of my favorite legs of the system. The hills are thrilling."

"I can't handle thrills right now. Can't you find a gentler route? Dad has a lot of good ones marked."

She slid forward even more and gripped the wheel harder. "I noticed he refreshed a lot of them when he got home. Even the route to Garnet Point."

Turning away from the window, I stared at her. "How would you notice that?"

"I suppose I could tell you that my gentleman friends take me out for a spin," she said. Her lips tipped up in a smirk. "That sounds plausible."

"It's obviously untrue. Which means you've been driving around back here often enough to explore Dad's old routes."

"There are so many of them. It brings back memories." She gave a nostalgic sigh. "We did have fun back in the day."

"Mom. What vehicle are you using for these joyrides? It can't be my truck because I'd notice. And Buttercup is still on blocks."

Her smirk turned into an enigmatic smile. "It isn't your truck, so you have nothing to worry about."

"Are you driving your dates around? Renting a car?"

"Darling, focus," she said. "Learn from what I'm learning. We're on the run from someone right now and my driving habits are the least of your worries."

In that moment we seemed to lift off. Then we landed with a bump that tossed Keats into the footwell.

"Take it easy on my dog," I said. "Your driving habits are my *biggest* worry right now."

She let go of the wheel with her right hand and thrust her thumb over her shoulder. "Lights, darling. We have company."

Keats got back on the seat and looked out the rear window, grumbling.

"Is it her?" I asked him.

His next mumble was an affirmative.

"Do you mind telling me who we're outrunning?" Mom asked.

"The reporter. Justine Schalow. She's been tracking me and getting in the way of both the rabbit rescue and the murder investigation. If she saw we were trespassing at Tizzy's, she could publish the news and impede Kellan's work."

"Which means it could impede the wedding." Mom's fingers tightened on the wheel. "What if she got a photo? We lost time as you were thrashing around in the grass."

I bit my lip to stop hot words from spilling out. She wasn't wrong. I was just embarrassed. "Justine wasn't close enough to get a good shot in dim light. That's probably why she's in pursuit."

"Well, it's a good thing I covered your plates, now, isn't it?" Mom asked.

"You covered my plates? With what?"

"Scarves. I always carry a couple in my purse in case I'm caught in a draught. The weather at this time of year is so unpredictable."

"When did you pull that off?"

"While you were negotiating with Brick House. It only took a jiffy and I suspected you'd be running around later. I'm surprised you haven't thought about it before."

I rubbed my forehead. "So we were driving around town with scarlet scarves screaming 'pull me over'?"

"It's one reason I thought we were better off back here," she said. "Either way, black trucks are a dime a dozen and that reptilian reporter will have a hard time proving it's you." Turning on the high beams, she peered up at the trees. "There it is! Your father's Champagne Trail, marked clear as day."

She switched off the high beams again and said, "Keats, can you help navigate, please? I don't want the lights to give us away."

He came through the seats with a reluctant mutter, which I interpreted for her. "He said, slow the heck down or the deal's off."

"I know what he said." She gave a tinkling laugh. "I don't like to think I speak his language but when I'm distracted, I tend to get the general drift."

With Keats sniffing the air through the crack and tapping the dashboard, we traveled a very circuitous route that anyone would have trouble following, not just a newcomer to the area. I started to breathe a little easier and my stomach settled.

"Why is it called the Champagne Trail?" I asked.

"Because it leads to Champagne Alley," she said.

"Which means what, exactly?"

"Let me focus, darling. I can't see her lights, but I think she's still back there. Call it mother of the groom intuition. That woman is trying to steal our wedding."

I fought a grin. Mom did consider the wedding her time to shine, perhaps because she never got the one she wanted. But it was motivating her highly now, and I appreciated her commitment to getting us out of this scrape. In fact, she seemed to have become one with the truck, gearing up and down seamlessly as the terrain changed. When she was in this mode, there was no question that she was a better driver than I was. And yet she had taken out more stop signs than everyone else in the history of Clover Grove combined. People were so complicated. It was one of the reasons I wanted to escape human resources, and most definitely the attraction of farm work. Managing livestock wasn't easy but it was a picnic compared to interpreting human behavior. Or at least a relief.

Keats mumbled his agreement to that.

"I can tell you two are talking about me," Mom said. "Thank you for keeping it private."

Reaching out, I patted her arm. "Maybe it's flattering. I'm astounded by how you're handling this trail. Even if I'm worried about how you've been training for it."

"Blame it on Edna. She turned me down for her stupid course and it got me thinking."

"You actually bought into the zombie uprising?" I asked, laughing.

"I bought into the perils of modern life in Clover Grove. How many murders have you seen come and go, Ivy? Too many, and it keeps me up at night sewing the worry away. We need to be able to take care of ourselves."

The trail expanded to a broad plateau and she geared up. Grabbing the handle, I braced Keats. "Mom, you're out in the open driving like a maniac. With the lights out."

"We've got a problem," she said. "Oh my!"

Two sets of headlights came directly at us, driving side by side at a speed that made me gasp first and then scream.

"Mom, look out!"

She hauled the wheel right and rolled the truck down an embankment into a creek. Keats jumped into the back seat and barked a warning.

"Switch places, darling," Mom said. "Fast."

I started to open my door and found her already climbing over the stick shift. Her elbows were on my knees and pinned me down.

"Wait," I said. "Let me run around the truck."

"You want them to find *you* behind the wheel, trust me. Get moving."

Easier said than done. Mom was barely 100 pounds, but the awkward position and floundering reminded me of being stuck under Wilma last year. Only the swampy pool was missing.

The thought made me laugh and then I was done for. I couldn't stop giggling as I tried to navigate under her flailing limbs. I yelped once as my injured ankle snagged on the passenger seat and again when her stiletto gouged my arm.

"Ivy, you're so stiff and inflexible. How many times do I need to recommend yoga?"

"If truck wrestling is going to be a regular thing, I'll give it a try," I said, shoving off the passenger door with my good foot.

Unfortunately, it was slightly ajar and the door flew open. In the meantime, my skirt snagged on the stick shift.

"One last try," Mom said, clawing madly at the dashboard to prop herself up.

"It's too late," I said. "Just play dead."

There was a pant of laughter that I first took to be Mom, but then realized it was Keats. He wouldn't be so amused if we were about to be ambushed by Justine, or worse.

Two sets of high beams shone over the shallow gully and a man's voice rang out. "Stay where you are. Do not move."

And so, when light flooded into the driver's window, my beloved found me lying across two seats half underneath my mother, with my dress hitched up beyond decency.

CHAPTER TWENTY-FIVE

One flashlight beam immediately flicked away, no doubt due to the state of my dress.

"Mom, are you kidding me?"

The voice was Asher's and I could tell he'd turned his back on the truck.

"Turn that light off, Kellan Harper," Mom said. "Ivy's tied up at the moment."

The light wavered and then bounced around. There was a clicking sound.

"Did you just take a picture?" I said. Shouted, actually. The window was partly open but my indignation was high.

Kellan didn't say anything. The flashlight continued to bounce around, returning again and again.

"It's not funny," Asher said. His teenaged squawk had returned. "With all due respect, Chief, that's my sister half-dressed under my mother. I don't even want to know what they were doing."

Kellan stopped trying to hold back. Leaning against the truck, he unleashed a bellow of laughter. He sounded young and carefree again, and my heart twinged a little remembering how often I used to hear that laugh.

Keats climbed over me and Mom to escape through the open passenger door. A moment later Kellan's laughter turned into a yelp as Keats ended the merriment.

The dog mumbled something and Kellan said, "Fine, fine, I'll get her out."

Mom released my skirt from the stick shift and left the truck under her own steam. Meanwhile, Kellan opened the driver's door carefully, slipped his arms under mine and half-lifted, half-pulled till I was upright. My ankle promptly gave out and I staggered into him.

"Ow, ow. My ankle," I said.

He swept me into his arms and carried me up the bank. It was nice to feel supported by a handsome man in his best leather jacket.

Mom had to manage without an offer of support, and she still passed us. Her golden boy's jeans and sneakers also disappeared swiftly over the top.

Asher's pickup and Kellan's SUV sat right above us, driver's doors open. When he got to his vehicle, my boyfriend set me down carefully where I could prop myself on the hood.

"What happened to your foot?" he asked, showing he was still in boyfriend mode.

Mom strutted up to him and inserted herself into his space and the conversation. "Ivy hasn't learned to run in heels. It's a valuable skill."

"We were doing some reconnaissance at Tizzy Cousins' house when Justine Schalow tracked us down," I said. "We tried to get away before she caught us in the act."

"And you led her out here again, when I asked you not to," he said, sounding more chiefly. "Where is she now?"

"I don't know." I glanced down at Keats and he raised his paw in a point. "Somewhere in that general direction."

"Which happens to be the direction of Potter's Bog," he said. "So I'm going to have to send officers after her."

"It wasn't my idea," I said. "Although I probably would have done the same thing. We don't need photos like that in her gossip rag at a time like this."

Kellan crossed his arms. "So you let your mother drive. After I asked you not to do that, too. And with the plates covered, on top of everything else."

"She didn't *let* me, young man," Mom said, putting her hands on her hips. "I fought for the wheel because she'd hurt her foot. I was protecting Ivy from the press. And protecting Asher from having his wedding cancelled."

"Don't bring me into this," Asher called. He was on the other side of his truck, using it as a shield against mortification. "I'm the one who seized your license, remember? And the one who detained you after you knocked down another stop sign a while back. Now you've put Ivy's truck into a ditch and tried to blame her."

"Asher, we're in this together," I said. "Family."

"I am *not* in this with you two," he said.

"You sound very pouty," Mom said. "No one likes a pouty police officer, son."

Kellan started pacing, perhaps to avoid the sheepdog as much as my mother. I sensed he was fighting both anger and laughter, and there was no telling which would win. "Mrs. Galloway, you can't flout the law and take a drive when the spirit moves you. No license means no driving. Ever."

Asher's mumble talk on the other side of the truck sounded like my dog's.

"Never mind," Mom said. She had very sharp ears for her children's mutinous insolence. "Let's stick to what happened tonight."

Kellan turned and said, "Officer Galloway. Please join us."

My brother's face was a mottled red when he stepped back into the overlapping circles of light. "I'm sorry, Chief. I can't control her, and I have tried."

"Are you aware of other driving incidents?" Kellan asked. All the humor had drained out of his voice now.

Asher scuffed the soil with his boot and then said, "I have reason to believe she may have been driving."

"Nothing you witnessed yourself," Mom said, "which invalidates any slanderous reports."

Kellan looked at me and I shrugged. "I only got wind of it tonight. I'm assuming one of her admirers has been lending her a car."

"Sutton," Asher said, still scuffing the dirt. "My nephew. I asked where he got the coin to upgrade to custom rims on his beater and the truth came out. I'd planned to bring it up with Mom after the wedding."

"My own grandson sold me up the river," Mom said. "I'll have a word with him."

"Leave Sutton out of it," Asher said. "In full disclosure, I bribed him for the information."

"He's extorted me, too," I said. "That boy will make a good living one day."

"Get into the car, Mrs. Galloway," Kellan said. "Back seat, please."

"I will not," Mom said, lifting her chin defiantly. "What I've done is no worse than what you two were doing back here in Champagne Alley."

Kellan backed away as if he'd been nipped, although Keats had walked away to surveil the darkness behind their vehicles.

"Champagne Alley," I said. "That's an odd name. What were you and Asher doing?"

"We were in pursuit of a suspect," Asher said, blue eyes darting around suspiciously.

"In pursuit of a high," Mom said. "Drag racing. Just like when I caught you both out here when you were fifteen. Unlicensed. In a stolen car. And drinking cheap champagne to boot. Buttercup had a heck of a time with the terrain, but we got here before anyone was hurt. Or arrested."

Kellan faded back even further and now he was the one scuffing the dirt. "It's not what you think."

"It's exactly what I think," Mom said. "Your very posture proves it, young man. Plus I have pulled my son out of more awkward situations than anyone knows about. I have a nose for these things."

"Mom," Asher said. "He's my boss."

"And I'm your mother. The one who gets nothing but flak for the way I raised you. But when you were in trouble, who drove to the rescue? Was it your father? Daisy?"

Asher paused for a few seconds. "You did. And I guess I owe you a thanks."

Mom shook her head. "That's what mothers do. I also take accountability for the reasons you used to come back here and risk your life with Kellan Harper and the other ruffians."

"And here I thought we got all the bad genes from Dad's side of the family," I said.

"Mine aren't all rainbows either," Mom said. "We do the best we can with the hand we're dealt. I will say, I never in a million years would have predicted you boys would end up in law enforcement."

Kellan finally came back, prompted from the rear by his black-and-white nemesis. "I wouldn't have predicted it either, Mrs. Galloway. And in consideration of the circumstances, perhaps we'll just ignore this violation. As long as you promise not to bribe Sutton for his wheels again."

I wanted to warn him that he was leaving three teenage loopholes wide open, but Mom pressed down on my good foot with one stiletto to silence me. "Agreed, Chief," she said.

"For the record, we never stole cars," Kellan said.

"We returned them clean every time," Asher added. "Not so much as a ding."

They looked like two sheepish schoolboys caught in Mom's glare.

"Why were you drag racing?" I asked.

"Men need to blow off steam sometimes," Mom said. "The pressure on Kellan and Asher is incredibly high this week."

"The wedding," I said, grinning. "This was your bachelor party."

"Bachelor party of two," Asher said. "We just wanted a bit of fun to commemorate our friendship. And now you've wrecked it."

"Hardly," Kellan said. "I believe you won, my friend. Something that didn't happen too often back in the day."

"Aw, Kellan let you win as a wedding gift," I said, looping my arm through my boyfriend's. "You guys have had a long bromance and I think it was the perfect way to mark the occasion."

"Can we not talk about this again?" Asher said. "Jilly wouldn't like it."

"You don't know her like I know her, brother," I said. "Now, would you mind backing my truck out of the ditch?"

"I'll do it," Kellan said, releasing my arm. "Officer Galloway is going to fish Justine out of the bog."

"Don't hurry," I called after my brother. "Let her stay gone till after the wedding."

"Someone's a little jealous because the reporter's a good sleuth," Mom said.

"If Justine manages to break the case before we do, I'll send her flowers," I said. "And not poison ones. My pride will take the hit for the sake of the wedding."

Keats mumbled to me and I looked down to find him in a point again. "It's okay, buddy. Asher's going to handle the reporter."

Stopping halfway down the bank, Kellan called, "Can we send Officer Keats with your brother? It'll likely take half the time and ensure the groom is back for the wedding. I don't trust Ms. Schalow not to turn this into gossip theater."

Keats trailed after my brother more reluctantly than I expected. Normally he loved special assignments where he got to show off his superdog powers. His blue eye pierced the darkness and locked onto mine. There was something I was missing, that much was clear.

"Tomorrow," I said. His mumbled response faded as he jumped into Asher's pickup.

That would be soon enough, I thought.

It was only two days till the wedding, so it had to be.

CHAPTER TWENTY-SIX

I was awake and waiting when Byron delivered his four a.m. status report, and took my cue to get up and going.

"Remember when I used to sleep like a normal person?" I said, digging through my drawer for long johns. I hadn't needed cold weather gear this year and just seeing them made Keats quake. Long johns meant his coat would soon come out for winter, the season of his discontent. "Right, you wouldn't remember my sleeping normally because that was before your time. Getting clocked by Skint wrecked my inner clock."

I chuckled at my play on words and all that got me was stares from my companions.

"Oh, cut me some slack. You boys manage to catch a few winks through the day but this is it for me. I'm going to be haggard in the wedding photos."

I pulled on the long johns and then my overalls. Getting a jump on the day had its upside but my metabolism took a while to catch up.

"We'll stop for coffee and pie later," I said. "I'm going to need the full force of Mandy's magic to get through our itinerary. Even for us, it's busy."

Percy let his fluffy tail settle over his eyes, letting me know he was still in a snit over being left out of the bachelorette party and all that came after. I'd never known a cat to hold onto a grudge so stubbornly. But then, I'd never known a cat like Percy. He was one of a kind. A feline hero.

The tail lifted slightly and he shot me a green-eyed glance that said, "you got that right."

"I'm sorry you missed the party, but you'll be at every other event till Jilly drives off on her honeymoon," I said. "And we've agreed you can split your time between us if you like."

He got up with a little purr-meow and came to offer me a head butt as I sat down on the edge of the bed. I wasn't sure whether he'd take me up on the offer to enjoy joint custody but it seemed he liked having choices.

It took a few minutes to ease a compression bandage over my foot. The swelling wasn't too bad and I wanted to keep it that way. I'd gotten off pretty lucky and still hoped to wear heels to the wedding. Today, I was happy to lace into my boots for stability.

"Listen, boys," I said, reaching for my jacket, "I'd really appreciate it if you could help me pull out all the stops today. I feel like we're getting close."

Keats' mumbled response ended on a questioning note.

"Nope, not a clue," I said. "Well, plenty of clues and motivations, but no real idea who poisoned Rosalie. I count on my intuition—and you two—to fill in some blanks." Staring down at them, I sighed. "To be honest, each time we get to this point, I doubt it will all come together."

I finished my autumn ensemble with a scarf and a wool toque. Keats snorted in disgust.

"It's overkill, but we're going to visit the rabbit colony and sitting with them drives a chill into my bones. Any more snarky remarks from you, and guess what?"

He backed away from me and shot through the bedroom door when I opened it.

Percy chose to ride out in style on my shoulder. "I'm glad you don't mind either baths or coats, my fluffy friend. It shows just how exceptional you are."

Our main chores were done by five, still well before the sun came up.

"It's too early for any of our errands," I said, as Keats herded me to the truck. "What did you have in mind?"

He didn't waste time responding. Evidently, I was to follow his lead without question, which I normally did anyway.

I ducked out of his path and headed back to the barn for what Edna called my "go-kit." It had started as a gym bag and grown into a military style backpack, complete with sleeping bag. Every time she came over, she seemed to add something new. Recently, she'd slipped a diagram and index into the front pocket so that I could find things in a pinch.

"Edna's a good friend," I said, heaving the pack into the bed of the truck. "I don't tell her that often enough."

Keats gave a teasing ha-ha-ha as he brushed past me and jumped inside.

"I know. Last night, I dropped kind words on Mom and now I'm getting sentimental over Edna. The wedding is making me soft. Or maybe it's the murder. Or the rabbits."

Once we were settled, I leaned over and dropped a kiss on the dog's head. He reacted as if I had doused him in cold water, which made me laugh. Percy, on the other hand, accepted a half dozen smooches and would have taken more if a certain hater of PDAs hadn't deliberately stepped on the cat's tail.

There was a heated exchange and Percy retreated to the back seat.

"Don't be mean to your brother," I said, driving down the lane.

"Next thing you know, he'll move and leave us behind. That cat has come through for us more times than I care to think about, Keats."

He put his paws on the dashboard and barked a command to drive on.

"Tone, buddy. Tone. My brain works much better when it's full of love and peace."

A cool blue eye didn't faze me and he ended up giving me a shot of the brown eye to make amends.

After that, it was indeed peaceful and I settled in for a long drive to a destination of my dog's choice.

We ended up on the back trails not far from where we had entered them after visiting Tizzy's yard last night.

"We're back so soon? I suppose you did try to tell me we had unfinished business. Lead on."

I didn't expect to miss my mother but she wasn't wrong about the driving taking a toll on my ankle. It was nothing a couple of painkillers wouldn't help, and I was confident Edna had put some in my kit.

When Keats pushed off the dash and spun in his seat, I knew we'd arrived. To me, it looked like most stretches of the trail, especially in the dim half hour before sunrise.

"I hope you're right, buddy," I said, getting out of the truck, "because I don't feel that safe out here alone. Should I call Edna?"

He mumbled a negative and guided me around the truck to the tailgate. I put two and two together and checked the index from the backpack.

"Collapsible trekking poles! Genius."

With those and the painkillers, I felt more optimistic about the rough terrain. The points gripped the grass and kept me from tumbling into a hole that smelled interesting to Keats. He looked back at it longingly and kept going. Today wasn't the day for gophers or badgers.

As it turned out, it was a day for rabbits. There were a few hopping around and I noticed they were far more cautious in the back country than they were in the cemetery or near their colony. Out here there were coyotes, foxes and who knew what else. But with the pickings getting slim in town, they needed to expand their territory.

Keats circled and herded me forward. Percy was a brilliant blob in the distance that seemed to snag the beam of my high-powered flashlight on purpose.

When the cat stopped moving, I stopped, too. Then he came back, in a slow, low crawl. It looked very much like Keats' stance when he was herding the livestock.

"What have you found, Percy?" I called. "Be gentle with those claws, please."

The cat gave up the game and decided to escort his guest properly.

"Opal!" I said, when I was close enough to see the familiar chink in her ear. "You've covered some ground, girl."

It was possible that other rabbits had scarred ears, but her ease around both me and the pets suggested it was the same one. Nearly all the others had shown at least some reservations, although nothing like a wild cottontail.

"My dog seems to think you've got something to show us this morning," I said.

It *was* morning, now. The sun had finally hoisted itself over the horizon, which made me breathe more easily.

Opal turned and hopped ahead of us to the tree line. I noticed she had slowed her roll from the night before and it almost seemed like she was accommodating for my limp.

"That's kind of you, Opal," I said. "Maybe I should text someone to say we're here." Glancing at the dog and cat, I saw they were in a hackles-neutral position. If there was a threat, it apparently wasn't anything a hobby farmer, dog, cat and rabbit couldn't handle.

That made me snicker. No cold-blooded killer would find our

foursome fierce, especially with me on sticks. But we'd give any attacker a good fight, no matter what.

Opal hopped along with determination and we followed. My heart rate picked up again when we entered the bush. Nothing good ever happened in the hill country bush, it seemed. The flourishing forests had probably always hidden flourishing crime, and still did in modern times. Anyone who knew how to navigate the trees and, more importantly, the swamp, could get away with, well... murder.

Luckily we didn't need to go far. Opal stopped a few yards in and if that weren't proof enough of something happening, Keats lifted one paw in a point.

I picked my way around the rabbit carefully and flashed my phone light in broad arcs around the still-dim bush. At first, it looked like a bust, but the rabbit sat like a stone garden sculpture and Keats kept his paw up, too.

It was Percy who finally cut me a break and delicately stepped over logs and branches till he came to an object I didn't recognize.

I followed slowly, and eventually the light hit plastic or glass. Percy's find turned out to be a full face respirator that was similar to one sitting on a shelf in my toolshed. Charlie, my farm manager, used it when he was dealing with dangerous chemicals.

"Interesting," I said, kneeling to take a closer look. "Why would someone be out here in a gas mask?"

Opal turned sideways and I could have sworn she fired a "duh" look in my direction.

"It may be obvious to you, lady, but I'm not piecing things together," I said. "Was Edna doing survival drills? It's not like her to waste a valuable tool like this."

Keats gave a mumble that told me to think harder, and yet again, it was Percy who came to my rescue.

His green eyes glowed in the flashlight's beam and once he was sure he had my attention, he gave an elaborate sweep of one paw over the mask.

When I didn't react immediately, he got busy with more swishes until I said, "Okay, Percy. Heard you loud and clear. Someone died because of this mask."

His tail went up and bristled, just to add an exclamation point to my conclusion.

Then he leapt away to let me do the dirty work.

CHAPTER TWENTY-SEVEN

We all went back to the truck, where I took more photos of the mask for Kellan before stowing it under a blanket in the rear footwell.

Once again, Keats herded me around to the tailgate and I reached for the backpack to see what else he thought I needed.

His next mumble was impatient. A little rude, actually. There was no gold star coming for this farmer-sleuth today.

"What? The only things back here now are the backpack and Percy's spare carrier."

He shoved his muzzle under my fingertips to get them moving.

"Why would we put Percy in the carrier? We only need it if we get time to visit Mandy later."

A mumble-sigh confirmed my lack of sleep was showing. He turned and lifted his paw into a point at Opal.

"Oh, Keats, we can't put Opal in there. Even if we caught her, it would be so traumatic. Mishandling rabbits can break their bones, you know. They're very fragile."

The white paw stayed up. He was adamant.

"No. I'm drawing the line, here. She's proven she can get where she needs to go just fine. It's probably only two miles back to the cemetery as the rabbit hops, and she already knows the route."

Still the white paw stayed up.

"I am not confining that bunny in a small space. She's been our special agent rabbit and deserves the dignity of making her own choices."

Percy was already inside the truck lying on top of the evidence. Opal may have discovered it, but the cat was taking credit.

Keats finally put his paw down but then he collapsed on his side. I knew this pose all too well. It was his most dramatic protest move, generally used in conjunction with his sworn enemies: water and coats.

"Fine, you win," I said. "I'll give Opal the option of riding with us. But if she turns it down, I will not force her. And *you* will not force her. Got it?"

I set the carrier on the grass in a brilliant ray of sunshine and opened the metal lattice door.

Stepping back, I wagged my finger warningly at Keats, who was now upright and firing his hypnotic sheepdog stare at Opal.

She didn't need to be persuaded.

A few hesitant hops brought her to the door and after a long pause, she went inside and turned around to face me.

"This rabbit isn't Zander MacBride's livestock," I said, carrying the crate to the truck and buckling it into the back seat. "She was someone's pet."

Keats mumbled something and I nodded.

"All the more reason to make sure she's safe." I took a last look around before climbing into the driver's seat. The rest of the rabbits had vanished. "Maybe we can connect with her owner. She deserves a cushy life."

Opal must have agreed because she started to make a noise inside the carrier that sounded a lot like purring. Percy was curious enough to get off the blanket and stare through the grate.

"Leave her be, Percy," I said. "It's her form of purring, only she makes the sound with her teeth. Apparently they hum, too. And scream, although we don't want to hear that."

Percy went back to guarding his evidence and I thought a little bit more about the mask as we drove back the way we came. It was tempting to drop in on Tizzy Cousins now and ask if she knew anything about it, but it was always better to confront potential killers in a cupcake shop if you could, I decided. Her car was already gone when we passed so that sealed the deal.

"Let's see what Kellan has to say about all this," I said, as Keats resumed navigation.

I couldn't tell whether my boyfriend or the chief picked up because his mouth was full when he said, "Hey."

"Hey? That's all you've got for me this fine morning?" I put the phone on speaker and slowed to a crawl, in anticipation of a lecture.

He spit and then said, "Toothpaste. I just got up. It's barely dawn, Ivy."

"We've been working for hours," I said. "No joke. And we found some evidence for you."

"Who's 'we'? Because I'd hate to think you were wandering around in the dark without protection." The sound of running water got louder suddenly. He must have put the phone on speaker. "Where exactly are you?"

"Driving. Where are you? In the shower?"

"Yeah." His voice got louder. "Gotta keep moving."

"Okay. Do you mind if I ask you a question?"

"Just as soon as you answer *my* question."

He was much harder to fool these days, unfortunately. "I'm not far from Tizzy Cousins' house, actually. Keats wanted to take another look around last night but you deployed him to find Justine. Tell me Potter's Bog got her first."

"I'm sure you already know from Keats that they found her in tears with a flat tire."

I looked at the dog. "You didn't mention the flat. That would have made getting up early so much easier."

"What about the tears?" Kellan asked. "Have you no compassion?"

I could tell he was smiling so I did, too. "Not for Justine. The tears were fake, guaranteed. Asher wouldn't know the difference."

"Well, the flat was real," Kellan said. "She didn't have a spare so he had to sit with her for half an hour till the tow truck arrived."

"I hate to think what she might have picked out of him. He's a vulnerable man right now. Maybe he cried, too."

Kellan laughed outright. "Nah. I gave him a huge shot of testosterone by letting him win that race."

"Only shot he ever took willingly," I said. "Edna used to run him down like a lion on an antelope for school vaccines."

"Which is a vivid memory that doesn't distract me from the matter at hand. I'm still wondering where you are and whether you were adventuring alone in the dark."

His voice sounded a little strained and I pictured him angling his face for the razor. The "ouch" that followed probably confirmed it.

"It's just us," I finally admitted. "We left so early no one was up. Besides, I didn't exactly know where we were going."

"I thought you and the dog shared one mind."

"It's not a perfect meld, although we're aiming for that. Mostly, I just trust him to steer me right." I left a strategic pause and added, "So do you."

The shower curtain scraped back. "Yeah, but wandering the back trails takes more than special canine woo-woo. Need I remind you that—"

"Someone killed Rosalie Roarke with rabbit poison? Oh right, you haven't mentioned that yet."

There was total silence at the other end and I pictured him standing motionless in a towel. It wasn't an unpleasant image.

"How did you know?" he asked, at last. "I only found out late last night."

"Opal told me," I said.

He groaned. "Tell me that's not the rabbit. *Your* rabbit."

"It's my rabbit. She was back here waiting for us and led us to a full face respirator. Then Percy called a litterbox time of death and I put two and two together."

"So you're driving around with the evidence now, instead of waiting there for me?"

"I was silly enough to go there alone but not silly enough to stay there too long," I said. "I took plenty of photos and I had everything I needed in my go-kit. Gloves, tarp... You name it, Edna packed it."

There was a puffing sound and I imagined him hopping while trying to pull on his socks. "And you're bringing it here?"

"To the station in a bit. Don't worry, Percy's keeping it warm. He's proud of it."

"And the rabbit?" He was in the kitchen now. I heard the clink of the glass coffee canister against the faucet and nearly started drooling.

"She's purring," I said. "Have you ever heard a rabbit purr? I can hear it over the motor."

There was another pause as he took this in. "The rabbit is with you?"

"Yep. She wanted a ride back to the colony, I guess."

"She wanted a ride? So she's loose in the cab, like the time you drove a goat around? Or the horse? We talked about this, Ivy. There are bylaws."

"You never did show me those," I said. "But Opal is chillaxing in Percy's crate."

"Purring."

"Purring. Or the rabbit equivalent." I lifted my nose and sniffed. "That coffee smells awesome."

He laughed. "If you hurry, I'll save you a cup. I'm guessing your tank is empty."

"Bone dry," I said. "But I've got an errand to run on the way downtown."

"With the evidence, which I'd prefer you deliver immediately. Much can happen on your errands."

"You're right, but Percy's got a lock on it, don't worry. Can you tell me the name of the poison the killer used?"

"Aluminum phosphide," he said. "It's a rodenticide that requires a license, but people manage to find it. Comes in tablets that combine with moisture to release deadly phosphine gas." He waited a beat and added, "Rosalie's lungs were toast."

I pulled over and sent him a close-up shot of the mask. "It looked like the rubber seal was damaged and the filter cartridge, too. I guess Roz was so riled up over the rabbits and losing the horticultural society seat that she didn't notice someone had tampered with it."

We were both silent for a moment. Rosalie's had not been an easy death, and despite her lethal plans for the rabbits, I didn't wish that on anyone.

"I'm sorry," Kellan said.

"About what?" I asked.

"The coffee. It's not fair that I have it right now and you don't. I know how much it means to you."

"So much. But I'm glad we're one step closer. Hopefully the killer left DNA on that mask. I assume someone went along with her to poison the warren. But how did she get inside the cemetery?"

"Dragged," Kellan said. "And artfully arranged as you found her."

"Using her own key," I said.

"Looks that way. We'll be checking for leads on aluminum phosphide in the underground market."

"Kellan, we've got to get those rabbits out of there. If this stuff is that accessible, someone will strike again."

"I know. Soon, Ivy. This new discovery means I need to comb the crime scene again. And far beyond, obviously."

There was a different sound from the back seat.

Not purring.

Growling.

"What was that?" Kellan asked.

"Opal's upset. Rabbits growl, you know. They can also be litter box trained. Just in case you were wondering."

"I wasn't. Thank you."

"Later you might be glad I told you. It's the kind of thing that might come up at a wedding. Perfect for making small talk."

Kellan sputtered over his coffee and then coughed.

"Don't waste that," I said. "Somewhere, an under-caffeinated farmer is crying right now."

"Ivy, just drop the mask at the station before your next errand. The sooner we're on it, the better."

"It won't be soon enough for the wedding, will it?" My voice went from cheery to teary in two seconds. "Poor Jilly. Poor Asher."

"I know." His voice was gentle—the same tone he'd used with the baby goats we delivered together. "Just come in and talk to me when you bring the mask to the station, okay? We'll figure something out."

Keats mumbled a cheeky suggestion. It sounded like he was advising the chief to let *him* figure something out. And maybe hand over his service weapon while he was at it. The dog gave another pant-laugh at his joke.

"What did he say?" Kellan asked.

"You don't want to know," I said. "But I'd keep a close eye on your gun."

CHAPTER TWENTY-EIGHT

I wouldn't have been surprised if Zander MacBride had been wearing a smoking jacket or at least a silk robe when he opened the front door. He had a Hugh Hefner quality about him, and knowing he'd married a young blonde wife underscored the image. When he stared at me through the screen, however, he was wearing a blue-checkered nightshirt.

He was drinking coffee out of a pewter tankard and I couldn't help wondering if it was spiked. There was a vague whiff of whiskey, but it may have been steeped into his bones. His throat, when he cleared it, suggested he was a smoker, to boot.

Not that I really judged. We all had our coping mechanisms. Maybe he drank whiskey for breakfast and smoked cigars after dinner. I drank too much coffee, ate too much pie and acquired too many animals. There was a very real risk of more than 100 rabbits joining me before long. The Mafia hadn't shared the specifics of their plan but often it included building a new pen on my property. I didn't want to say yes but I didn't know how to say no.

Keats mumbled something, and I muttered, "Boundaries. Got it."

"If you understood boundaries, you wouldn't be standing on my porch at the crack of dawn," Zander said. "Or at all for that matter. I tried quite hard to make you feel unwelcome on your first visit."

"And succeeded, sir," I said. "Don't fault yourself on that."

"Yet you're here." He leaned sideways and stared at the truck. "And without the saving grace of Edna and Gertie. Fine women, both of them. Don't pass that on. Their egos are big enough."

I laughed and even Zander cracked what passed for a smile. "It's another lady I've come about," I said, "and I do apologize for the early visit."

"If you're talking about the reporter, she was no lady," he said. "Assertive women I appreciate. Abrasive, not so much."

"What did Justine want? Did she figure out you were ground zero for the rabbits, too?"

He snorted. "Ground zero. I bet you think you're clever."

"Nope, but I'm surrounded by brilliance." I gestured to the dog and cat. "How did Justine know to come?"

"Fishing expedition, from what I could tell. She said she was looking for 'color' for her follow-up article. Someone told her I had rabbits and she seemed mighty disappointed when I snared her."

"Snared?"

"Simple leg snare. Had it rigged to a siren behind the barn. She was fighting like a rabid badger when I got there."

"Oh man, I wish I'd seen that." Keats gave a pant-laugh and I added, "My dog does, too."

Zander eyed me up and down. "Maybe you can. I've got it on my security feed. But before I share, tell me why you're really here. The truth, now. You can't fool someone like me."

"I wouldn't even try," I said, beckoning. "Come down to the truck and I'll show you."

Taking another swig out of the tankard, he set it on a shelf and opened the screen door. I was somewhat alarmed to see bare legs under the nightshirt, which wasn't as long as I'd expected. The day was cool and windy so he probably regretted his decision even before he started down the stairs.

I certainly regretted mine when he strode ahead of me and a breeze picked up the tail of his nightshirt and gave me a peek at his pale backside. Keats mumbled something that was far from flattering.

"What's with that dog?" Zander said. "Mine never made noises like that."

"Well, your dog was just a farm implement, as I recall. Like a tractor, you said. Keats is more like my—"

He turned on me so fast I nearly caught a glimpse of the other side as well. "Do not say your child. I cannot stand the modern penchant for humanizing animals."

I cut my eyes aside in case the wind worked against me. "Penchant is such a good word, isn't it? I won't deny my penchant for humanizing my animals, but Keats is far more than a child to me."

Now he shook his head. "Please don't say 'husband,' because a girl like you can do better. I heard you *have* done better, for that matter, with the chief of police."

I just smiled. "Keats is my comrade in arms, as is Percy, my cat. I don't expect people to understand. It's complicated."

Pulling a pack of cigarettes out of the pocket of his nightshirt, he confirmed one suspicion. "Dogs aren't complicated. People aren't even that complicated when it comes down to it."

I started opening the rear passenger door of the truck and turned. "My experience suggests otherwise. I've nearly been killed a dozen times."

He stuck a cigarette in his mouth and stared at me as he lit it. After taking a deep drag, he said, "Maybe you're the one who's complicated. Ever think about that?"

Keats gave a ha-ha-ha and Zander glanced at him, startled.

"The thought has occurred to me," I said, opening the door. "As well as my dog, apparently."

In the rear footwell, Percy was still stretched out on the blanket that covered the gas mask. His hackles lifted but I figured that had more to do with protecting our find than with Zander himself. Keats was enjoying the visit too much to worry.

"What's in the cage?" Zander asked. "Another comrade in arms?"

I nodded, listening to another strange noise emanating from the crate. It sounded like rhythmic thumping, and after leaning in for a second, I realized that's exactly what it was. Opal was sounding an alarm. "It's okay, Opal," I said. "You're fine and it'll only take a second."

"Opal?" Zander peered into the truck as I turned the crate to face him. "Hey, that's my rabbit."

"Not anymore," I said. "Finders, keepers. Anyway, how would you know she's yours?"

"The V in her ear. Don't ask me how she got it. Point is, she's the only one of mine that had a scar like that." I waved my hand to clear the cloud of smoke and he blew more in my direction. "I gave this one away."

"Why? And to whom?"

"Daughter of my handyman took a fancy to her, and I couldn't say no to a kid. That was a couple of years ago. Surprised the rabbit's still kicking, let alone running wild in the cemetery."

"Can I get this guy's name?" I said. "If Opal wants to go home, I'll make it happen."

"You'll consult with the rabbit?" he asked, as I closed the truck door. "That's what you do with your comrades?"

"Exactly. Although if this family deliberately turned her loose, they don't deserve her." I gave him a bright smile. "Now, if the offer's still open, I'd love to take a look at your security footage, Mr. MacBride."

I half-expected him to turn me down but he led me back up the stairs.

"You're as strange as everyone says, Ivy." He flicked his cigarette into the bushes beside the porch without even butting it out. "But I like oddballs."

"Thank you, sir," I said, going back down the stairs. "Then you won't mind if I put that butt out for you."

He laughed as I stomped on the cigarette and then continued to the door. Just before he went inside, the breeze presented *his* butt for one last viewing. By then, it had lost its shock value, which probably would have disappointed him.

Gesturing to the coffee pot, he told me to help myself and then went into another room. I was relieved when he came back wearing jeans under his nightshirt.

"Take a seat," he said, setting a laptop computer on the kitchen table. "And don't drown yourself, now."

I had practically buried my face in the big mug I found in the cupboard. "Best coffee ever," I said, coming up for air.

"Coffee's important. One of life's great gifts."

"I could not agree more." Sitting beside him, I grinned. These days, finding common ground with people didn't particularly surprise me, but I would have thought it unlikely with a man who "farmed" rabbits and considered his dog a tool.

It turned out Zander and I shared more in common than coffee, too. We both laughed so hard over the images of Justine's struggle in the snare that I literally spit coffee on his computer screen.

"Careful now," he said, using his sleeve to buff the laptop dry. "There's more to see."

He increased the magnification so that I could watch Justine release herself from the snare with what appeared to be a penknife. She ran with a clumsy gait that reminded me, to my great regret, of my own.

A loud sound from the laptop made me jump.

"Fired a shot over her head," Zander said. "Just to motivate her. That'll teach her to trespass on my land. And that's not even all."

In the video, Justine spun in a full circle and then fell into a large mud puddle. She crawled out of camera range on her hands and knees.

Sitting back, I thanked Zander. "That was so satisfying. I'm not going to lie."

He got up and poured more coffee into his tankard. "Raising rabbits was a mistake," he said. "I'm a big enough man to admit that now. When it came time to... well, harvest them, I kept putting it off. And then there were more. It was becoming a problem I didn't know how to handle."

"Until someone handled it for you," I said.

He took a sip and nodded. "I secretly thanked them, if you must know. Told myself the rabbits were living a great life out there. Never saw one around here again so I had no idea where they landed."

"I can understand that," I said. Keats' posture told me Zander was telling the truth, and as I watched the dog, he directed his blue eye toward the laptop. "You really have no idea who set them free?"

The old man shook his head, and then sat down again. "But I've got some older footage."

CHAPTER TWENTY-NINE

Kellan waved from the doorway of the police station as I drove away. He usually saw me in and out of the building so that I wouldn't have to face Bunhead Betty alone. In our first encounter, the receptionist had judged me as unstable, and worse, unworthy of Kellan, simply because I arrived with a cat and a dog, and a femur under my arm, asking to see the chief. I rarely considered myself unworthy of Kellan anymore, but with Betty, the feelings came rushing back. What would it take to lose them for good? A ring on my finger? Or hand-to-hand combat with Bunhead herself?

Keats mumbled something reassuring.

"I know I could take her in a fist fight," I said. "And Percy would have a heyday with his signature scalp massage." I turned onto Main Street and trolled the strip slowly. "That bun is probably a wig. Or at least one of those clip-ons. What do you think?"

His next mumble was kind but firm. Now wasn't the time to muse on the quality of Betty's hair.

"I should have picked up Jilly after we dropped Opal near the cemetery," I said. "She cares about hair."

He turned his cool blue eye on me.

"She *does*. Even at a time like this, she still cares about things like that. It's one way we kept each other sane all those years in corporate misery."

His eye got frostier.

"Who stole your funny bone?" I asked. "You were all chuckles at Zander MacBride's house earlier."

He turned away with a canine sigh and left me to draw my own conclusions.

"I know it's frustrating. I hoped Kellan would recognize the person lurking around Zander's barn, too. But we watched the clips a dozen times and there was literally nothing to identify them. Man, woman, old, young. A black hoodie and sweatpants disguise anyone of average size, it seems. The balaclava and the shadows certainly didn't help. This person knew their way around. Unlike Justine."

Percy jumped up on my shoulder and blocked my view of the disgruntled dog. His warm fur and warmer purr were reassuring.

"Thanks, Percy. I'm doing my best in a bad situation. Normally, I love it when the plot thickens, but this time it's tough. We're getting down to the wire with the wedding. Even if the gas mask is the clincher, it probably won't reveal its secrets in time."

Keats stuck his nose out the window and took in a deep snort. It seemed to restore his equanimity and his next mumble was considerably cheerier.

"That's the spirit, buddy. We're down but not out." I pulled into a parking spot that was big enough for a yacht. That hardly ever happened on Main, so it had to be a good omen. "How many times have we pulled out all the stops at the last minute?"

By the time we were outside First Frost, his tail was fanning lightly.

"Let's just get in and out. I want to spend some time with the rabbits at the colony before heading home to help set up for the rehearsal dinner. We're still going full steam ahead until otherwise. The out-of-town guests are on their way."

A waft of warm, cotton candy air greeted us as we walked inside.

Tizzy's puff of copper hair peeked up over the counter. I didn't know if she was reaching for something under the cash register or hiding.

"Morning, Tizzy," I called. "It smells like heaven in here."

It actually smelled too sweet, even for me. Fake, like Bunhead Betty's hair. Or Tizzy's, for that matter.

"Oh, hi Ivy," she said, as her eyes rose over the white counter. "Are you in the market for cupcakes for the rehearsal dinner?"

Her cheeks were as pink as the cupcakes on a three-tiered glass stand in front of her. That suggested she'd been hiding, but perhaps she was just having a hot flash. Mom, for all her denial, worked up a lot of color and heat sometimes. I hoped I got a chance to use my hormones for the greater good before they turned traitor on me like that. Babies had crossed my mind more than once lately. Even farmers had ticking clocks, it seemed.

Keats poked my fingers in a blatant bid to get me to focus. Given his earlier frustration, I was lucky it wasn't a nip.

"Yes, please," I said. "I'll take a couple of dozen."

She pulled out a flat cardboard box and started folding up the sides. "Pick and choose what you like."

"Whatever's popular," I said. "It seems like everything is popular. You have a constant stream of people in and out."

A red ringlet bobbed as she nodded. "I can't keep up with the demand. Some days, I bring in my friends to lend a hand. Aubrey mans the ovens and Lita is a whiz with frosting. Would you like one to eat while you wait?"

"Sure, I'm starving. The ones you brought to Rosalie's store on the day she died were amazing. Do you have that flavor?"

"Red velvet with vanilla bean frosting," she said, sliding one across the counter to me on a napkin. "Always a crowd pleaser."

Picking it up, I took a big bite and chewed. "Scrumptious! A baker with a green thumb. I admire both of those talents."

"You're multitalented, too," she said. "Have you had any luck getting rid of the rabbits?"

I surreptitiously signaled for Keats and Percy to fan out and do reconnaissance. "Not yet, but the mayor's on it."

"What they did to the cemetery is tragic, and I hear they've been sighted in Clover Grove Gardens as well." She watched me through heavy false eyelashes. "I'm sure you'll be sad about that."

My trysts with Kellan were clearly the talk of the gardening community, but who was going to complain about the chief of police keeping the place safe?

"I am sad about that, and about the rabbits who will soon be displaced through no fault of their own." I set the cupcake down because it was too cloying even for my palate. Or maybe the terrible taste in my mouth was a result of her disregard for her so-called friend's passing. "I guess flowers and rabbits are nothing compared to the loss of Rosalie, though. You two went way back."

"Way back," she agreed, counting the cupcakes in the box. "Seven, eight, nine years."

"Were you on good terms when she passed? I heard you both competed for the same spot on the Hill Country Horticultural Society. It's a hard gig to get, from the sounds of it."

She set a blue frosted cupcake in the box and lifted heavy lashes to give me an even heavier stare. "There was no real competition. Edwin and Goldie approached me and many vouched for my skills." Her lips tipped up in a sly smile. "I think it was my roses that sealed the deal. They're so fickle in our soil but I found the magic formula to keep them blooming all season." She plucked a pink cupcake off the stand and added it to the box. "Roz was probably more jealous over that than my getting the society nod. Her roses would never rise to the occasion."

That seemed like a harsh and unnecessary jab at the dearly departed Rosalie, and it disappointed me. In my experience, anyone who shared her animosity that openly wasn't the killer.

"It doesn't sound like you shared much of a bond," I said. "And yet you gave her a monogrammed cupcake on the day she died."

"I gave a cupcake to everyone. This is my art and I like to share it."

"But she wouldn't touch it," I said.

"I'm sure she did later." The smile came back. "I like to think she ate something delicious before... you know."

"Before eating something toxic. Like ricin, from castor beans."

The box tipped and the cupcakes collided in colorful chaos. "What are you talking about? Roz died with yew berries in her mouth. That's what killed her. Everyone says so."

"I suppose castor bean plants are hard to come by around here. But there are plenty of other poisonous flowers. I had no idea, and now I'm worried for my livestock."

She turned and put the box of crushed cupcakes on the back counter and started folding another box. Her hands trembled now.

"I'm sorry about the mess, Ivy. I've been a nervous wreck all week, for obvious reasons. If someone came after Roz, they could come after any passionate gardener."

"But why?" I asked, taking the empty box from her hands and assembling it for her. "You already got the coveted seat on the horticultural society."

"That's not public yet," she said. "Anyway, put the blame where it belongs: on the rabbits. Once they're gone the threat will vanish, too."

"I don't understand."

My hands stopped moving and she took the box back. "Then you're not as bright as everyone says."

Keats came back to my side with a loud grumble. His hackles were up but it was merely an amber alert. If Tizzy had been lacing Rosalie's cupcakes with ricin from her own castor plants, as I suspected, there was no proof on site. Regardless, ricin wasn't what had killed Roz. It was just an important part of the puzzle. For all I knew, two or more people could have been trying to put her out of commission with different strategies.

I pulled some bills out of my front pocket and tossed them onto the counter. "That's for your trouble, Tizzy, but I don't think we can wait."

"But what about your red velvet cupcake?" she called after me. "It's half eaten."

I rubbed my stomach and frowned. "Bit queasy today. Pre-wedding jitters, I guess."

"Oh Ivy, the wedding won't happen," she said. "Resign yourself to that now."

The taste of the cupcake stuck to my lips and I rubbed my mouth with my sleeve as I said goodbye.

My phone pinged as I left.

And then again.

And again.

And yet again.

It was a symphony of alerts and it could only mean one thing.

CHAPTER THIRTY

Pulling up outside Daisy's house, I rested my fingertips on Keats' ears for a moment. "If you've got a little extra to give, I'll take it, buddy. After that cupcake, I could have done without a Butter Tart 911."

The family code red had summoned us all at a run. Even though I had been nearby, most of my siblings' vehicles were already there. They'd probably deployed from the farm, where they were setting up for the guests, and come over in a convoy.

Keats cast his blue eye down the street and I saw my father's truck turning the corner.

"Let's beat him inside," I said. "Mom's going to throw a connniption. Somehow these crises usually turn out to be about her, even if they aren't about her. It's amazing how that happens."

Percy flitted up the front stairs ahead of me, determined to be first through the door. He wasn't usually pushy, but my nephews' two ferrets had a magnetic hold over the cat.

"No ruckus, Percy, okay? The last thing we need is a ferret landing on someone. I don't know what it is about the weasel family, but they push the wrong buttons and it really isn't their fault."

Keats mumbled something that sounded less charitable. He was probably worried the ferrets would land on the farm one day, and I wouldn't put it past the twins—or Daisy—to offload them. All four of the boys still seemed fond of the ferrets, however. It gave me hope they'd turn into fine men.

I kicked off my boots in the front hall and joined everyone in the kitchen. Mom was in her usual spot on a stool at the counter, sipping from the colorful mug Daisy assigned her to mask lipstick stains. Pulling a tube from her purse, Mom applied a new layer of scarlet to her lips. It seemed like overcompensation for her attire. She was wearing her only pair of jeans and an old plaid shirt that belonged to Poppy.

"Mom, what's wrong?" I said. "Where's the satin? And your heels?"

She stuck out a sneaker and frowned. "Can you believe Daisy put the mother of the groom to work? I had me-time scheduled at the spa and she sent me to do hard labor in the yard."

Daisy slid a white china cup across the counter to me. "Can you believe the mother of the groom doesn't know how to use a rake? I didn't expect the leaves to start falling so soon."

"If you were all at the farm why did we need to meet here?" I asked, accepting the coffee gratefully. My only cup had been at Zander's and that left me several below my normal threshold. It would be tough to hold my own without the joy juice.

"I don't know," Daisy said. "Ask Asher. He called the meeting."

My brother was in uniform, pacing restlessly around the kitchen, rather than lounging against the fridge per usual. "I didn't call the meeting, you did," he told Daisy.

She held out her phone, presumably to prove the first message had indeed come from him. His brow furrowed and he looked at Jilly.

"Don't ask me," she said, from her spot at the kitchen table. "The message came from you and everyone jumped like they'd been struck by lightning. And here we are."

Asher pulled out his phone. "It must have been a butt dial."

"A butt dial that specifically said Butter Tart 9 1 1?" I asked. "Just how talented is your butt?"

He tried to frown but ended up laughing. "Very. It has a fan club."

Jilly raised her hand. "Fiancée 9 1 1. I don't want to hear about your backside's other admirers on the eve of our wedding. Or ever, for that matter."

"Did we come at a bad time?" a man asked from the front hall.

The voice startled Mom so much she slid off her stool even without the hazards of satin. She reeled as if her coffee were spiked and then landed in Iris' lap.

"Sorry, darling," Mom said, as Iris pushed her upright. "Mother! Dad! What are you doing here?"

Gardenia and Albert Swingle stood in the doorway, while Calvin hovered behind them, looking as if he wanted to flee. Instead, he slipped into the living room and appeared in the other kitchen doorway.

My grandmother raised her fine gray eyebrows. "Your father got a message on his cell phone to come over here directly. That thing never stops pinging."

"It's mostly me checking on Clippers and Bocelli," I said. "He sends me photos every single day."

I went over to hug my grandfather and stopped short. We hadn't quite gotten to the spontaneous hug stage, but a handshake felt too formal. We both settled for an awkward clap on the back, which made Poppy giggle. I fired her a dirty look. After all, we only discovered we had grandparents a few months ago. There was no fast-forwarding a relationship like that, but I'd given them two of my favorite animals as tokens of my affections. Or at least intentions to have affections.

"They're enjoying some downtime with your emu and alpaca now," my grandmother said. "We only stayed long enough to unload them before riding over here with Calvin. These had better be some good butter tarts."

Now I laughed. "Unfortunately, these meetings aren't always so tasty. It's usually a family emergency of some sort. This time it's a false alarm. Asher butt-dialed his distribution list."

Albert touched Gardenia's arm. "She just means Asher sat on his phone and contacted everyone by accident."

Mom got back on her stool, clearly determined to avoid PDAs with her parents. "Well, I, for one, appreciate the break."

"What on earth are you wearing, Dahlia?" my grandmother said. "Are those blue jeans? We dress like ladies in our family."

"Tell it to my daughter," she said, pointing at my overalls.

"That's different. Ivy's a farmer," Gardenia said. "You're a seamstress and every outfit sells your skills."

Mom opened red lips to argue but realized in time that she actually agreed. "It's good to see you, Mom. Have some coffee."

It was the closest she could come to telling her own mother to back off, and the comment was understood. Gardenia accepted a white mug from Daisy and smirked a little before sipping.

Asher was staring at his phone. "I don't have a distribution list, and no matter how talented, there's no way my butt could have messaged all of you. Something strange is going on."

"A prank?" I asked. "Cop on cop humor?"

"No one knows our code, except..."

We all turned at the sound of heavy footsteps and saw Kellan walk around my grandparents into the kitchen.

"Sorry to crash the party, folks."

"Methinks you *called* the party," I said, going over to him. I was about to kiss his cheek and saw his shoulders stiffen slightly. He must be here in a professional capacity. As I drew back, he grabbed my hand and squeezed—a gesture that reminded me how difficult it was to walk the lines between the many relationships here. This kitchen was jammed with personalities, including the sheepdog shoving between our shins now. For the moment, it wasn't a game, according to a deep and prolonged grumble. Keats was calling the meeting to order for Kellan.

"Thank you," Kellan said, with a flicker of a smile toward the dog. "I'm sorry I hijacked your family's private channel, but I wanted to speak to all of you at once, and as soon as possible."

"What's wrong?" Mom said, fiddling with the top button on her plaid shirt. I knew she was wishing she were better dressed to receive the news, whatever it was.

"It's the wedding," Jilly said. Her voice was flat. Emotionless. "He's calling it off."

"Not me," he said. "But you're not wrong. Mayor Martingale called me an hour ago and she's unwilling to risk community safety with the killer still at large. I'm sorry, Jilly. And you too, Asher. I really hoped we'd be able to get this resolved in time."

Asher slumped against the fridge now, and if my grandfather hadn't prodded him in the ribs, I think my brother might have slid right down into a uniformed heap of misery.

"It's just a wedding," the old man said. "Barely the beginning of your life with this beautiful woman. I guarantee you'll face many worse challenges together, so you'd better stand up straight and take it on the chin."

I stared up at my grandfather. "This probably just looks like a party to you, but it's more than that to Asher. To our entire family. We've had a challenging year and he was looking to celebrate getting everything on a more stable footing." I turned my eyes on Asher. "Am I right, brother?"

Asher's blue eyes were full of sorrow. "I really wanted it to be great. For Jilly and everyone else."

Daisy pushed Kellan aside to give my brother as much of a hug as his contact with the fridge allowed. "It will be fine, Ash. You've been through worse and come out the better for it. Right?"

He tried to meet her eyes and failed. "I guess. It was supposed to be a turning point. Instead, it's a bad omen."

"It's not a bad omen," Kellan said. "There's no such thing, Officer Galloway."

Asher turned away from his boss. "Having a murder derail your wedding is a bad omen. I think the world would agree with me."

"Not to mention the rabbits," Mom said. "A rabbit army is a bad omen, too."

My grandmother's eyes widened. "A rabbit army? What on earth?"

I looked down for Keats and found he'd left my side to join Jilly at the kitchen table. Her fingers touched his ears and then rested on his back while he stared up at her with his warm brown eye. Instead of slumping like Asher, her back straightened and she gave me a little smile. She was all right. More than all right. Jilly was actually relieved. Not that the wedding was cancelled, I was sure, but that the pressure was off. The big community affair had never been what she wanted.

"I have an idea," I said, as Jilly sent Keats back to me with a gentle shove. "If I understand Kellan correctly, we're only barred from an outdoor wedding in the orchard. Why don't we just move the reception inside?"

"Because the inn only holds fifty people max," Daisy said. "And thanks to the combined efforts of Asher and Mom, the guest list is getting close to four hundred. I'm sure it's grown even this morning."

"I did invite the barista at Berry Good Café earlier," Asher muttered.

"Four hundred?" I said. "We can't even get a turnout like that at the fall fair."

"It's supposed to be bigger and better than the fall fair," Asher said. "I thought it would bring the community together. So they'd stop..."

His voice drifted off so I finished his thought. "Killing each other?"

"Something like that." He started sliding down the stainless steel again and my grandfather gave him a harder poke in the ribs.

"It's a worthy goal, but not achievable, Officer," Kellan said. "The roots of hill country crime go back to before your grandfather's time, and you can't heal the culture with one wedding."

"The chief is right," my grandfather said. "That's too much weight for one wedding. Mine with Gardenia was small but mighty, and our marriage has been strong enough to withstand the winds of time and crime."

Gardenia looped her arm through his and gave him a fond smile. "A wedding with four hundred people is silly. You'd never find your bride in the crowd, and it's supposed to be about the two of you." She glanced at my mother and her eyes narrowed. "I never thought I'd say this, but you could just elope, like Dahlia did. Problem solved."

Keats mumbled something at my side. "Has anyone thought of consulting the bride?" I said. "Other than Keats."

The dog gave a pant-laugh and all eyes turned to Jilly. Her cheeks were pale but her eyes sparkled. "Kellan, can we have a small wedding inside?"

His lips pressed together and I knew the mayor had put the kibosh on any event at all.

"Just immediate family," I said, reaching for his arm. "Please."

"The killer isn't after any of us," Mom said. "What do we have to do with Rosalie's death?"

"We have a lot to do with what happened after her death," I said. "I probably know too much, even though I don't know enough."

"Ivy's right," Kellan said. "Asher, Jilly and Ivy, among others, know more than the killer would like and there's a chance they would take advantage of a party's hubbub to eliminate a risk. We simply don't have enough resources to keep an event of any size safe."

My grandfather faced Kellan and I noticed for the first time that he was just as tall and even more imposing than my boyfriend. "I can get you resources, young man."

Calvin spoke for the first time from the living room doorway. "Me too."

"Don't insult the chief, you two," Gardenia said. "Let's give him the respect he deserves for doing his job."

He gave her a grateful smile. "The mayor wouldn't be satisfied with other resources, as much as I appreciate the offer."

"I have another idea," I said. "But I need time to work my wiles."

"You have wiles?" Mom said. "How can anyone in dirty overalls have wiles?"

"Dahlia." My grandmother's voice was severe. "According to Daisy, Asher invited half the town and you invited the other half. Were you trying to have the wedding you never had?"

Mom's face burned with the power of a million hot flashes. "Of course not."

"Then be happy Jilly might get her wish for an intimate affair," Gardenia said. "Anyone can see that's what she wanted in the first place. It's not about the show, is it Jillian?"

"Small is fine," Jilly said. "Ivy does have wiles, so let her work them."

Mom opened her mouth once more but instead of lecturing me, she screamed. Percy was climbing the curtains after the ferret, who leapt onto my mother's shoulder, and then slipped into her collar and moved down to squirm around her midriff. She jumped off the stool and did a jittery dance to dislodge him.

"Oh goodness," my grandmother said, with a wider smile than I thought she had in her repertoire. "Good thing you wore denim after all, Dahlia. Ferrets make short work of satin, I'm sure."

"Meeting adjourned," Asher said, clapping me on the shoulder as he walked over to Jilly.

Keats had already called it quits by nipping off Kellan's bootlaces. When my boyfriend looked down, four black sections sat in a neat row.

"Seriously?" he said.

"That's what you get for being a party pooper," I said, smiling as the dog herded me out.

CHAPTER THIRTY-ONE

"Flats flatter no one," Mom said, as I came down from my bedroom for what was supposed to be the rehearsal party but was now just a welcome to out-of-town guests who'd already been en route before Kellan's kibosh. We'd spent the afternoon calling hundreds of people to cancel the wedding. If it came off at all, it would be a very small affair. "They make anyone's legs look thick."

"Ivy's legs are not thick," Jilly said. Normally the peacemaker and chief handler of my mother, my best friend had had enough. "She looks very nice, and I told her to be careful with her foot. She sprained her ankle doing brave work for this community."

"I was there, remember?" Mom said. "Doing brave work in heels. It's all about practice, Jillian."

The beautiful dark-haired version of Jilly came up beside me. Janelle, Jilly's cousin, was wearing the steepest stilettos I'd seen off a runway and an equally fashionable green dress. "There's a time and place for flats," she said. "Or so I'm finally learning. Speed is of the essence in my line of work."

"Running a gift store?" Mom said. "I would think heels were an asset."

"It's no ordinary gift store," Janelle said, with a sly smile. "And I don't dare leave it alone. My dog, Mr. Bixby, stayed back to keep an eye on the place." She looked around the small crowd, which included my grandparents, Uncle Sterling, Edna, Gertie, four cops and the rest of my family. "Where's Aunt Eva?"

Jilly looked up, down and all around before answering. "I caught Mom right before her flight and told her not to come. For her own safety."

"For her safety or yours?" Janelle said, grinning.

"Yours, actually," Jilly said. "She doesn't like either of us, but you're the one with the failing grade."

"That's ridiculous," Mom said. "I have five girls and I love them all equally. Except for the rare moments I love Ivy more."

"That's on the first of the month when the rent would be due anywhere else," I said.

"Dahlia, are you freeloading?" my grandmother asked. "You make a decent living with that salon, from what I've heard."

"And extra coin from her sewing," I said.

"I pay the rent on my apartment in town," Mom said, which was now often true. "But I want to be close to my favorite daughter."

"See?" I said. "I really am her favorite."

"I meant Jillian," Mom said. "She'll still be here at the inn for work."

"And likely the first to give you granddaughters," Gardenia said.

"No promises," Jilly said. "That's not up to me."

"Grandsons are fine, too," Mom said. She smiled fondly at Daisy's eldest boys, which was a rare enough event. The twins had found the key to her heart. Literally.

"Oh, right," I said. "Especially boys who let you drive their cars illegally."

"Hush now," Mom said. "That's never been proven."

"Check out their phones," I said. "No way could they afford that model without extorting their sweet grandma."

"Extortion? Please," Mom said. "Family helps family. End of story."

I left her and walked across the room to talk to Sutton, who was standing alone. "What's in your shirt, Sutt?"

He grinned at me. "That's a personal question. Mom always says we need to protect ourselves if we feel uncomfortable."

"I would think you already feel uncomfortable. When your grandmother sees that ferret, she's going to flip her lid."

Sutton touched the lump at his waist. "This poor guy was upset about what happened earlier. She practically squished him with her flapping. I couldn't leave them at home."

"Them?" I circled him. "Are there two running around in there?"

"Weston has the other," he said, pointing to his twin. "Ferrets like parties, you know."

"This isn't just any party, Sutton. We're all on tenterhooks and a ferret incident could blow the whole thing up." I pointed to Percy and Keats. "They're well aware you brought prey along to divert them."

"They're all friends," he said. "What are tenterhooks, anyway?"

"The kind of thing that gets me in trouble all the time. Now, am I still your favorite aunt?"

"And role model," he said, grinning. Sutton had Daisy's eyes, Asher's teeth and his father's cleft chin. How did I have nephews old enough to be heartbreakers?

"Then I'm asking you to stop accepting bribes from your grand-mother to drive your car. It's upsetting the chief and he has enough on his plate. Do you have any idea how hard it is for him to deal with our crazy family on top of the crime in this community?"

"That's one reason I decided to become a renegade like you instead of a cop," he said. "Too many rules."

"You've already got the evasiveness down pat," I said. "Answer my question."

He shifted awkwardly to let the ferret climb into his armpit. "She pays well, Aunt Ivy. I gave up my job at Donut Delight. There are bills to pay."

"So that's where her money's going." I glanced over at Kellan. "There's only one thing to do about this."

"Don't tell the chief," Sutton said. "Please."

There was a note of urgency in his voice that told me Kellan had spared my nephew from at least one infraction.

"I won't, as long as you meet my conditions," I said. "First, you take both ferrets upstairs and put them in the cat carrier in my bedroom. Second, you let me out-bribe your grandmother."

He brightened immediately. "You'd do that?"

"Sure. I was going to offer to help with your college tuition but if I need to invest early, I can do that."

"I don't want to go to college anyway," he said. "Renegades don't need an education."

"I have an advanced degree, Sutt, and it made me what I am. For better or worse."

He started backing away. "You don't seem all that smart, sometimes, Ivy. No offense."

"None taken. A head injury messes with basic cognitive functioning, sometimes. But I can still run rings around you."

A covert gesture sent my clever dog to run rings around Sutton, herding him to the stairs.

"Don't even think about fanging these jeans, Keats," he said. "Cost me two hundred bucks."

"Add it to my tab," I said. "And the Band-Aids, too."

"Band-Aids?" he called, from the bottom of the stairs.

"You'll find the disinfectant in the bathroom vanity," I called back. "You never know where"—my nephew gave a startled yip—"a dog's mouth has been."

"Ow! Ten bucks for every bite."

"Done," I said. "Rack it up, Keats. And then come back for the other twin."

I didn't get to enjoy the full experience because the front door opened and Meryl Martingale let herself in. Kellan left Asher and the two cop groomsmen and went to the door to speak to her. I gave them a moment.

She waited till conversation in the room quieted to speak but her smile already told me my wiles had prevailed. I'd called the Dog Town mayor directly to talk rabbits and weddings. Isla McInnis was both a former Rescue Mafia member and a true romantic. I knew she would help if she could.

"I come bearing good news," Meryl said. "Dorset Hills police department has agreed to send most of their force over tomorrow to provide security for the wedding."

"It's back on?" I said. "In the orchard?"

The mayor nodded. "Capped at sixty. And you need to stay within the hazard tape."

"That'll ruin the photos," Mom complained.

Asher stepped right in front of Mom and eased her backward into a wall, where she squeaked unintelligibly. Perhaps his status as golden boy went down a notch or two, and she most certainly regretted feeding him so much in his ravenous teen years.

"Thank you, Mayor," he said. "I hope you'll still do the honors."

Meryl smiled in relief. She was a good woman in a difficult situation. "Absolutely. But now I need to steal the chief to discuss logistics."

I waited till I saw their taillights heading up the lane before making my way to the back door. Just as I was about to slip out, Jilly grabbed my arm and asked, "Where are you going?"

"To put the livestock to bed," I said. "Just like I do every night."

"Let me come with you. Kellan wouldn't like you going alone."

"You can't leave your own party. You're the guest of honor."

"Edna then," she said. "And Gertie."

"I'll come," Janelle said, joining her. "You really shouldn't be alone, Ivy."

When Janelle cautioned me, I usually listened. She was the most intuitive person I'd ever met.

"It's just the barn. I'll be fine," I said, slapping the pocket of the jacket I'd thrown on over my dress. "I've got my phone, and more importantly, Keats and Percy."

Both animals slipped between us and pressed Jilly and Janelle away.

"Excuse me," Jilly said. "I'm not your sheep to herd around, buddy. And Percy, you're my baby."

The cat blinked at her with big green eyes and then delivered his sonorous purr-meow, clearly designed to put her fears at rest.

Janelle stepped around the pets, gave me a hug and whispered, "Call me if you're at all worried. I've got a bad feeling about... well, everything."

I nodded and Keats forced his way between us, more assertively this time.

"Why is he so set on your being alone?" Jilly asked.

"Because manure time is think time. Remember what Kellan said earlier? I know more than I actually know right now. And it's going to take some peace and quiet to let the pieces come together."

"Got it," Jilly said. "Be careful with your fertilizer, my friend. With my mother out of the picture, I'd like you to give me away tomorrow."

I smiled and then shook my head. "I'd jump in front of a stampeding llama for you, Jilly, but I can't give you away."

She must have sensed the emotion welling up because she pushed me through the crack in the door. "Go, before your mom sees."

I stuck my head back in. "If she causes any trouble, mention the ferrets are in my bedroom. Waiting for her."

CHAPTER THIRTY-TWO

The livestock had already been fed and bedded, either by Charlie, now gone, or Calvin, who was inside at the party.

As it turned out, the boys had other plans for us, anyway. Percy led me to the truck and Keats urged me on from behind. The dog had gone from being in a party mood to being grumpy. Sometimes that happened when we hadn't checked off everything on our to-do list. Especially if it was something he liked to do. He was good at keeping me on top of my busy life.

"The rabbits," I said, letting them inside and hopping behind the wheel. "I promised to head over and check on them, but after the family meeting, I lost track of time. If we hurry, we could still get the last light."

Keats managed a ha-ha-ha at this. It was already dusk and unless we teleported, we would be tromping around in the dark. The bush was always dark anyway.

"What about parking at the cemetery and going in that way?" I said. "It would cut nearly an hour off the mission, but you boys would need to get us past at least two cops."

Keats pounded the dashboard and Percy lashed his fluffy tail. I took that as confirmation.

"Probably won't be too hard," I said. "Kellan had to pull some staff off today. If all goes well, the Mafia will be able to begin the extraction on Monday. I can't wait to see the rabbits safe and sound in the sanctuary Remi found."

We'd be joining a convoy down to a Texas rescue designed specifically for rabbits. Initially, they'd balked at the number, but the Mafia's generous donation threw their gates wide open. Money made hoppily ever afters possible.

"Maybe our luck is turning," I said as we drove down the road leading to the cemetery. "The wedding may have been downgraded, but Jilly's happier that way. By tomorrow night, she'll be on her way to that swanky honeymoon resort upstate."

I reached out to touch Keats for comfort and got a handful of hackles.

Uh-oh.

"What's the matter, buddy? I mean, other than that we're visiting a cemetery at night. I'm not thrilled about that, I won't lie. Ever since we saw that weird stuff happen with Janelle at the Briar Estates I've been a little more touchy about the woo-woo. I don't really believe in ghosts but that doesn't mean I want to get too close to the earthly remains of Clover Grove's past in the dark. Some of those people were scary enough while alive, by the sounds of it."

Keats gave a decidedly grumpy grumble. It was almost like he was telling me to shut up. Rude, even by his liberal standards.

"Drop the attitude," I said, slowing at the entrance to the cemetery. "Musing out loud often helps me make connections."

His paw came up and his blue eye cut my way. "Connect that," he seemed to say.

I hit the brakes and stalled the truck. "Oh, for pity's sake. We don't need another problem just as we're managing to get the ones we have resolved."

I'd planned to park in the bushes nearby and walk but there was no point now. Someone else hadn't been shy about leaving her car in full view.

Cajoling the truck into moving, I drove into the lot and parked beside Justine Schalow's sedan. It was still filthy from her rumble on the back country trails but there was a shiny new set of roof racks.

"Why is she here again?" I asked. "It can only mean bad news for the poor rabbits."

We all got out and I walked around to the back of the truck. Looking down, I sighed. While I'd worn flats, I was in a narrow skirt with a short slit at the back.

"Maybe Edna put battle gear in my go-kit," I said. "It would be the sensible thing to do."

Evidently, Edna thought dressing for action was a given, and normally I did. Tonight, I would just have to make the best of it. At least I had the trekking poles, which would help ease the load on my sprained ankle. I wanted to recover in time to participate fully in the rabbit extraction.

"We'd better see what Justine is up to, first. I don't want her following us to the colony if she doesn't already know the location. Where is she, boys?"

Both tails puffed as the two pets trotted ahead of me along the brick wall. We passed the place where Justine got stuck and I started to wonder if she had gone straight to the colony.

At the very end, however, we came upon her ladder. It was shiny and new, like her roof racks.

"She's still searching for the rabbits, and this time, she made it inside," I said, staring up at the iron spikes that topped the wall. "Boys, I can't do it. Even if I took my skirt off, I'd probably never get over there alive. Not with this bum foot."

Keats mumbled his agreement.

"I'm sorry. It's not like me to back away from a challenge but Justine would probably catch me stuck up there in my underwear and make me front page news. I could handle the embarrassment, but it isn't fair to Kellan."

Keats was already herding me away, so I guessed he couldn't handle the embarrassment either. He guided me around the corner of the cemetery and then took the lead again. I pulled my phone out of my coat pocket but it was next to impossible to light the way while using the trekking poles. I decided light was more likely to keep me upright, so I tucked the poles under my left arm. They kept sliding around, so it was probably only a matter of time before I took a header. Hopefully I didn't end up stabbing myself with them.

My speed was a disappointment to Keats and he circled back again and again. I thought Percy had gone on ahead until he gave a quiet hiss from above. He was picking his way around the spikes on top of the wall and his sharp eyes had found something he didn't like.

"Is it Justine?" I whispered. His green eyes caught mine and he made a few litter box sweeps of his paw. Now that he realized the power of that maneuver to command attention, he used it more often. It didn't necessarily mean someone had died anymore. Mind you, here at the cemetery, he could sweep all night long and still be right.

"I guess we'll try the back door," I said, "but Kellan would never have left it unlocked."

Keats came around and gave me a sharp poke with his cold nose, probably sparing the teeth only for fear I'd scream. I almost did anyway.

The back door wasn't just unlocked but ajar.

"Maybe it's the groundskeeper," I said, passing through the door. "He alibied out, but maybe he's just tracking Justine."

Inside, there were a couple of old lamps on high poles that seemed more about atmosphere than functionality. Still, they shed enough of an eerie glow that I slid my phone back in my pocket and used the poles to help me move along more quickly. There was an unmistakable urgency to Keats' gait. His belly was low and he darted ahead, ducking behind tombstones and then making another move. Percy was doing the same on my opposite side. I'd never felt so clumsy and obvious, and it upset me. I felt unworthy of my amazing pets.

Once more, Keats circled back, this time just to infuse me with confidence, it seemed. My hands were occupied so he stared up at me with his warm brown eye and then gave a whine so high I could barely hear it.

That whine said we were in trouble. What's more, it reminded me to tell Kellan we were here. I should have done it the second I discovered Justine's car. After texting, I stared at the phone, hoping he'd reply right away. When he didn't, I texted Edna, too. This wasn't an official emergency. Yet. All I had to go on was a very bad vibe and two wary pets.

I stuck the phone in my pocket and plodded on. Vanity had kept me from wearing a compression bandage tonight and I regretted that now. There was a lot to be said for work boots and overalls. No matter what Mom said, they were remaining my uniform of choice.

A dozen or so headstones later, I stopped on Keats' unspoken command. He sank to the ground and I crouched behind one of the taller monuments. We were still in the old part of the cemetery, where Jilly and Asher liked to canoodle before it was razed by rabbits.

Rabbits.

That's when I finally noticed Opal and my other long-eared friends had joined us. Or more likely, we'd joined them. Once I actually started looking I saw dozens of rabbits, and it seemed like they were ducking behind headstones just like we were.

Opal took a few hops toward me and then turned back. It seemed we had our orders to follow.

On Keats' cue, I moved ahead, stone by stone, wincing over every step until we came upon Justine. Her predicament sent adrenaline coursing through my body.

After that, my foot didn't bother me at all.

CHAPTER THIRTY-THREE

No one would choose to die in a graveyard, even knowing they would end up there soon enough. It just seemed pointless. Moving you out and back would be a waste of time.

Yet it looked like Justine was going to be facing that inconvenience very soon. She was tied to a tall headstone. At first I thought the lower half of her face was covered in blood, but then I realized she'd been gagged with a red bandana. Whoever captured her must have gotten tired of hearing her, too.

I told my limbs to move. At first, they ignored me. The paralysis of fear was temporary, I knew, and soon enough it faded to mere pins and needles. The pain in my ankle stayed gone. There was a lot to be said for a jolt of adrenaline.

Keats turned back to get my attention and lifted his paw in a point. Not for the first time, I was grateful for his white flags. The paws and the tuft of his tail were often as good as a flashlight.

I scanned in the direction he signaled and saw a dark, misshapen bump on the ground. It looked like a bear, but that didn't make sense. Then the shape rose up in the dim light and I saw it was just a regular human, if regular humans tied up reporters to tombstones.

My eyes darted back to Justine. Her eyes were closed and it wasn't clear whether or not she was still alive.

Her assailant wore a black hoodie and pants, and a balaclava. It was very likely the same person who'd been caught on Zander MacBride's security feed, some time earlier than Justine herself. Were they connected in some way? And what did it have to do with Rosalie Roarke? Or the rabbits, for that matter? They had to be linked somehow, and a tickle in my brain told me I already knew.

For the moment, I stayed down, watching. I seriously hoped Kellan or Edna would arrive as backup before I had to intervene. In fact, if Justine didn't move, I wouldn't intervene at all. Instead, I'd just film whatever strange ritual was already underway.

The black-clad person walked over to Justine and she flinched. Her eyes opened and she murmured pleadingly around the gag.

I cursed mentally, knowing I now had no choice but to take action to save her. I wished her gone, but not that gone. All I wanted was for her to pack up her ladder and move to the next newsworthy town.

The first thing I needed to do was figure out the assailant's plan of attack. My only weapons were Keats and Percy, but they were highly potent ones.

Both turned to me now, two gleaming green eyes and one blue one.

Keats lifted his paw again and I looked back at the attacker. I was pretty sure it was a man, now, from the way he moved. But he wasn't tall, and there was a reasonably good chance we could overpower him together.

If he was unarmed.

For the moment, all I could see was a device of some kind hanging from one hand.

That numbing chill passed over me again.

It was a respirator, and there was a canister hooked to his belt.

Turning away, he yanked up the balaclava and then stretched

the mask right over his face. Then he pulled a silver tube from his pocket that glittered in the weak beam of light.

Aluminum phosphide.

The rodenticide that killed Rosalie. I'd looked it up online.

Seeing the poison in the man's gloved hand triggered a memory. Where had I seen that tube before?

I stopped filming and started scrolling through my camera roll. Sure enough, there was an aluminum tube just like it sitting among chunks of green florist foam under the counter at Twig Master. I remembered the stench in the store that day. Edwin Masters may have been dealing with pests there. Or perhaps there was more to it.

Keats crept over to nudge my hand, as if to tell me to keep going.

I scrolled back even more. This week alone I'd taken nearly 100 photos.

My finger slowed. There it was again! A silver tube sat among condiments beside a fancy espresso machine and an even fancier mixer.

Aubrey Wagner? It was hard to believe he could gas anyone, and I knew he had an alibi. Edwin Masters, possibly. His wife, Goldie? More likely.

Maybe it was a woman after all. Goldie was as tall and imposing as this figure in black.

I lifted the phone and started filming again. Someone had to find out which garden fanatic fit the gas mask. It was like a murderous take on Cinderella.

Exchanging another glance with the boys, I moved forward carefully. This situation could turn terminal very quickly, not only for Justine, but also the rabbits. And even us.

When I was within striking distance, I sent the boys out to circle around and be ready if we got our chance.

Then I put my phone on record, dropped it into my pocket and stumped forward on the trekking poles. Maybe if I looked infirm, he'd underestimate me.

Or maybe I overestimated myself, considering my current infirmity.

"Hi there," I called, when I was just a few yards away.

The person turned quickly but I couldn't make out any features through the mask.

I studied the posture. The nervous twitching of the deadly tube. Then the mask swiveled to scan for the rabbits. The person waved them away.

That was all I needed to see. No way would Edwin and Goldie scatter the enemy of gorgeous gardens everywhere when there was poison on hand. The man who called his long-eared neighbors "floppers"? Possibly.

"Aubrey?" I said. "It's me, Ivy. Just out walking my pets."

When he didn't answer I wondered if I'd guessed wrong. But the nervous twitching got worse and said I was right. He was a flight animal, like a rabbit. I'd have to be careful not to startle him further, because there was no predicting what he might do.

"Are you and Justine playing a game?" I asked. "Trying to spice things up a little?"

Justine tried to speak. Her words were swallowed by the bandana but her tone had a brazen edge. I had to give her credit for having spunk in extremely difficult circumstances.

"Oh, don't worry, Justine," I said. "Your secret's safe with me. As far as I can tell, you and Aubrey are single, consenting adults. Others come here for dates, too, so far be it from me to stop you from enjoying a nice evening of role playing."

I started to turn around and that galvanized Aubrey. "Stop, Ivy."

Turning back, I saw he'd lifted the gas mask.

"Aubrey, I've got to get home to my guests. You know I called earlier to cancel Asher's wedding but now it's back on. Consider yourself reinvited. You too, Justine. I know you twisted my brother's arm into putting you back on the list when he saved you from the bog."

It was unlikely Aubrey would be attending any events tomorrow. He'd either be in jail or keeping a low profile. Hopefully the former.

"Come over here and sit down," he said. "Other side of the headstone, where I can tie you two nosy parkers together."

"Don't lump me in with Justine," I said. "I'm just here checking on the rabbits. You know how I am about animals."

"I know you're in the wrong place at the wrong time," he said.

I decided to light a match under him and see what sparked. "Looks like I got here at exactly the right time to stop you from killing the rabbits. That's all I need to know."

"Killing them!" His voice notched up. "I'm not killing them, she's killing them."

He aimed a kick at Justine and hit the tombstone instead. I took advantage of his momentary distraction to come closer.

"What do you mean? That's rabbit poison in your hand. I looked it up."

"Rabbit poison that belonged to Rosalie Roarke," he said. "She came here to 'eradicate a pest problem.' I was just along to help. Or so she thought."

"So you eradicated a florist problem instead?"

"The damage wasn't the rabbits' fault." His voice sounded tortured now. "They're innocents."

"I know. You were only trying to help them. After all, you freed them from Zander MacBride's farm to give them a better life."

He took the mask right off and stared at me. "Yes! You understand. No one else would."

"I assume you took his dog, too. There was a crate in your basement."

"Zander didn't value that dog at all, but the stupid thing kept trying to go back to the MacBride farm."

"That's a shame. I bet you would have given him a great life."

"In the end, I did. I found a new farm down the range. He's happy there."

"That's wonderful. Good for you."

If I could just keep him talking, help would arrive. Oddly enough, Aubrey and I had something profound in common. He wasn't the first person I'd met who'd gone off the rails over a love of animals. That might very well happen to me, were it not for a strong community keeping me grounded.

"I wanted the best for the rabbits, too," he said.

"I guess they sort of got away on you?"

He nodded. "I thought they'd disperse, you know? After being jammed up and hurting each other at Zander's why wouldn't they scatter to the winds? Instead they congregated here. I didn't even know for months, and when I found them I—I—"

"Didn't know what to do," I said. "Who would? That's a lot of rabbits."

"Word got out and other people started setting their pets free, too. It made me so mad. How could they survive the winter?"

"So you delivered food. And toys," I said. "I saw them playing. I didn't know rabbits did that."

"No one gives rabbits enough credit. They're smart and sweet when you handle them the right way."

"I couldn't agree more. I've become quite fond of one who came to the farm. I named her Opal. When all this is over, I plan to keep her. If she wants to stay, that is. She's a free agent now and deserves a choice."

Aubrey smiled but it fled his face just as fast. "That isn't going to happen, Ivy. Although if you tell me how to find Opal, I'll look after her."

"We're on the same side, Aubrey. The side of the rabbits. Because of us, that entire colony is moving to a safe haven. You did it!"

"That's good news," he said. "Very good news. But I still can't let you or this one"—he kicked at Justine and connected this time—"spread the news. She's not like us."

"No, she's not. But that doesn't mean she deserves the hand you dealt Rosalie. Justine is just looking for a good story, whereas Roz was killing the rabbits, and even enlisted your help."

"I didn't want to kill her," he said. "At first I just baked poison into her favorite banana bread. I've got a little greenhouse downstairs, you see, with plenty of goodies. I spiked a cupcake at Tizzy's, too."

"The one I nearly nabbed," I said.

"Exactly. Too bad the poison made Roz lose her appetite. It slowed her down a little but she was still bound and determined to go big with the aluminum phosphide. Take out the whole colony in one fell swoop, she said. So I had to go even bigger. Roz had already found the warren so I went along with her to make sure she got a taste of what she was doling out."

"You tampered with her mask." It was a statement. I'd seen the damage when I collected it from the woods.

He nodded. "I counted on her being too worked up over losing the horticultural society seat to notice, and she didn't disappoint." He looped his mask over his arm and then patted it. "Luckily, mine held out nicely."

"No rabbits harmed?" I asked, remembering Opal sitting among bits of aluminum near the colony.

He shook his head. "Roz didn't realize you need to plug all the many entrances to a warren for the gas to work. She dumped all the tablets into one hole, added water and... poof. She was gone. Happened so fast I had to drag her into the cemetery when I'd planned on her coming on foot. I was going to dig a hole for her among the other wicked folk of Clover Grove."

"But then we came along and interrupted you."

He nodded. "Had to leave in a hurry. I went down to The Tipsy Grape to be sure I had an alibi. No one ever keeps close tabs there."

"What I don't understand is the yew berries and other plants you stuffed in her mouth," I said. "Was it a statement?"

"They came from the gardens of Tizzy Cousins and Edwin Masters. Gardeners grow all kinds of toxic plants that are bad for animals." He rubbed his forehead and then his eyes. "I hoped your boyfriend and the mayor would follow that trail someday and do the right thing. But you can never count on cops or politicians, so I left no leaf unturned."

"Wow, Aubrey. That was very well executed."

I regretted the word the second it was out of my mouth because the animation faded from his face and his hands fell to his sides. Aubrey didn't think of it as an execution, but a noble mission.

"Maybe so, but now you know too much, Ivy. If it's any consolation, the poison is very fast. I bet it doesn't hurt a bit. I was almost disappointed Roz didn't suffer more. She killed dozens of rabbits in her yard. It was torture. For me and for them. Have you ever heard a rabbit scream?"

I shook my head. "I hope I never will."

"You won't," he said. "That's one thing I can spare you, Ivy."

It was a promise he couldn't keep.

CHAPTER THIRTY-FOUR

In the same instant that Aubrey lunged for me, the most horrific sound I'd ever heard rang out in the cemetery. It wasn't just one rabbit screaming, but dozens upon dozens.

Suddenly, they were underfoot, a writhing mass of multicolored fur. He tried to run after me as I backed away, but he didn't want to step on the rabbits, and there was no path through them.

Reeling around, he screamed, too. It was a howl of rage, frustration and despair.

I thought it would be easy for Keats and Percy to take him down, but the rabbits disoriented all of us. Aubrey finally started kicking out at them, which forced me to get creative.

Climbing on top of a tombstone that read "Henrietta Tavish," I swung a trekking pole at Aubrey. I aimed for the shoulder but he moved and it hit him hard in the chin. As he staggered backward, Keats managed to gather himself to launch at the man's chest. Then Percy piled on to give a little claw love to the balaclava that was still on Aubrey's head.

That was enough to take him down, and the rabbits zipped out of the way.

Jumping off the tombstone, I held the point of the trekking pole to Aubrey's jugular and pressed.

"Here's how this works, Aubrey. You can't love one animal and kill another. That includes humans. Even Justine."

With Keats on his belly, Percy on his face and a sharp point at his throat, I thought we'd be fine till someone made good on that clanging screech in the distance. It sounded like metal on metal.

I shouldn't have let my attention wander for even a second because Aubrey managed to shove my pole aside and roll away. He kicked me hard in the leg and my ankle gave out. Soon I was the one down with a point to my throat.

His grimace told me he was going to press hard enough to send me under the grass with Henrietta Tavish. But then he gave a little yelp. And another. I looked sideways and saw rabbits gathered around him, biting his legs. It wasn't much but he cried out as if he were being stabbed in the heart. Perhaps this betrayal by the rabbits he'd tried to help felt exactly like that.

Keats used the moment to take another leap and toppled Aubrey.

Meanwhile, Percy yowled and sent the other trekking pole rolling away from Henrietta's tombstone. I managed to clamber to my feet and grab it.

Pinning the man this time was going to be tougher because he was thrashing wildly.

"Ingrates," he yelled. "After all I did for you."

Keats saved me the trouble by locking down Aubrey's earlobe.

The man's scream wasn't nearly as eerie as the rabbits' but it, too, echoed through the cemetery and beyond.

I sat down harder on Henrietta than I would have liked, but the strength went out of my limbs suddenly as another, familiar roar reached me.

"Dagnabit, Ivy, can't a soldier get a night off for once?"

Edna and Janelle jumped off the ATV and ran over.

Unsheathing a sword, Edna said, "This blade's never killed before, Aubrey, but trust me, it already knows how."

Aubrey went limp and within seconds, Edna had him roped up on another tombstone. She handed me the sword, pulled out a bandana and gagged him.

Janelle bent to remove Justine's gag but Edna stopped her. "I don't want to hear from either of them. Ivy, you get your butt off Henrietta Tavish right now. She was a classy lady. Baked cookies for the neighborhood kids until she was a hundred."

I heaved myself off Henrietta and gave Edna a little bow. "You got here so fast, Edna. Thank you."

"Thank Janelle. She stuck a tracker down your blouse before you left. We were on the road before your text."

I patted my chest. "Is that even legal?"

Janelle grinned at me. "Where I come from, it is. I told you I had a bad feeling. This bought me a minute to change into something more casual."

She was wearing my overalls and sneakers, with one of my baseball caps. Yet somehow she still looked gorgeous.

Edna took over the story. "I wasn't sure my chainsaw would work on the gates, but it sliced through iron like butter. We were going to climb over but I wanted my whole arsenal with me."

"Well, I'm sorry I took you away from flirting with Sterling to save me yet again."

"Flirting! Soldiers don't flirt, Ivy. But I'm glad the wedding can be the spectacle Asher and Dahlia wanted."

I shook my head. "There's no going back now. Jilly was happier with small-scale." I leaned over Justine Schalow and said, "You're uninvited again."

"Should we cut her loose?" Edna asked, taking back her sword. "Who knows what she'll say about us in her rag."

"She'll say we saved her life, if she has any sense at all," I said. "And if we're lucky, she'll move on to the next town."

Justine's eyes narrowed, and I knew she wasn't going anywhere. Moreover, she was planning to be the bane of my existence for some time to come.

Sirens stopped and there was the sound of boots thumping on grass. The rabbits dispersed.

When Kellan arrived, I went to step into his arms and nearly collapsed.

He carried me back to Henrietta and set me on the tombstone despite Edna's protests.

"It's just her foot, Chief. Don't go getting emotional," Edna said. "And for heaven's sake, show some respect for Henrietta. Put Ivy on Gerhard Peckins. He was a piece of work."

Kellan actually did as he was told, glancing at the various stones till he found Gerhard Peckins. Leaning over me, he pushed the hair out of my eyes. "You okay?"

It was such a gentle gesture that I wanted to cry. Luckily, Justine's presence was sufficient to stop me. So I just nodded and filled him in, instead.

"I thought it might be Edwin Masters," I said. "Or Goldie. There was aluminum phosphide in their store."

He nodded. "I sure wouldn't be using a toxin like that to kill vermin—even if it was approved for use. But their alibis checked out."

"Didn't you have rabbit officers on patrol?" I asked. "What happened to them?"

"Clobbered from behind. They'll be fine." Kellan glanced at Aubrey. "Doesn't look like much, but he sure packs a punch."

"Aubrey was trying to save the rabbits," I said. "I guess he became deranged."

"That's what happens to animal huggers left to run amok," Edna said. "I'm trying to save you from that fate, Ivy. You're one hoof short of a crack-up."

I laughed. "Fine. I'm capping my livestock at sixty. Nothing comes till something goes." Peering around, I found Opal sitting on Henrietta's stone. "Except Opal. She led an insurrection."

"See, that's your problem," Edna said, sheathing her sword. "There's always an exception."

Kellan gestured to Justine, who was now on her feet surrounded by officers. "You might want to run before the gag comes out."

"Run?" Edna said, handing me the trekking poles. "More like hobble."

"They came in handy," I said. "I like your go-kit."

Janelle decided to stay with the police, so I limped after Edna to her vehicle.

I had suffered many an indignity in the pursuit of justice, but getting lifted aboard an ATV by an octogenarian was one of the worst.

"If this is going to become a thing, I'll have to ask you to ease up on the pie," Edna said. "My back isn't what it used to be."

Keats gave a hearty pant-laugh as I got myself settled, but he didn't join me.

"You're staying behind, Officer Keats?" I asked, as Percy jumped into my lap.

He mumbled an affirmative and loped back to join Kellan.

The last thing I saw as we drove away was my dog snipping off Justine Schalow's shoelaces, and that put a smile in my heart.

CHAPTER THIRTY-FIVE

The bride wore army boots.

So did the maid of honor, both bridesmaids, four sisters-in-law and, most shocking of all, the mother of the groom.

When Edna bound up my ankle and declared boots my only option to get up the aisle without crutches, Jilly decreed that we would all do the same. As it happened, Edna had boots in every size for her future militia, so it was a simple change. My mother and grandmother pinned up our floor-length gowns to make sure the show of solidarity was noticed.

It was most certainly noticed by Justine Schalow, who roamed around the orchard taking photos of the guests, and just about every-thing else. She tried to get sneak shots of Keats and Percy, but they evaded her lens every time. Finally, Keats charged her and she sat down hard on a folding chair, looking rattled. The episode in the cemetery had drained off some of her defiance, but not much.

"What's she doing here?" I asked. "I told her she was off the list."

"I put her back on it," Mom said. "She nearly died, Ivy. Besides, this is the event of the season. It deserves to make the news."

The private and intimate affair had swelled again to more than 100 people, but it was still markedly less than the original 400. The groom's phone had been confiscated by the chief of police to make sure it stayed that way.

"I'll give Justine points for spirit," I said. "That was a terrifying encounter, yet she's here drinking more than her share of sparkling wine."

"There's plenty of wine," Jilly said. She looked absolutely radiant in her stunning dress and veil as the wedding party gathered in an informal holding area. "Far more than we could ever need. Maybe if she's tipsy, Justine will leave you alone."

"She won't," Edna said. "She's obsessed with Ivy. That's why she's here, you know."

"Here at the farm, you mean?" I asked.

"Here in Clover Grove," Edna said. "She wants to sell your story to some big-name magazine and then write an exposé about rising crime rates in hill country."

I stared at her. "Where did you hear that?"

"From the reporter's own lips. I went back to the cemetery last night and offered to see her home. She availed herself of my emergency flask and dagnabit, that girl can talk." Edna grinned at me. "I made sure my ATV hit plenty of rocks."

"That young lady will get herself killed," Uncle Sterling said, joining us. "That's exactly what used to happen to gossips in my day."

"Sterling, go and sit down," Mom said. "This is the bride's waiting room and it's not the right time to worry about the future."

We were at the base of the old orchard, which was strung with thousands of twinkle lights among the remaining apples. There was a plywood "aisle" to keep us from making apple sauce with our army boots as we made our way to a beautiful arch made of twigs and non-toxic flowers by our artist friend, Teri Mason.

"Dolly, it's exactly the right time to worry about the future," Sterling said. "Anyway, my place is here with the bride. I have the honor of giving her away to that rapscallion son of yours."

Mom took the news in stride. "Asher did very well, didn't he?"

Sterling gave Jilly a courtly bow. "He most certainly did. I've never seen a more elegant bride, and she has wisdom and wit to boot." He winked at me. "Did you see what I did there? With the boots?"

"Cleverly done," I said. "Are you really worried about Justine Schalow?"

"I told you a month ago that trouble was brewing, and next thing you know a reporter pops up," he said. "Aren't *you* worried?"

"Oh relax, both of you," Edna said. "We'll take care of Justine just as soon as the wedding finery is put away."

"And the rabbits rescued," I said.

"Be careful how you 'take care' of her, Edna," Sterling said. "In my experience, reporters are like those Terminators in the movies. They just keep on coming."

I laughed. "She's a survivor, for sure. I'm going to try to ignore her and enjoy the day."

The ceremony was about to begin. After that, there would be cocktails, followed by a sumptuous meal among the trees, and finally, dancing under the stars. It really *was* the event of the season. More like the decade.

Daisy was pulling all the strings now, and she signaled Sutton to cue up the music.

We shuffled into position and accepted our bouquets from Iris, the flower wrangler. They were modest and classy, just like the bride. There wasn't a garish blossom in the bunch. Kevelyn Welsh might win herself a place on the Hill Country Horticultural Society yet. Especially when word got around that cupcakes had been poisoned under Tizzy's watch. The rumor mill wouldn't care that Aubrey had done the deed. There were toxic plants in her garden and toxic thoughts in her head. She deserved to be taken down a bloom or two.

I bent over to have a word with Keats and Percy, each of whom was adorned with a festive bowtie that matched those on the grooms-men. There was a ring box attached to each collar.

"No funny business, you two," I said. "This is a formal occasion."

Keats mumbled something sassy. He was still on a high after our cemetery takedown, and it was hard reining it in.

"Just for fifteen minutes," Jilly told him. "Then you can cut loose."

He offered her a bow even more elaborate than Sterling's, white tuft waving.

And with that, we were off.

Keats and Percy began the procession, marching side by side. The crowd made such a fuss over them I was afraid there'd be nothing left for the bride.

About halfway to the altar, Opal hopped out from under some chairs. She was carrying a half-chewed corsage and her arrival brought a round of applause.

I had looked for her when I visited the colony in the morning but it seemed that she had already made her way here. Soon, the rabbits would be moving to new pastures. I would visit daily until then and hoped Opal would choose to stay.

The rabbit's journey up the aisle was erratic enough to annoy Keats. Despite my hissed command, he broke formation and started herding her. Once the rabbit arrived at the altar, he came back for the rest of us. The dog wasn't satisfied until he delivered the bride herself to the groom. Sterling came along for the ride, but it was ulti-mately Keats who gave Jilly away.

Family took up the entire first row of folding seats and the Rescue Mafia and their men took up the second. Since most of our meetings were about work, I had never seen my friends in their full finery. Cori was wearing a fitted black shift that sparkled, kitten heels, and dramatic eyeliner. Her signature gloves were missing, but she gave me a thumbs-up. At first I thought she was commending me on a job well done the night before, but when she added a wink, I wondered if there was more to the message.

Meryl Martingale stood under the arch, wearing a stylish blue suit and a smile that wavered between solemn and delighted. My brother stood to one side, flanked by Kellan and the two other groomsmen from the police force. They were a handsome bunch, no question about that. I tried to catch Kellan's eye but he was intent on his duties. Asher was twitching nervously and his blue eyes spilled over before Meryl began speaking.

Kellan leaned over and offered my brother a handkerchief. And then another. I wondered if he had a pocketful, like a magician. He whispered something in Asher's ear and my brother's shoulders straightened. Another comment brought a grin. And by the third, my brother's teeth flashed. I had a strong feeling there was teasing, perhaps about future illicit drag races.

With Asher settled, Kellan was able to turn his attention to me. His face lit up with obvious admiration that quickly turned to amusement when he saw my boots. His eyes came up and locked on mine and it seemed like the music soared.

Actually, the music really did soar, and Sutton ran over to turn down the volume. That's when I noticed the ferret on his shoulder.

My nephew was blatantly wearing a ferret on Jilly's big day.

Bending, I whispered to Keats and Percy, "Keep an eye on them, please. I don't want to lose any guests to heart attacks."

Keats mumbled back that it would be his pleasure. His tolerance for boring ceremony was almost at a max already.

As unnerving as the sight of the ferret had been, it kept me from getting too emotional. I'd worn waterproof mascara, but there was no need. My tear ducts stayed stitched, which was a relief. I wanted to keep up a good front for Justine Schalow.

Would everything hereafter be about staying ahead of Justine?

"Smile, darling," Mom hissed from the front row. She was staring at the back of my dress, so she must have known from my posture.

I straightened my shoulders and shivered. The dress was strapless, but I was determined to get through the ceremony without resorting to a shawl, or worse, a cardigan. Even a farmer knew when to doll up.

The vows were witty and wise on Jilly's part, and sweetly stumbling on Asher's. My friend's tone vanquished the last doubts I had about her decision. She was quite certain about embracing our messy and imperfect life as Galloways.

I blinked a few times, fighting tears, but as always, warm, soft ears anticipated my need. Keats leaned against my leg to inject a little extra oomph into the job.

It was all over quickly, and after the bride and groom delivered a kiss worthy of all the clicks and flashes, they walked the plywood plank into their new life together. Kellan offered me his arm with a smile and Keats circled behind to drive us forward.

"Next job, boys," I said. "See to the ferrets."

"Ferrets?" Kellan's chin was up, smile in place. He looked like a movie star.

"The twins," I said. "I saw one ferret and have no doubt the other is here."

His smile slipped away. "It'll end in tears, Ivy."

"If pet ferrets are all we have to worry about, then it's a good day."

He draped his arm over my bare shoulders and half-hugged me. "It's a good day. A dress rehearsal."

Another shiver ran through me. The good kind. The excited kind. Kellan was saying that we'd be making a similar walk someday soon. Plywood was plenty good enough for me. Combat boots even better, although I wouldn't say no to heels on my wedding day.

In the clearing beyond the orchard, all the guests mingled and a battle began between voices and music. The louder the crowd got, the more the boys hiked the tunes. It was time for me to have a word with them about their contributions.

The Rescue Mafia had bunched up, clearly waiting for the right moment to pounce.

"What's wrong?" I asked. "The ferrets will be fine. I'll ask the boys to take them up to the inn."

"Don't," Cori said. "I asked the twins to bring them."

"Why?" I said. "Just to cut the bliss with some shrieks?"

She gave me a mischievous grin. "I like the way you think. But even I'm capable of nobler causes. We're going to extract the rabbits now, while people are distracted, either by the wedding or what happened last night."

"Now? Dressed like that?"

Bridget laughed. "We'll change in my van. Happens all the time."

"We have at least twenty volunteers on site already and more to come," Remi said. "This may be our most complicated operation yet."

"Where do the ferrets come in?" I asked.

"We'll send them down into the warren to flush out stragglers," Cori said. "Sutton says the ferrets are good with rabbits and they're wearing trackers. This is actually where ferrets really shine. They're underestimated, you know."

Would animals—including Cori Hogan—ever fail to surprise me?

Keats assured me with a mumble they would not.

"That reminds me," Cori added, "we need Percy and Keats, too."

"Keats will get dirty," I said, holding out my bare arm to show scratches on the underside. "Do you have any idea how hard it was to bathe him this morning?"

Cori rolled her heavily lined eyes. "Sheepdogs are bred to work, not preen. But that doesn't mean he shouldn't suck it up when you ask him." She stared at Keats. "Welcome to my training school, buddy."

He literally shrank under her gaze and then shuddered.

She gestured with her index finger toward the parking lot. "That bowtie isn't doing your ego any favors. Time to build you back up with an exceptional mission."

"I'm coming," I said, hitching up my dress.

Bridget shook her head. "You're the maid of honor. We wouldn't do that to Jilly."

"She has my permission," Jilly said. She was standing behind me with Gertie and Edna. Even at her own wedding, she was committed to our animal cause. "I wish I could come, too."

"Officer Sobby would need another hankie," Edna said. "Gertie and I have a change of clothes in the van and we'll meet everyone there."

I hugged Jilly. "Thank you. We'll be back in time for dinner."

She gave me a little shove toward the house. "Just as long as you're here for the bouquet toss. Mine has your name on it."

"Maybe I want it," Cori said. "I'd win it, too."

"Don't be so sure," I said. "A sprained ankle won't stand between me and my rightful claim."

"Gertie and I have designs on that bouquet as well," Edna said, grinning. "And there are three Galloway girls who've been in training. The competition could be fierce."

I laughed. "Bring your best game, ladies."

CHAPTER THIRTY-SIX

The pets went ahead with Cori, but Kellan was leaning against my truck when I came out of the house in overalls. I was surprised to see he'd replaced his suit with jeans and a lumber jacket.

"Did you already know about the extraction?" I asked, as he opened the passenger door for me.

"I suggested it and both mayors agreed," he said. "There was no better time to get them out. By tomorrow, the gardeners would unite again and the whole thing could start over." After walking around the truck and getting in, he added, "I asked your sisters to keep an eye on Justine. If she makes a move of any kind, the other groomsmen will detain her."

"Thank goodness," I said. "I wouldn't want her to ruin a perfect wedding."

Kellan laughed. "This is your idea of a perfect wedding? Leaving the reception to chase rabbits?"

"It doesn't need to be rabbits, per se. My idea of a perfect wedding—a perfect life—is combining all the good things. Family. Friends. Animals. *You.*"

He laced his fingers through mine. "Sounds good to me. I just hope Keats doesn't puncture my suit or eat my shoelaces at the altar."

"He's on Cori's radar for booster training," I said. "With all that's happened, we've gotten lax."

"Understandable. And it may get worse before it gets better, I'm afraid."

I looked up at him, startled. "Worse? How could it get worse? We can barely stay ahead of the murders as it is."

His lips pressed together as if deciding whether to ruin the moment with bad news.

"If your uncle and his old friends are right, someone has filled in the vacuum left by Vinnie Swenson and his criminal organization. Right now, they're running the show from afar, like a puppeteer. But I rather expected them to show up at the wedding today, so I kept the Dorset Hills detail."

"At the wedding? Why? Don't tell me Asher invited this new crime lord, too."

His lips pressed together even harder.

"He did?" I said. "Is he crazy? We could all be in danger."

"Family," Kellan said. "Reckless and dangerous in so many ways. It's a minefield of blood ties."

I stared at him, waiting for him to clarify. Did he mean Asher was reckless? Or that the new crime lord was, well... family?

Maybe it was lucky timing on his part, but he turned into the cemetery before I could press for more information. The only thing that could distract me from a bombshell like that was an animal cause, and we certainly had a big one.

Cori was waiting for us with Remi and Bridget. Other than the eyeliner, the tiny trainer looked like herself again. She was in jeans now, with her black gloves and orange middle fingers flashing as she choreographed everything with the help of two rabbit experts who'd driven up from Texas.

When I tried to join in, she shooed me away rather rudely, especially since she'd commissioned my pets.

"No offense," she said, smirking.

Remi countered Cori's orange finger with a shake of her index finger. "Ivy, with your injury, you need to take care. We can handle rabbits, but not the other critical missions you take on."

"Not yet, at least," Cori said. "But some of us might be interested in learning the ropes."

"Forget it," Kellan said. "If I need an auxiliary team, I'll be the first to speak up."

Cori turned her smirk on him. "Chief, this is a rabbit matter, not a police matter. No offense."

He rolled his eyes and looked at me. "Why does she bother pretending to be anything but offensive?"

"Good point," Cori said. "I prefer to be authentic, so if you could deploy yourself to the clearing, Chief, I'd appreciate it. Make that Kellan, since we're on my clock."

Shaking his head, Kellan kissed my cheek and left at a jog.

It took me a while to hobble to the rabbit colony using trekking poles. The clearing was lit up with so many police lights that it looked like noon instead of dusk.

I followed Cori's directions to stay out of the way, although being sidelined frustrated me no end. Keats, alongside his fellow sheepdog, Clem, responded well to casual flicks of Cori's gloves. Percy did his own thing, but it was always the right thing, it seemed. Rabbits darted here and there with no idea they were being driven into one of four big holding pens. The twins stood close to the warren, shouting commands to the two ferrets, who popped in and out of burrows, looking for stragglers.

It was well over an hour before Keats went into a point. I was pleased to see he offered that courtesy to me, instead of Cori. "That's it," I called. "You've got all you're getting, at least for today."

Cori took him at his word and sent the dog back to me. His whites were grimy, but at least we got formal photographs at Clover

Grove Gardens before the ceremony. There wasn't much left in the flower beds, but the Japanese maples made a nice backdrop.

Leaving some of the others to catch and transport the rabbits to a temporary safe house, Edna, Gertie, Remi and Evie Springdale drove back to the farm with Kellan and me.

Dinner was underway when we arrived, so we all slipped into our designated seats wearing our casual gear. Avoiding my mother's stare, I admired the twinkle lights that lit up the orchard. The tables scattered around the clearing were covered in white linens, tea candles and bouquets of pink peonies. It was exactly as I'd imagined it, down to the last petal.

"Ivy Rose Galloway, where on earth have you been?" Mom said.

"And what exactly have you been doing?" my grandmother said.

I took a long sip of champagne and felt the bubbles go straight to my head. "Rabbit business." Beaming at my grandmother, I added, "Tell me all about living with Clippers."

The decoy worked and I was able to relax fully and enjoy the rest of the evening. The younger twins took over the music and by the time the dancing began, Kellan and I were in appropriate wedding apparel again. His hair was tousled from rabbit herding and there was a muddy streak on one cheek that I didn't bother telling him about. I liked him even better that way.

The smell of apples past their prime hung over the makeshift dance floor as the bride and groom took their first turn. I hadn't factored that part into my wedding vision, but a slightly sour note made the rest all the sweeter.

My mother waited demurely on the sidelines until Calvin bowed and offered his hand. The two whirled off, perfectly in step, as if they hadn't had a decades-long gap in their dancing career.

Kellan and I joined them, followed by Janelle and one of the groomsmen. Edna declined the other in favor of Uncle Sterling, and they gave Mom and Calvin a run for their money. Both couples shamelessly eclipsed the bride and groom, but Jilly and Asher stepped aside to enjoy the spectacle.

"Is it all you hoped?" Kellan asked, as I rested my head on his shoulder.

"And more," I said. "Knowing the rabbits are one step closer to their hoppily ever after frees me to enjoy this to the fullest."

"It's good to be off duty with you," he said, into my hair. "It doesn't happen often enough."

That was a request for me to stand down on questioning him about what he'd said earlier. It was unnecessary. I was determined to wring every bit of joy from the event before the inevitable sadness followed.

"What's wrong?" he asked, tightening his hold on me.

He could pick up my emotions as well as my mother, it seemed.

"Just that Jilly's leaving. I'm thrilled for her but it's the end of an era."

He nodded into my hair. "I understand. Better to think of it as the start of a new one. We can have our own era."

I laughed and lifted my face for a kiss. "I like the sound of that."

It would have been nice to savor that moment but my beloved gave a sudden jump and his eyes hardened. "Tell him, Ivy. Tell him now."

Drawing away, I looked down. "Keats, don't you dare puncture Kellan's suit. It needs to be perfect for his own wedding."

After a pant-laugh, Keats mumbled something about beauty being in the imperfections. At least, that's how I chose to interpret it.

The last hour of the reception passed far too fast, and soon we stood outside the inn waiting for Jilly to emerge in her "going away" outfit. She'd shown me a green dress and jacket weeks ago that looked great, but when she came down the stairs, she was wearing overalls, the combat boots, and a big grin. Asher came out right after her in jeans and a lumberjack shirt.

Everyone laughed, with the notable exception of my mother and *her* mother. There was such a thing as taking a joke too far, in their view.

I hugged Jilly hard and said, "Thanks for joining me in the country and showing it suits you."

"Best decision I ever made," she said. Pulling away, she added, "Don't think bagging another murderer gets you out of buying me a wedding gift."

"Aubrey ruined it," I said. "I wanted to get you a state-of-the-art espresso machine like his."

"Maybe his will be on sale since he's going to the big house," she said.

"Please. I would never bring bad vibes like that into your home." My eyes finally turned traitor and welled up with tears. "I want your home to be happy always."

"Yeah, about that," she said, beckoning my brother. "We were going to wait till after the honeymoon to ask, but..."

"No need to ask," Asher said. "We're family. Mom just moved herself in here, so I don't see why I can't."

My mouth dropped into a gape until my brain made the necessary calculations and sent the signal for a sloppy smile. "You're staying here?" I asked.

"If you'll have us," Jilly said. "Asher's going to rent out his house and we'll use that extra room here nobody wants because of the constant donkey carry-on. I find it soothing. Plus, you need someone to cook for you or you'd never stop working to eat."

I stared at my brother. "Are you sure?"

His brilliant smile confirmed it. "You need more help with the livestock and I need more time with my other girl." He glanced at the alpaca pen, and sure enough, Alvina was straining against the fence, watching him yearningly. "We can dance every day."

Despite the happiness filling my heart, a sudden suspicion made me turn to Kellan, who was staring at Alvina just a little too hard. Had he assigned Officer Galloway to serve and protect the inn?

Keats mumbled at me from below. It sounded like, "Take the win."

So I pulled them both into a hug and let the dog herd them off to Asher's truck. It had been decorated in the classic style, with tissue flowers and tin cans. The artistry smacked of Edna because under "Just Married" it read, "Officer Sobby."

People blew bubbles and threw birdseed in place of confetti, and a wave of goodwill sent the newlyweds off with a rattle of cans.

The brake lights came on and Jilly stuck her head out the window. "I expect a fancy-pants espresso machine to be waiting when I get back, Ivy Galloway. There are no free rides."

"Tell me about it," I called after her, as Keats tied me into a sheepdog love knot with Kellan.

All the tears I'd expected to shed as they drove off turned into stars in my heart and lit me up from within.

I signaled Keats to disperse the guests back to the orchard while Kellan and I walked up the stairs to the porch.

"Welcome to a new era," he said, lifting his head and sniffing loudly. "Still smells like manure."

I listened to the rattle of tin cans fading into the distance and then smiled. "Smells like promise to me."

Wondering who caught Jilly's bridal bouquet? Join my newsletter at **www.el-lenriggs.com/bouquet-bonus** and read the bonus scene!

RUNAWAY FARM & INN RECIPES

Mandy's Better-Than-Cupcakes Triple Chocolate Layer Cake

Ingredients for Cake

- 4 cups white sugar
- 3½ cups all-purpose flour
- 1½ cups cocoa
- 3 tsp baking soda
- 3 tsp baking powder
- 2 tsp salt
- 4 eggs
- 2 cups buttermilk
- 1 cup vegetable oil
- 4 tsp vanilla extract

2 cups hot coffee or boiling water

1. Preheat the oven to 350°F.
2. Combine the sugar, flour, cocoa, baking soda, baking powder, and salt in the bowl of a stand mixer fitted with the whisk attachment. Blend on low speed for 1 minute, or until well mixed.

3. With the mixer stopped, add the eggs, milk, vegetable oil, and vanilla, then beat on medium speed for about 3 minutes. Stop the mixer twice during that time to scrape down the sides of the bowl.

4. With the mixer stopped again, pour in the boiling water. Blend at the lowest speed until combined, stopping the mixer once to scrape down the sides of the bowl. The batter is fairly thin.

5. Butter three 9-inch cake pans and line with parchment paper.

6. Bake in preheated oven for 30-35 minutes, until tops spring back when lightly touched. Check to make sure the center is cooked.

7. Let the cakes cool in the pans completely before icing.

Ingredients for Frosting

12 oz brick-style cream cheese, at room temperature
½ cup salted butter, at room temperature
⅔ cup cocoa
4 oz 70% Belgian chocolate, melted and cooled to room temperature
4 cups icing sugar
1 tsp vanilla extract

Instructions

1. Place the cream cheese and butter into the bowl of a stand mixer and, using the whisk attachment, beat on low speed until combined, about 3 minutes. Stop the mixer twice to scrape down the sides of the bowl.

2. Add the cocoa, melted chocolate, 1 cup of the icing sugar, and vanilla and mix again on low speed until blended.

3. With the mixer on medium speed, add the rest of the icing sugar 1 cup at a time. Stop the mixer twice to scrape down the sides of the bowl, folding from the bottom until everything is blended together. This should take about 5 minutes in total.

4. Increase the speed to medium-high and beat the icing for an additional 4 minutes until fluffy.

5. Apply icing sparingly between layers and generously to top and sides.

More Books by Ellen Riggs

Bought-the-Farm Cozy Mystery Series

A Dog with Two Tales (*prequel*)
Dogcatcher in the Rye
Dark Side of the Moo
A Streak of Bad Cluck
Till the Cat Lady Sings
Alpaca Lies
Twas the Bite Before Christmas
Swine and Punishment
The Cat and the Riddle
Don't Rock the Goat
Swan with the Wind
How to Get a Neigh with Murder
Tweet Revenge
For Love Or Bunny
Between a Squawk and a Hard Place
Double Dog Dare
Deerly Departed
Think Outside the FoxMouse of Ill Repute
Bee All and End All
Sheep with One Eye Open
Roo the Day

Bought-the-Farm Mysteries - Boxed Sets

Bought the Farm Mysteries - Books 1-3
Bought the Farm Mysteries - Books 4-6
Bought the Farm Mysteries - Books 7-9
Bought the Farm Mysteries - Books 10-12
Bought the Farm Mysteries - Books 13-15
Bought the Farm Mysteries - Books 1-10

Mystic Mutt Mysteries Paranormal Cozy

I Want You to Haunt Me
You Can't Always Get What You Haunt
Any Way You Haunt It
All I Haunt Is You
I Only Haunt to be with You

Books by Ellen Riggs and Sandy Rideout

Dog Town Series

Ready or Not in Dog Town (The Beginning)
Bitter and Sweet in Dog Town (Labor Day)
A Match Made in Dog Town (Thanksgiving)
Lost and Found in Dog Town (Christmas)
Calm and Bright in Dog Town (Christmas)
Tried and True in Dog Town (New Year's)
Yours and Mine in Dog Town (Valentine's Day)
Nine Lives in Dog Town (Easter)
Great and Small in Dog Town (Memorial Day)
Bold and Blue in Dog Town (Independence Day)
Better or Worse in Dog Town (Labor Day)

Dog Town Boxed Sets

Mischief in Dog Town - Books 1-3
Mischief in Dog Town - Books 4-7
Mischief in Dog Town - Books 8-10
Mischief in Dog Town - The Complete Series